Spellbound

a horror anthology with 27 stories from 16 authors
The Box Under The Bed Book 4

COMPILED BY USA TODAY BESTSELLING AUTHOR
DAN ALATORRE
EDITED BY DONNA DAVIS WALKER AND ROBERTA EATON CHEADLE

Spellbound

A horror anthology with 27 stories from 16 authors.

This is a work of fiction. Names, characters, places, and incidents either are the product of the authors' imaginations or are used fictitiously, and any resemblance to actual persons, living or dead, businesses, companies, events or locales, is entirely coincidental.

Warning!

American *and* British spelling ahead. It's not typos.
Probably.

A few Aussie stories might have snuck in here, too, and one from the Great White Canadian North. It happens. They're sneaky.

To enhance your reading experience and prevent confusion, I have noted the country of origin for each writer. I agree, it's sad I had to do that.

Each story appearing in this anthology is meant to be a complete, stand-alone short story. If you enjoy the piece and want more information on that author or their other works, a link has been provided near the title of the story.

Other Books In This Series:
Nightmareland
Dark Visions
The Box Under The Bed

If you like a story in Spellbound, leave a review on Amazon.

It's okay to post a review for only the stories you read.

TABLE OF CONTENTS

ACKNOWLEDGMENTS

I'd like to thank the other authors
for making this anthology
so much fun to do.
An especially big THANK YOU goes out to
MD Walker
for efforts above and beyond the call of duty
and to Roberta Eaton Cheadle
for her amazing assistance.
You all rock.

Dan Alatorre

SPELLBOUND

Dan Alatorre
Tampa, Florida, USA
Copyright © 2020 by Dan Alatorre. All rights reserved.
geni.us/DanAlatorreAuthor

The tall blonde woman swept back her robe and put her hands on her hips, glaring at the young girl in front of her. Frowning, she eyed the child's adult companion. "How far along is she?"

The room was dark, barely allowing the two visitors to make out much beyond the rows of thick, old books jammed onto sagging bookcases. Dried herbs and flowers had been tied in small bundles and stacked on shelves, giving the space the faint aroma of a health spa. Other than that, the room was dark and still.

A cat stepped through an entrance in the back somewhere, yawning and stretching as its green eyes flashed in the candlelight. Its shiny black coat made it nearly invisible as it turned and wandered off.

"The child is early in her learning." The trembling woman stepped forward, her voice wavering. "But she sees well. Visions of future events, at times, and without the aid of a potion or fire."

The blonde woman narrowed her eyes. "This is what you've been told?"

"No, mistress. As her mother, this is what I've witnessed from Madeline with my own eyes for ten years."

"Is it?" The instructor picked up a worn, leather-bound book with a dusty cover, an embossed pentagram adorning its front.

Curvaceous and toned, she sent her long, rose gold-colored hair over her shoulder with a flick of her head. The silvery, white and pink-tinted edges bounced and swirled to the middle of her slender back. "Let's find out."

Turning, the leggy blonde walked deeper into the darkness of her gallery, passing through a doorway and into a large chamber with a warm, roaring fireplace.

The mother followed as far as the doorway. "I was told—"

"Be silent or be gone, woman!" From the fireplace, the blonde's eyes flashed at the mother. "Do not insult me with talk of payment. One cannot offer money for my services. If my terms are agreed to, we proceed—and the price will be whatever I require." She looked at Madeline. "The training is intense, child. Grueling. It will break you down and wear you down. It will age you beyond your years. But already, you know—the gift must be used, or it will destroy you. Are you prepared to commit?"

The mother nodded. "She will." She glanced at the fireplace.

The instructor was no longer there.

"Silence!" The mistress appeared at the mother's side, waving her hand.

The woman's head snapped back. She howled as she dropped to her knees, putting a hand to her red cheek. Her mouth hanging open, she peered up at the instructor.

"I speak only to the child!" The witch hissed, her chest heaving. "You cannot commit for another. Not for this. The decision is hers and hers alone. The child must decide."

Madeline's mother cowered on the floor, her cheek red and hot. "Yes, Madam Chanticlaire."

As the dark robe flowed around her, the instructor swept in front of the child. "You will forego your youth and beauty for my instruction. Your friends and the comfort of your life—such as it is—all this and more I will demand, for what will be gained at my side cannot be learned anywhere else. You will agree or you will leave now, just as I had to when I was your age."

"Your youth and beauty were sacrificed?" The child stepped forward, gazing at the instructor in the glow of the fireplace. "But . . . you are beautiful, mistress."

"Am I?" The witch took a deep breath and let it out slowly, stretching her arms out from her sides. Closing her eyes, she leaned her head back.

A low groan escaped her lips. Winkles etched themselves into her firm forehead and neck. Full, supple breasts pouted and sagged, drawing close to her caving ribs. Her back arched, hunching and curving as a long, withered cane stretched down from her hand. As the haggard instructor leaned on the walking stick, moles grew from her cheek and lip. Bags appeared under her eyes, dragging her withered, spotty flesh downward. Pale white eyes now stared out at the child between strands of thin, matted white hair.

The elderly woman smiled at them through worn, yellow teeth, her knotted fingers stretching out from the black robe.

"We of the coven learn to allow the outsiders to see what we want them to see." The witch's smooth, vibrant voice was now weak and warbling. "I am but thirty-three years on this earth. The powers take their toll."

Inhaling deeply again, she closed her eyes.

Her former state reappeared. Young and full of vitality; firm and powerful. Her long, smooth fingers brushed a lock of hair from the girl's face. "This is your fate, child. You must accept it willingly. How do you choose?"

Madeline looked down, shifting on her feet. "I must follow where the powers lead." Her eyes met her instructor's. "They brought me to you, so I will listen and learn as best I can to all you will care to show me."

Thunder rumbled outside the room's thin wooden walls.

"She's polite, I'll give you that." The witch strutted around Madeline, looking her over. "And smart. That's a plus."

Chanticlaire walked to a large cauldron boiling over the fire. With a short wooden catch, she hoisted the huge pot from the flames, carrying it to a stone pedestal. Placing it there, she stepped away and let the steam rise in front of her.

"Come, child. Look into the cauldron. Tell me what you see."

"I can tell you from here," the girl said. "It is a man. He works on a construction site."

The witch's eyes widened. "Go on."

"He . . . finds a book. It is like yours, the one you hid under a silk scarf before we entered. It has the same circle and star on the front, and the same markings." Madeline looked at Chanticlaire. "It is a forbidden book, like the many others you've hidden here. The one he found has been burned, but only the outside."

"Yes! Yes!" The witch nodded, licking her lips. "Go on—what else?"

The girl stared at the instructor, looking past her, *through* her. "He puts it in the wrong . . . I don't know what it's called."

"Describe it."

The child sighed. "I see a big metal container, for trash. Heavy, and long. But the book . . . can't go in there. Wood with nails and broken drywall go in there."

Chanticlaire nodded. "What does he do?"

"He . . . his friend calls to him. It's lunchtime. The first man throws the book into a different big container. It's nearly full. The book sits on top. Their boss sees, and takes the book out."

"Show me."

Madeline's gaze focused on Chanticlaire. "What?"

"Show me." The witch strolled across the room to stand by the far wall. "Close your eyes and put it here. View the demolition site. The men are on a street corner. The charred remains of the old shop stand behind them. There are many containers for the construction debris." She swept her hand out. "Imagine it here, on the wall, and it will be so."

Madeline shook her head. "I . . . I can't."

"You can." The witch was at Madeline's side, grabbing the child's hands and putting them to her young temple. "Think. See. Show me."

Madeline squeezed her eyes shut, pursing her lips.

The far wall glowed, turning from black to brown to orange. Reds and yellows appeared, forming the man's hard hat and his safety vest. His husky friend sat on a milk crate, opening a lunchbox.

"Paper always goes in the red bin, Tommy," the fat man said. "But not if it's burned. All the burned debris goes into the gray bin."

"Okay." Tommy held the book up, staring at its charred cover. Running his finger across the embossed leather, he glanced at his friend. "This is old. Seems like it might be valuable."

4

The fat man shook his head. "Everybody went through this place and took anything valuable a long time ago. If it's here, it's garbage—but we still have to sort it into the right container."

In the dark hall, Chanticlaire leaned down close to Madeline's ear. "What is the name of the fat man?"

The child looked at the wall. "Charles."

"And their boss?"

"Mr. McCloskey. The man—Tommy—is new. He lost his job and Charles is helping him make ends meet."

"Yes!" The witch clapped her hands. "What else do you see?"

"A boy took the book," Madeline said. "And he—"

"Not yet." Chanticlaire shook her head, whispering. She put her hands on the girl's shoulders. "Show me all the steps."

Madeline nodded. "I see Tommy. He takes the burned cover off the book as a joke. Then he throws it into the bin for the burned things."

"And the book? The pages?"

Madeline glanced at the witch. "Is that what you want? He tossed the pages into the recycle container. That's where she got it."

"Slow." Chanticlaire panted. "Go slowly. Tell me all the steps so we can follow its path and know it is the same book."

Madeline looked into the witch's deep brown eyes. "His daughter came, and the book fell out of the bin. It was on the top and it slipped off as she approached."

Chanticlaire gasped. "It fell? Or did it go to her."

"I . . ." Madeline shrugged. "I don't know, mistress."

"Doesn't matter," the witch whispered. "Go on."

Madeline narrowed her eyes. Sweat formed on her brow. "She asked—well, she was bringing him his lunch. She's . . . his daughter. Her name is . . . Tiffany." She was panting now, as if each word weighed twenty pounds and had to be lifted from deep inside her, one by one, using only her rail-thin arms. "She has brown hair, like his, and wears red sneakers."

"Are her clothes dirty?"

"No." Madeline shook her head. "She looks friendly, and very clean."

"Focus. Why is she there?"

"I—I said." The child's breath was heavy. "To bring his lunch."

"You must look deeper." Chanticlaire shook the child. "Why is she there?"

Madeline scanned the wall, gazing into the images. "The book."

"Yes." The witch's eyes widened. "Yes!"

"It—I . . ." Madeline quivered. "I don't know."

"You do. Say it."

"It . . . called to her."

The witch gasped. "The book speaks?"

"No." The child was gazing through the wall now. She was on the street corner in front of the burned-out shop, standing next to Tiffany as the girl turned her head and spied the book out of the corner of her eye. She reached down and picked it up, flipping through its old, yellowed pages.

"It's not like a voice," Madeline said. "It . . . it's more like . . . a feeling. She was drawn to it."

The witch kneeled at Madeline's side, her eyes locked on the child. "But she doesn't keep it. Why?"

"She was afraid." Madeline swallowed hard. "It made her feel strange. Sick."

Chanticlaire nodded, her voice a whisper. "So, she is not of the coven." She glanced at Madeline. "Why did the book call her?"

"To bridge the gap." Madeline stared at the wall. "That's where the boy gets it—from her trash. He rides his bike past her house and sees her in the kitchen window, doing dishes—but the book beckons to him."

The witch put a hand to her mouth. "And why does he take it?"

"The book called to him." Madeline breathed hard. "It spoke to her, and it spoke to him." She broke her trance, looking at Chanticlaire. "But why? I don't understand."

The blonde witch stood, sweeping her hands out and casting lights and shadows over the wall. The images of Tiffany's house disappeared. "Because the power of the book isn't contained on its pages," Chanticlaire said. "It is spellbound, an essence unto the paper, permeating it the way the smell of smoke lingers in a cold, empty fireplace. The pages are mere representations so *we* can understand. The real power of the book is as mine is—beyond what we can touch or hold. It stirs inside those who speak its language, calling us and guiding us to where the spirits on the other side want us to go. You and I, we are merely vessels for the energy to pass through, directing us in its path to its destinations."

Madeline stood, her shoulders heaving but her eyes on Chanticlaire.

"The boy." The blonde witch gazed into Madeline's eyes. "He takes the book. And?"

"He reads," Madeline said.

"And?" Leaning forward, Chanticlaire faced the child. "What happens if he reads?"

Madeline shook her head. "I don't know."

"You do!" The witch grabbed the child by the shoulders. "See it. Tell me."

Madeline's gaze darted around the room. "He .. he . . ."

The witch leaned closer. "Yes?"

"I can't tell." Tears welled in the child's eyes. "It's not there."

"It is!" Chanticlaire gripped the girl's collar. "Tell me!"

"He sees . . ." She swallowed hard. "He reads the stories on the pages, and that, it . . . they . . ."

Thunder rumbled overhead. Chanticlaire shook Madeline. "It makes them turn real, doesn't it?" She shouted. "It makes the stories come true!"

"Yes!" Tears ran down Madeline's cheeks.

Chanticlaire's mouth hung open. "An innocent must be the pathway. He is the innocent." She released her grip on the girl.

Madeline sagged to the floor, sobbing. "But I don't understand. The girl . . ."

"A transporter, nothing more." Chanticlaire paced back and forth. "The boy will unleash what is contained within the pages because he will read them without knowing what he is doing."

Gasping, Madeline looked up from the floor. "And the stories?"

Chanticlaire raised an eyebrow. "You tell me. Your mother says you have the sight."

Pushing herself up on her elbows, Madeline stared at the wall again. "The book is the mate to yours—the one you hid under the scarf. When he reads the stories, some will come true. Others will not. Many are simply spells disguised as fables or folklore, so those who aren't learned in our ways can't discover them and look for those who write such things or practice our arts. So . . . we hide?"

Chanticlaire rushed to the shelf and yanked back the scarf, revealing her book. The circled star and strange letters matched the one displayed on the wall, held in the boy's hands.

"We hide in plain sight." Chanticlaire folded the scarf and laid it on the shelf beside the book. "As our kind has done for seven hundred years."

Madeline nodded.

"And now we begin our lessons." Chanticlaire handed Madeline the book. "Read the stories."

FATE AND MOONLIGHT

Dan Alatorre
Tampa, Florida, USA
Copyright © 2020 by Dan Alatorre. All rights reserved.
geni.us/DanAlatorreAuthor

The man lowered himself into his dark leather desk chair, gesturing for his adult children to join him.

Margarita, Gianni Mannaro's eldest daughter, brought him a glass of water and set it on the desk. He glanced at it, nodded, and took his daughter's hand, holding it to his cheek.

His two other children took seats in the antique chairs in front of the massive wooden desk.

Mr. Mannaro sighed, leaning back and looking at them, bags under his eyes. "Today, I buried my wife of twenty-nine years. But you . . ." He pointed to his children. "All of you lost your mother."

Janielle dabbed her eyes with a handkerchief, sniffling. His youngest, Peter, leaned forward in his chair, his head hanging as he put his elbows on his knees and clasped his hands.

"She leaves us." Mr. Mannaro cleared his throat. "But only physically. A mother's love, it doesn't fade. You carry it always. When life delivers a challenge to you, try to remember what she would say or do. The things she taught you, pass on to your children. Every day, make sure they know they are loved, and give them the guidance and protection she always wanted you to have."

He reached into a drawer and withdrew a heavy wooden box. It had been painted black, and red tissue paper pinched out between the lid and the sides. Mr. Mannaro slid it to the center of the desk.

"Before she passed—before the long night that took her from my side   we talked. She knew she didn't have long."

He sighed, grasping the brass knob on the top of the lid and opening the box. Removing three bundles, each wrapped in the red tissue paper, he glanced at his son. "On the first wedding anniversary after you were born, I gave your mother a ring with three diamonds—one for each of the beautiful children she gave to me. A few weeks ago, when she knew her time was nearing, she asked me to take the ring to Sonia Vitelli's shop and have her cut it up, melt it down, and make these." Mr. Mannaro unfolded the tissue and held up a gold necklace with a diamond pendant. "The stones from your mother's ring are here, one diamond for each of you."

His daughters stepped forward, taking their pendants. The setting sun shined on the gemstones, twinkling and casting tiny bright flashes in all directions.

His oldest child kissed her father. "I'll keep it for Marcella, Papa. Until she's old enough to keep it herself. She'll love it, as I do. Thank you."

"It's beautiful, Daddy." Janielle hugged her father, burying her face in the lapels of his black suit. "One day I'll have a daughter to give it to. It will be a keepsake, to be cherished. Passed on from mother to daughter."

"Good." He stroked his daughter's hair. "Good."

As Janielle returned to her seat, Mr. Mannaro's son stood, stepping forward.

"Thanks, Pop." Peter glanced at the high, wood paneled ceiling. Two centuries of oil lamps and cigars had stained it nearly black, but the craftsmanship was still visible in its delicate, carved features. "And thank you, Mama."

"You're the most like her." Mr. Mannaro wagged his finger at his boy. "You'll need her watching over you the most. The real value of a family heirloom is never in the stone or the gold. This pendant is a blessing from your mother. It's sacred."

"I know, Pop. Don't worry." He lifted the pendant by its thick gold chain, admiring the stone it held. Tiny rainbows reflected off every sharp line, every corner of its crisp, polished cut. "I don't remember it being this big in the ring. How many carats is it?"

"Enough." His father put his arms on the sides of the leather chair, turning to view the cars lining up on the street outside. Past the giant, candlestick-shaped Italian cypress trees, the villa's long driveway was full, and the road outside the tall stone wall was bumper to bumper, all the way down the hillside. Beyond the cars, rows of lavender waved in the breezy fall twilight. "Come on." Gianni rose, the old wood floors gently creaking under his feet. "We must see to our guests."

"Papa, there's no rush. Donato is in the entry hall, and Jacitti is taking the overflow crowd to the courtyard." Margarita patted his arm. "They'll take care of things, as always. Your friends understand."

Nodding, Mr. Mannaro looked around his dark, ornate office. Tiffany chandeliers cast light over heavy bookcases stuffed with first-edition books and their faded, cracked leather bindings. Chippendale end tables held generations of framed family photos. "So much business. So many things. What does any of it matter now?" He walked past antique vases and hand-carved mahogany walls filled with painted portraits, his oldest daughter escorting him. At the door, he stopped, gazing at the portrait of his bride. The gilded frame reflected light from the candles burning on the table beside it. The contessa's dark eyes and long black hair that he loved so much—the look that she had passed along to each of their children—stirred his heavy heart. He admired her long neck and milky white skin, captured well by the artist, and the soft and gentle smile that gave no hint of the sharp tongue inside.

Mr. Mannaro's voice fell to a whisper. "Your mother was more beautiful than any diamond, children. Rare and precious, and now she's gone. But her heart is your heart. Her blood is your blood. You carry her with you, always."

His children at his side, the widower stepped out of his office and into the anteroom, preparing to greet his guests.

Many hours and many bottles of wine later, the last of the visitors was shown to the door. The crystal glasses were stacked in boxes; empty silver platters were gathered from the tables by the servants and loaded with dozens of wilting bouquets, carried to the back of the kitchen and tossed into the compost. When the long tables were wiped down and the floor was swept, the lights of the room were turned out. Only the three massive fireplaces shed light into the room.

Gianni stood by the tall windows, gazing into the courtyard as the servants doused each of the tall lanterns lining the perimeter. Jacitti went to each table, holding the cup of the long, brass snuffer over each delicate candle flame until a gentle trail of white creeped out from underneath and floated upward to the skies. Carla followed with her stepstool, reaching up to pluck each thick candle in the row, taking them down from the heavy candelabras and returning them to their wooden boxes.

"It will rain tonight," Gianni said.

Pulling his phone from his pocket, Peter pressed the weather app and shook his head. "Pop, the forecast says it'll be clear."

"It will rain. The wind will pick up soon."

A gust by the stone wall sent a smattering of leaves across the manicured grass. Carla's skirt fluttered around her calves. Two servants lifted a table and flipped it upside down, setting it on top of the table next to it and stacking them on a trailer. Half a dozen young men followed them, piling wooden chairs onto the flatbed truck and driving them to the storage barn on the far side of the estate.

Within minutes, the courtyard was empty and dark.

The first of the heavy raindrops fell.

"The sky cries for the loss of your mother." Gianni turned away from the window.

Donato jerked the heavy rope cord and the curtains swooped shut, plunging the hall into shadows. The light from the three fireplaces cast an orange glow over Mr. Mannaro. Outside, a gust of wind sent leaves tapping against the leaded glass.

"Will you be okay tonight, Papa?" Gianni's eldest took his arm. "Should I have Carla bring you a sleeping pill?"

"I'll be fine." He patted her hand. "Will you be staying over?"

"We need to get home. Marcella's at that age where she can only sleep in her own bed. I'll come back in the morning. I can see if Janielle can stay. I don't think Haven will mind."

"No, she should be with her husband. You all should go home and sleep in your own beds." Thunder rumbled outside, rattling the windows. "Go, before the rains make it impossible. Kiss your loved ones and hold them tight."

"I'll see you in the morning. I'll ask Carla to make eggs benedict for you. She's been wanting to do something nice for you all day."

"Eggs benedict." Gianni managed a smile. "Your mother's favorite."

His daughter kissed his cheek. "Try to pretend to have an appetite."

As Margarita's family departed, Donato locked the big door behind her. Gianni headed off to the room he hadn't slept alone in for twenty-nine years.

* * * * *

Peter passed his father in the hallway. Shoving his phone in his pocket with one hand, the young man twirled his car keys with the other. "Goodnight, Pop."

"Go home, boy. Go to bed."

Peter sighed. "I won't be out late. Hunter is meeting me in town."

"Tonight's not a night for being in town." Gianni huffed. "Especially not with Hunter. That boy will be the death of you."

"We won't be drinking. We'll be talking. He knew Mama, too. I haven't seen him in months, and he wants to catch up."

Gianni narrowed his eyes. "When's the last time you two caught up without getting drunk?"

"We'll probably have a few beers." Peter shrugged. "But that's it. I'm not in a party mood."

"See that you behave." Gianni hugged his son. "Show your mother some respect."

Kissing his father goodnight, Peter walked down the long hallway. Light and shadow flickered across the walls. In the great hall, Donato stoked the glowing embers in the fireplace. Orange sparks leaped and popped.

Turning, Peter reached for his phone, his fingers brushing against the pendant in his pocket.

His mother's face appeared on the old front door.

Gasping, Peter jumped backwards, his mouth hanging open. He clutched one hand to his abdomen, the other reaching backwards for the wall so he didn't fall.

"Stay in tonight," his mother said. "Go home to your wife."

Her voice was strong and calm—not weak and wavering as it had been in her last few months—but still a whisper, obscured by the growing gusts on the other side of the old door. Her skin was firm and full, her eyes alight with life.

"Keep the pendant with you and be safe." Her words echoed in the wind like they were far away and close, all at the same time. In front of him, behind him, and then gone.

Peter reached out, his trembling fingers sweeping through the air as the image of his mother faded. As the last of the orange embers sparked and died in the fireplace, her stark face disappeared from his view.

He stared at the old door, the wind howling on the other side. Massive hinges. Thick, rustic planks. Wood and iron, nothing more.

The grains in the wood played a trick in the light, that's all.

He exhaled sharply, shaking his head.

And that's before I've had a drink.

Peter's Maserati hugged the dirt road as the rain turned it to mud. Down the hillside and out to the main avenue, he gripped the steering wheel and leaned close, squinting through the thick drops as they flashed white in front of his headlights. The wipers batted back and forth, sheets of water filling it the moment the rubber blades passed.

He slowed the car to a crawl, looking for the cross street.

A lone Italian cypress arched over the road, bending and swaying in the grip of the storm. Raindrops rattled across the roof of his car.

He spotted the oak tree near the tumbling remains of the neighboring villa, and between them, the paved road that led to town. His headlights swinging onto the asphalt river, he turned the wheel and raced away to make his appointment.

Hunter Dallenfield was a college friend, smitten with Peter's expensive cars. When he saw the sprawling family estate, as well as the sweet wine grapes he found there and the fragrant fields of lavender, he decided Peter should be his best friend. He liked to shoot game in the family's private woods on his visits and was allowed to the villa almost one fourth of the time he asked to come.

But Peter's mother never liked Hunter.

The contessa was schooled in the art of keeping everyone as her close acquaintance, allowing all to consider themselves friends while never letting on to those she mistrusted or feared. But she had a list, and she kept it close. Hunter Dallenfield was on it, as were many others.

In fact, Peter was quite sure everyone in the town outside the villa had made mother's list at one time or another. Such was her madness.

As he drove, lightning parted the sky.

His mother's face flashed white against the dark clouds. Peter's breath caught in his throat as he pressed himself backwards into the seat.

Scowling, the contessa glared at her son. "Keep the pendant with you, and be safe."

His heart pounding, Peter gripped the wheel and squeezed his eyes shut. "Madness!" He slammed on the brakes, sending the car sideways on the road.

When he opened his eyes again, his mother was gone. The rain slashed at the windshield, his wipers swatting it away in vain. Silhouettes of trees swayed in the distance.

Peter swallowed hard as he stared at the black sky. "You're raving mad, just like your mother was, with all her paranoid suspicions and ridiculous superstitions."

* * * * *

The *Proiettile D'Argento* was weathering the storm well. The stone tavern's tiny, painted wooden sign swung violently in the rain, barely hanging onto its post over the door. Despite the hour, the light in the windows said ale was still being served. A decked-out, shiny black Ford F-250 was parked in front of the ancient establishment; the big pickup truck's oversize tires and the gun rack in its rear window was all Peter needed as confirmation that Hunter was waiting inside.

Peter found a place to park around the corner; the downpour eased up just enough for him to dash into the tavern without needing a towel afterward. Hunter was at a table in the corner, a pitcher of beer, four glasses, and two young ladies accompanying him.

"Peter!" Hunter waved his friend over, standing.

Peter crossed through the half-empty room, past a dozen small tables. Some were littered with dominos, checker boards, or playing cards, and almost all had at least one empty beer glass. A few patrons huddled together in booths or smaller tables in the corners, quietly consuming their drinks.

"Petey babes." Hunter shook Peter's hand, then laughed and wrapped Peter in a bear hug. "How long has it been?"

Peter slapped Hunter on the back. "Too long, buddy. It's good to see you."

"It is, it is. But I wish it wasn't under circumstances like this. The rain and . . . I'm sorry about your mother." Hunter leaned back, clapping Peter on the shoulder. "We'll drink a toast to her. Several, in fact. *La forte contessa.*"

Peter glanced at Hunter's companions.

"Oh, and forgive my lack of manners." Hunter sat, glancing to the young ladies. "This is Trudy." He nodded at the cute, brown-haired girl sitting next to him, then to her raven-haired friend. "And that is Katy."

The young ladies giggled. The brown-haired girl extended her hand. "I'm Katya." As Peter shook her hand, she nodded to her friend. "That's Hildie."

"Katya and Hildie?" Hunter frowned, putting on an overly exasperated face. "What happened to Trudy and Katy?" He looked around the bar, then leaned over to peek under the table. When the cartoonish charade was finished, Hunter shrugged his shoulders. "Okay. Hildie and Katya it is."

Peter shook his head and sat down. "I'm sorry for this vulgar creature. We met at Stanford and I've been stuck with him ever since. He's like mud on my shoe."

Katya smiled. "You're American?"

"Yeah," Peter said. "My sisters and I were born in the States, and we all went to school there. But when my grandparents died, Mom needed to return to take care of things, so here we are."

Hunter glanced at the young ladies. "Petey lives in the castle."

"The one . . ." Katya's jaw dropped. She pointed to the window. "That big one, up on the hill right here?"

Peter nodded. "In Lupacchioto. Yeah."

"Wow, it's beautiful." She leaned closer. "And the whole family moved?"

"Lock, stock and barrel." Looking around the tavern, Peter kept his voice loud enough to be heard at the table, but not loud enough to carry. Advertising his family's situation wasn't as well received in some places of the world as it was in others. "Dad's business was mostly over here anyway—Mannaro Wine Import-Export—and we all work there, so it wasn't much of a sell. We always visited the family villa in Lupacchioto a couple of times a year anyway, ever since I was a kid."

"Mannaro." Katya nodded. "I like that red wine you sell—'Sangue Lupo.' It's really good. Expensive, but delicious."

"It's very popular," Peter said. "It was named for this area. The soil is very unique here, imparting deep, mellow tannins that linger at the back of the tongue."

"Yeah! It lingers. I like that."

"Mm hmm. Lots of people do. It's one of our best sellers."

She clasped her empty glass, hovering over it as she looked into his eyes. "And do you speak Italian, Peter Mannaro?"

"Some," he said. "Your English is very good, by the way."

Katya and her friend laughed.

"It should be." Hunter smiled. "They're from Cleveland."

"Oh." Peter's cheeks grew warm. "What brings you here?"

"We." Katya took Hildie's hand. "Are graduate students doing research for our thesis. We got a grant to tour parts of Europe and establish the roots of ancient folklore."

"A grant." Peter nodded. "Nice."

"A semester to hike the Tuscan countryside—among other places, when it's not raining." She glanced at Hunter. "We met your friend on the road."

Hunter shrugged. "Couldn't very well pass up two pretty hitchhikers when there were storm clouds on the horizon."

"Yeah, it kind of came out of nowhere. That's unusual for this time of year." Peter looked at the dark-haired girl at the end of the table. "What about you, Hildie? How are you enjoying your semester in *Italia*?"

She glared at him and turned away.

"Hildie . . ." Katya frowned at her friend, then turned to Peter. "She doesn't talk much."

"I talk when I have something to say." Hildie's tone was curt. "Unlike some people, I don't flirt with married men."

Katya sighed. "We are just talking. Anyway, being an introvert goes well with English Lit majors studying ancient folklore. We thought we'd see the lands where the stories we study originated.

Hunter says you know some of that."

"He did, huh?" Peter scooted his chair closer to the table, eyeing the tavcrn door again. "Well, my friend may come off as a bit of an intellectual and a rogue—and he works hard at fostering the latter part of that reputation, I can tell you—but he's mostly harmless. Unless you're in my mother's garden. Then . . ."

"Hey." Hunter sat upright. "That was an accident. You were there."

Katya's eyes widened. "What happened in your mother's garden?"

"Oh, not much." Peter lifted the pitcher of beer and filled a glass. "He got drunk and nearly shot her."

"Shot her!" Katya laughed, slapping Hunter on the arm. "You villain. Was she okay?"

"She survived the episode." Peter nodded. "She passed away recently, so that particular villain won't get another chance at her."

"Oh." Katya said. "I'm sorry to hear of her passing."

"Thank you." He looked away. "It had been coming for a while. Speaking of villains . . ." Peter set a brimming glass of beer in front of Katya, then poured one for Hildie and one for himself. "Has he been by yet?"

"Turino? On the way." Hunter pulled his phone from his pocket and checked the time. "Do you, uh . . . have his money?"

Katya cocked her head. "Money?"

"My friend is like a lot of rich people." Hunter took a sip from his glass. "He's loaded, but he never seems to have any actual cash on him. On top of which, he's a notoriously bad gambler—which causes him to have a dicey relationship with my boss." He eyed Peter. "So? Do you have his money?"

"No." Peter set his glass down, staring into the amber liquid. "I may have something he'll like better."

Frowning, Hunter sighed and looked down. "Well . . ." He glanced at the young ladies. "These nice *americano* ladies needed a ride. I thought maybe you could help them out. It's too late to get a cab out here."

"Wait." Katya put her hand on Hunter's. "Tell us the story about the garden first. Why did you almost shoot his mother?"

He smiled. "You are an absolute folklore fiend. But this isn't one of those stories."

"Sure it is." Peter took a sip of his beer. "All folklore has its start in reality." He looked at Katya. "But I'm sorry, he wasn't *trying* to shoot her—and I'm sorry again, because I can't give you a ride, if that's where this conversation was headed."

Hunter cleared his throat. "Well, you *could*."

"How?" Peter said. "I need to be here."

"Let them borrow your car."

Katya sat up straight, pushing her beer away. "I'm a good driver. And I haven't had anything to drink."

"I'm sure you're a terrific driver." Peter nodded, then glared at Hunter. "But when Turino sees my car outside, he'll know I'm here, that I'm not late or hiding this time. But . . ." He sighed, lowering his head. "If he doesn't like what I brought him, he might decide to just take my car instead. Crap."

"He won't take the Maserati." Hunter waved a hand. "If Turino took your car, he knows your father would kill you—thus ending my employer's most reliable source of income. One day he hopes you'll gamble the deed to the estate, so he can move to the top of the hill and live like royalty." Hunter chuckled. "But anyway, he'll see my truck when he arrives, and he knows I'm here to meet you. So, you could let the girls borrow your car and I'll take you to the hostel to pick it up when we're done with our business."

Peter looked at Katya. "Which hostel?"

"Mrs. Ostia," she said.

"Mm." Peter nodded. "Yeah, she's a tight one for rules."

"And it'll be curfew soon." Katya looked at Hildie, then back to Peter. "If we aren't there in thirty minutes, she'll lock the doors and we'll be sleeping in the front yard."

Hunter took a gulp of his beer. "And you know old Signora Ostia won't listen to a word I have to say if I drive them and get them there late. But if they took your car . . ."

Katya winced, jabbing her thumb at Hunter. "He had a dead pig in his."

"It's a small hog." Hunter snorted, raising his chin. "And it's in a cooler. But the truck bed was full of gear, so I put it in the cab, and . . ." He faced Peter. "I guess I got some blood on the seat and floor, so—"

"I'm kinda squeamish," Katya said.

"No, no, I'll take you." Peter placed one hand on the table and hooked his other arm over the back of the chair, glancing toward the tavern entrance. "My business with Turino shouldn't take long. Even if we're late, Mrs. Ostia won't turn you away if I'm with you. She likes me."

"And your daddy's company sends her a lot of business," Hunter said.

"And that." Peter sighed. "But we'll be okay." He sat up, looking at Hunter's guests. "Have you ladies eaten? If you want to wait at another table while I take care of a few things, feel free to grab a bite. I shouldn't be long."

"They can eat here," Hunter said.

"It's probably better if they aren't sitting with us when Turino shows up."

Hunter raised his eyebrows, lifting his glass for another swig of beer. "Good point."

"By the way," Peter said, looking at Katya. "My car is a two-seater, so one of you will have to sit on the other's lap."

Hunter chuckled. "So don't eat too much."

Katya rested her elbows on the table, biting her lower lip. "We'll, uh . . . move to an open table. No problem. But . . . would you tell us that story? The one about Hunter and your mother's garden? What happened?"

Peter stared at her. The din of the half-full tavern was enough to keep patrons at other tables from hearing too much. And the girls seemed nice enough—eager and interested, with a chance to get first-hand knowledge of things they'd only read about in textbooks. He knew the restlessness that caused.

He took a deep breath and let it out slowly, looking down at his glass. "Hunter almost shot my mother. He was drunk—we'd been drinking a lot while we were out looking for game in the woods. On the way back, it got dark. As we approached the villa, he saw something and took a shot, but he missed. There's really not much more to it than that."

"Thought I saw a bear. It was growling and—"

"A bear!" Katya put her hand to her mouth, covering a wide grin. "In Italy!"

"They have them." Hunter frowned, tapping the table with his index finger. "Marsican brown bears. They get in trash, eat things left for compost . . ."

"You said you were a good shot, Hunter." Katya stifled a giggle. "How did you miss?"

Hunter nodded at Peter. "He shoved my arm. My shot went over the villa wall and into the brush." Shaking his head, Hunter lifted his drink to his lips. "I swear, that thing was five feet tall, with big yellow eyes."

"Well, your eyes were red. That may have played a role" He glanced at Katya, enjoying her smile. Peter made a fist, sticking his thumb out and tipping it toward his mouth. "Too many sips from the flask that day."

"Anyway, it turned out to be his mother," Hunter said. "She never explained what she was doing in the garden at night."

Peter crumbled a napkin and tossed it at his friend. "That's what people do in a garden. They sip wine and enjoy the flowers, idiot."

Scowling, Hunter drained his glass and set it on the table.

"Was she mad?" Katya said.

Peter shook his head. "She said her ring saved her. The one my father gave her after I was born."

"A magical ring!" Katya elbowed Hildie. "See, that's what we came here to learn. The local stories that become folklore."

"It's just superstition." Peter peered at the door again. "My mom was always very superstitious. She believed America was too dangerous for our family. Too many guns, she said—and then she almost got shot in her garden in Italy."

"She was partly right," Katya said. "Hunter's American."

Peter looked at her, blinking a few times.

"It makes sense he landed here, in Lupacchioto. This whole area is rich with stories. Like, did you know even the word 'lupacchioto' literally means—"

The tavern door banged open. The gusting wind swept wet leaves into the room.

A short, fat man in a trench coat walked in, his hat pulled down low over his eyes. Behind him, another, taller, man stood, eyeing the room.

The fat man's gaze landed on Peter. *"L'oca d'oro."* He smiled, approaching the table. *"Buonasera, ragazzo."*

Katya stood. "Come on, Hildie. Let's change tables."

"No, no, bella." Turino put his hands out. "Sit. Stay. I'm not here to interrupt your party. I only want what's mine."

Katya took Hildie's hand, backing away. "We were leaving."

He glared at them. "Sit."

Swallowing hard, Katya lowered herself into the chair.

"Now, boy." The fat thug rubbed his thick fingers together. "I'm told you have something for me. Pay me quick, and you can get back to these *vagabondi Americani.*

Staring Turino in the eye, Peter slipped his hand into his pocket and withdrew the diamond pendant. It shimmered in the dull light of the tavern.

"Oh, ho!" His mouth agape, Turino held his hand out, gazing at the pendant. *"Fammi vedere,"* he whispered. He reached out and slipped it from Peter's hand.

The howling wind blew open the tavern door again. The bartender rushed to slam it shut. In the fireplace, the flames flickered.

Turino's round, sweaty face was dotted with tiny dancing rainbows as the diamond rocked back and forth at the end of the gold chain. He swept his fingers over his chin, staring into the sparkling gem, his eyes fixed to its beauty.

The windows of the old tavern creaked as the stormy winds picked up again.

Turino glanced at Peter, his voice a hoarse whisper. *"Quanti carati?"*

"At least three carats," Peter said. "With the chain, it's worth more than twice what I owe you."

"Ah, si." Turino nodded, his hand dropping to the base of his throat. He massaged his thick neck, staring at the jewel. *"Molto bello. Molto bello."* Blinking, as if waking from a dream, Turino straightened up and cleared his throat. "But it is not what we agreed." He leaned close to Peter, scowling as he pushed the pendant into Peter's palm. "I prefer cash, *Signore Mannaro."*

"Look again." Peter stared into the fat man's eyes, raising the gold chain and the heavy diamond on the end. "Your money is here—and then some. Plus a little left over for me. Say, five thousand."

Turino's eyes went to the diamond, his mouth hanging open. Sparkles from the stone streamed across his cheeks. He licked his lips, reaching for it. "American dollars?"

"*Si, signore.*" Peter pulled the pendant away. "What do you say? *Abbiamo un accordo?*"

Turino growled. "Such arrogance, to ask that of me." He stiffened his back, adjusting his shirt collar with both hands. "*Grandi palle.* I'm not a pawn shop. I have to take your jewelry, find a *gioielliere*, pay him . . ." He frowned, raising his bulbous nose into the air. "It's a lot of trouble for me."

Peter's gaze remained on the fat man, his voice low and calm. "Sonia Vitelli knows the piece. It's her work."

"Vitelli? Your father had this made?" Turino leaned forward, pointing to the piece, his eyes darting to Peter. "*Questo era di tua madre?*"

"*Si*, it was hers. And now it can be yours. You always wanted a piece of that castle, of its mystique and power. Here it is."

"Today . . . was her funeral."

"That's right." Peter held the pendant a little higher, letting it swing, like a tiny pendulum marking time for an eternity. "That's why I'm confused enough to sell an heirloom from her castle."

Turino turned his face away, rubbing his chin—but watching the diamond out of the corner of his eye. "It's bad luck to sell a family jewel. Such things are . . . sacred."

"That's my problem." Peter held the pendant out. "Take this and give me five thousand dollars. I'm taking a loss, but we'll call it even."

Turino's *scagnozzo* nudged him, gesturing to a nearby table. Playing cards and dominos were scattered between the empty beer glasses on the surface. "*Gioca a carte per questo. Una mano di poker. È americano. Non può resistere.*"

"*Ah. Si, si.*" Brought back to reality, the fat man narrowed his eyes. "Your offer is inconvenient to me, but I'm a generous man. What do you say we play cards for it? One hand of poker. If I win, I take the pendant and pay you nothing, but your debt is cleared. If you win, I'll accept the jewelry as payment of your debt in full and I'll pay you five thousand American dollars."

Peter's face was firm. "Ten."

"Bastardo!" Turino slammed the table with his fist. "No!"

Katya jumped, grabbing Hildie's arm. A hush fell over the tavern. The other patrons stopped drinking to view the scene unfolding at Peter's table.

"Look at the diamond," Peter said. "It's perfect. Powerful. It's worth over thirty thousand dollars. I'm giving you a deal."

Turino stared at the diamond, then at Peter. With a grunt, he turned and took a chair from the adjoining table, pulling it over and sitting down. Facing Peter, he smiled. "Your luck has always been lousy. That's why you're always in my ear." He reached for the cards on the other table. "We'll cut the deck for it. High card wins."

Peter set the pendant on the table. "Shuffle, you *grasso stronzo*."

Turino gritted his teeth, frowning.

"Petey." Hunter leaned forward, reaching for Peter's hand. "Maybe—"

Turino blocked Hunter's arm, his eyes remaining on Peter. "Let young Mannaro have his fun. In a moment, I'll be having mine." He shoved the cards into Hunter's hand. "Shuffle the cards."

Hunter quietly separated the deck and fanned the halves together. After two more shuffles, he placed the cards on the table. "Who goes first?"

Turino swept his hand outward. "Be my guest."

Peter eyed the deck, drawing a breath slowly. As he moved his hand over the cards, his heart raced.

Turino rubbed his thick fingers across his chin. Outside, the wind howled. The windows of the old tavern creaked.

Closing his eyes, Peter lowered his hand onto the deck, pressed his fingers into the sides, and lifted. He turned his hand over to reveal his card.

The three of spades.

Turino burst out in laughter. His bodyguard smiled.

Hunter winced, looking away as the girls put their hands to their mouths. A collective groan went up from the tavern's other patrons.

The breath going out of him, Peter slumped forward and laid his cards face up on the table. He forced himself to look at the smiling fat man sitting across from him.

Turino rubbed his hands together, chuckling. "After I beat you, maybe we'll go play again for your car. I always wanted a Maserati. Well, I always wanted *your* Maserati." He snorted, dropping his hand onto the deck and sliding his thick fingers over the sides. Lifting, he smiled as he turned his hand over to reveal his card.

The two of hearts.

"Peter won!" Katya shouted. "He won! He won!" Bouncing up and down in her chair, she hugged a smiling Hildie.

The tavern's other patrons cheered. Turino's face fell, his eyes wide. Hunter exhaled sharply and put his hand on his chest.

Frowning, Turino slammed his fat fist onto the table. His face red, he gritted his teeth, his curses unable to escape his mouth. He stood up, growling, knocking his chair over backwards. As he reached down and snatched the necklace from the table, he turned and pointed to the exit. *"Pagatelo!"*

Peter's heart settled back into his chest as Turino stormed away from the table. The eyes of the other people in the tavern returned to their drinks as the fat man passed. Rushing forward, Turino's henchman pulled a thick wad of bills from his coat and counted out Peter's money, then ran after his boss.

When the tavern door slammed shut behind the thugs, Peter's table erupted in cheers—along with the rest of the room.

"Unbelievable!" Hunter said. "Maybe your luck has turned. I can't believe it. That was incredible." He mussed up Peter's hair.

"Maybe my luck *has* changed," Peter said. "Life in Lupacchioto doesn't often work like that."

"Congratulations, Peter." Katya came around the table to hug him. "That was intense."

Peter sat in his chair shaking his head. The other bar patrons took turns slapping him on the back.

"I hate to spoil the celebration," Hunter said. "But Katya and Hildie still need to . . ."

"Right." Peter sat up. "You have to go." He glanced at Hunter.

"I'd better check on my boss." Hunter stood. "And make sure he doesn't have a change of heart in the parking lot. I'll meet you over at Mrs. Ostia's. There's a pub near there—Bellini's. It'll be open. We'll meet for that drink and toast your mother's memory."

"Yeah, check on Turino." Peter gathered up the thick wad of cash from the table and shoved it into his pocket. "I'll see you at

Bellini's."

Hunter headed for the exit. "Drive safe."

* * * * *

Ten minutes later—his boss no less angry but happy with his diamond and willing to abide by his deal—Hunter was on his way. The heavy downpour had let up and turned to a light, Tuscan drizzle. Half a mile from Mrs. Ostia's, his headlights fell upon Peter's yellow Maserati sitting sideways on the narrow road. Both the doors were open; water dripped slowly from the roof onto the side of the driver's seat.

As he slowed down, two shadows rushed out from the woods.

"Help!"

Katya and Hildie were drenched, with mascara running down their cheeks and their hair glued to their foreheads. Waving their hands, they raced towards Hunter's pickup.

He hit the brakes hard, putting down the passenger window. "What happened?"

"There's a wild animal out here!" Katya jerked the door open before the truck came to a stop, leaping inside. Hildie climbed in after her. Slamming the door shut, they sat with their feet on the cooler and their knees under their chins.

"A what?" Hunter said, eying the road.

"A wild animal!" Katya pointed to the Maserati. "Out there!"

"A wild . . ." Hunter thrust himself closer to the windshield. "Where's Peter?"

"Gone. He wrecked." Katya's voice quivered. "He—he said he felt sick, and then he lost control of the car."

"I couldn't see," Hildie said. "Katya was sitting on my lap. But he just slammed on the brakes and jumped out of the car."

Narrowing his eyes, Hunter stared out into the dark night. "So the car's okay?"

"Yeah, but he's not in it," Katya said. "He ran into the bushes, grabbing his head and making all these loud noises, like he was going to vomit or something. But the next thing I knew, there was this giant animal on the road—like a big pit bull or one of those giant Cane Corso dogs. It was huge, drooling and growling at us, and coming toward the driver's door of the car. When I saw that, I bailed out of the Maserati. I screamed for Hildie to run, and we bolted up the hill into the woods. I grabbed the first tree branch I could reach, and climbed as high as I could. We stayed there until we saw your headlights."

"It didn't follow?"

"I—maybe it did, I don't know. I was just running to get away. I heard it crashing through the brush after us, but I don't know where it went after that."

Hildie swallowed hard, water dripping off her chin. "There was screaming."

"Was it . . ." Hunter gripped the wheel. "Do you think the screaming was from Peter?"

"It—it had to be." Katya shuddered. "I'm sorry. We were so scared. You should have seen that thing. It was huge, and howling . . . It wasn't like anything I'd ever seen before."

Hunter scanned the road, chewing his lip.

"I hope it didn't get him, but . . . there can't be anyone else out here," Katya said. "It's been quiet for ten minutes, at least. We haven't seen anyone. Not the dog or Peter. When we saw your headlights, we ran for it."

Hildie quivered. "I've never been so scared."

"It's all right. You're safe now." Hunter unclipped his seat belt. "In all this rain, he probably hit an animal on the road, and when he got out to check, it attacked him. I've seen injured animals do that. They can—"

"No!" Katya shouted. "That's not what happened!"

Hunter eyed the empty road, jutting his jaw out. "Doesn't matter. If Peter's out there, he needs help." He unlocked a rifle from the gun rack and put his hand on the door latch. "I'm going to have a look."

Katya grabbed his arm. "Don't leave us!"

"You'll be fine. Use this." He opened the glove compartment and took out a pistol, thrusting it into Katya's trembling hands. "If you see that dog again, or whatever it was, empty the gun into it. Don't hesitate."

Katya gazed at the weapon in her wet hands.

Hunter looked at Hildie. "Do you have a phone?"

She blinked, looking up at him. "Yes."

"Call for an ambulance." He stared out into the night. "I'm going to look for Peter."

"No!" Katya cried.

Putting his hand on the door latch, Hunter peered up and down the road. "Stay here."

As Hildie steadied her shaking hands, she pressed the buttons on her phone. Hunter opened the truck door and stepped outside, gazing toward the Maserati. A thin trail of white emanated from the tail pipe as the powerful motor hummed. Holding his breath, Hunter inched forward. Overhead, rain clouds obscured the moon. Its dim, gray light filtered down to the darkness below. A chill wind swept through the trees, sending droplets of water cascading onto the brush.

A howl pierced the silence of the woods. Distant and horrible, as if a man were being eaten alive, the demonic screech filled the night air.

Hunter gasped, stepping backwards. The scream had disappeared as quickly as it came. The woods were silent once again.

His heart thumping, he cocked his weapon and raised it to his shoulder, creeping closer to the car.

The truck's headlights illuminated the scene in front of him. The Maserati's doors were open; the engine was running. A gentle chime from the dashboard indicated the door had been left ajar.

Aside from the wet interior, nothing seemed to be amiss. The ladies' story checked out—so far.

He flinched. *But if they did something to Peter, I just gave them a loaded gun.*

Hunter shook his head. *No. That wasn't acting. That was stark terror.*

Another howl came from the woods. This time, from the right.

Hunter's breath caught in his throat. The howl was closer this time.

The headlights cast his shadow onto the bushes at the edge of the pavement. Italian country roads were often close to being overgrown with brush out in the hills. He stepped forward gazing at the foliage, clutching his rifle tightly.

The leaves were dark in places, spotted and splattered dark against the green. He leaned forward, standing sideways to allow the truck lights to make the contrast more visible.

Red.

Blood.

A twig snapped to his right, barely audible above the car engine. He whipped around, staring into the woods, scanning the foliage for shadows, movement . . . anything.

Drips of water fell from leaf to leaf in the brush, causing a skinny tree limb to bounce, or a bush to shudder. The quiet Tuscan night was silent except for a few leftover raindrops that slipped from the leaves higher up, and the engines of the two vehicles far behind him.

In the greenery, a dark shadow moved past the trees.

Hunter jerked his rifle upwards, jamming it into his shoulder and dropping his eye to peer down the barrel. Holding his breath, he stared into the brush.

Nothing moved. Nothing sounded. A thin drop of rain fell onto the rifle barrel, splattering white in the distant headlights.

Hunter took a step toward the bushes, staring into it.

The shadow was gone.

Had he even seen it? Big and wide, like a bear in the—

Crashing through the bushes on his left, a black beast jumped out. It lunged forward over the road, the thing's yellow eyes wide with rage. It bared its fangs, growling with the voice of Hell.

Hunter thrust his finger onto the trigger and swung his rifle around to shoot.

The massive animal crouched, huge and dark, rippled with muscles under its wet black fur—then it sprinted toward him like a tiger.

Hunter aimed his weapon at the charging beast, and fired.

A tuft of hair went up from the animal's shoulder, but it didn't stop. As he cocked the rifle again, the beast was twenty feet away, then ten.

Hunter shot again and again, aiming for the massive maw that grew larger in his sights. The flash from the barrel turned the beast's huge eyes and fangs white.

He cocked the rifle again as the beast leaped toward him. The blast caught the animal in the chest, spraying red everywhere as it landed on Hunter, knocking him to the ground.

The rifle skittered across the muddy asphalt, disappearing into the weeds on the other side of the road. Gasping, Hunter rolled to his side, his heart pounding. He jumped to his feet, bracing himself and holding his arms out, readying to fight the beast by hand.

It laid there on the road, massive and dark, curled into a ball. Its thick chest heaved, one leg twitching outward as a low growl escaped the horrid beast's mouth.

Hunter swallowed hard, inching closer. He unbuckled his belt and slipped it free from his waist, wrapping the leather around his hand and letting the buckle dangle free. Stepping nearer, he prepared himself to thrash his makeshift whip into the animal's hide.

In the truck lights, the beast's chest lifted lower, a gurgle mixing with each forced breath. Overhead, the lower, darker clouds parted—but hazy skies still cast a fogginess over the moonlight. Its whiteness filtered down, displaying the blood that ran freely from the beast's wounds and over the wet road, streaming down across the gravelly edge and disappearing into the mud that seeped from the woods.

The beast shuddered, cringing as its chest lifted again. "Hunter."

He recognized Peter's voice. Glancing around, he looked for his friend.

The dying animal quivered again, whispering. "Hunter."

It was asking, not saying. A question from a dying man who could no longer see those around him.

The animal's fur was gone. Peter lay wet and naked on the road, covered in blood.

"Peter!" Hunter dropped to his knees, turning his friend to him.

Peter's pale skin was streaked with red, a massive wound in his shoulder and another in his chest. He fought for air, the red, gaping hole over his ribs hissing with each breath.

"I'm here, buddy," Hunter said. "An ambulance . . ." He swallowed hard, looking over the dying flesh that had been his friend. "There's an ambulance on the way."

Peter shook his head, almost imperceptibly, blood spilling from the corners of his mouth. He stared up at the sky. "Father . . . said you'd be the death of me."

"I'm sorry. I—I don't know what happened. There was an animal, and then . . . you."

Peter nodded at the sky. The last of the rain clouds drifted away, revealing the full moon. "She tried to warn me. I should have listened."

"Who?" Hunter leaned in close. "Who warned you?"

Peter gagged on the blood, coughing weakly. "I should have kept her pendant. I thought the stories were made up, but it really did protect us. Those of her bloodline."

"Stay with me, Petey babes. There's—there's . . . An ambulance is probably on its way right now. The girls—Hildie—she called."

"It was Mama, Hunter." Peter's fading eyes looked into the face of his friend. "In the garden. You . . . weren't seeing things." He choked again, sending blood streaming over his chin. "She was always afraid after that. She . . . she always thought you knew."

Hunter shook his head. "Hang on, buddy."

Peter's face sagged, his eyes staring off into the distance. Heavy drops of a new rain began to fall. The next wave of the storm was coming.

Hunter lowered his head and slowly got to his feet. His hands covered in red, he gazed down at his dead friend as the low whine of a distant ambulance came up from the far valley road.

Spellbound

MERCY

MD Walker
Breckenridge, Texas, USA

Plotmonster.wordpress.com

"You must see with your own eyes what evil lurks in this world."

Father insisted that I accompany him to the Greensmith house on this wretched night. I pulled the brim of my hat over my eyes as Father dragged me through the doorway into the storm outside. Fat drops of rain pelted my face and body. Water gushed off rooftops, sloshing into rivers on the ground as we made our way to their home.

It was little use to fight him. I had no interest in viewing the evil he spoke of, but I didn't have a choice. Father always got his way and those that clashed with him usually had a steep price to pay for their insolence. This, I knew well. My recent forays into town were unsettling to him but if he knew of my true nature, I would never be allowed under his roof.

The moon hid behind storm clouds and the wind howled, swirling, and lashing at us as we made our way through the darkness. For a man his age, Father was swift on his feet and he pulled me along, careful to make sure I maintained my footing.

The house sat on the edge of town, small and worn with neglect. Nathaniel Greensmith had died years before, leaving the care of the home to his wife. Goody Greensmith worked as a seamstress to provide for herself and her daughter but the house was showing signs of age and disrepair.

A fire with bright orange flames greeted us as Father barged in without knocking. We shook the water from our clothes, placing our jackets and hats on a table near the hearth to dry. Goody Greensmith sat in an old, wooden chair by the fire, quietly weeping and rocking back and forth.

Two men, Dr. Shaw and Magistrate Young, stood beside a cot in the back of the room. With a tight grip on my upper arm, Father ushered me beside them so that I could better witness the scene before us.

My breath caught in my throat and I squirmed out of his grasp, backing away from the bed.

Mercy Greensmith, small for her ten years, was dressed only in a thin cotton nightshirt and tied to the bed with thick leather straps. Her shirt was slick with sweat and her long blonde hair was a knotted mess. Blood oozed down her arms and legs where the leather had sliced into her skin.

Bile rose in my throat.

Why is she tied up?

I opened my mouth to question Father, but he shook his head. My jaw snapped shut and I turned back to the bed. The little girl was writhing, pulling at the straps causing them to cut her arms and legs more deeply. She was groaning in agony and every now and then a few clear words could be made out – unholy blasphemy the likes of which I had never heard in all my fifteen years.

Dr. Shaw stepped close to Father and whispered something in his ear.

Father shook his head. "Let's begin." The room quieted and the only sounds left were the crackle of the fire and the soft sobbing of the girl's mother. Father took a deep breath and moved to the bedside, holding a crucifix in his hands. "Mercy Greensmith!"

She ceased moving. Her big, blue eyes flashed bright with anger and she met my father's eyes without flinching. I took a seat beside her and began to smooth her tousled hair. My heart was overflowing with emotion; confusion, anger, sadness. I wanted to soothe the wounded child. My father took a step toward me and as I diverted my attention to him, the girl bit at me. She snarled and hissed as I stood, stepping back out of her reach.

"Mercy Greensmith," my father repeated. Mercy once again turned those hate-filled eyes toward him. "You have been accused of witchcraft."

The girl refused, or perhaps was unable, to answer the allegation but kept wailing and thrashing about.

Father's voice softening, he knelt by the bed. "Have you been bewitched child? Tell us who did this to you."

The girl spat at Father. A large trickle of saliva dribbled down his chin and he clenched his jaw. He got to his feet.

A strangled sob escaped her mother's throat and the sound of heart-wrenching cries filled the room. A tight ball of anger welled in my chest, giving me the courage to confront my father.

"She is only a baby," I cried. "Who would accuse an innocent child?"

"Silence, Josiah! You are here to observe. Goodwife Garren swears that she saw Mercy practicing witchcraft. Would you call her a liar?"

I bowed my head.

"No, sir."

Dr. Shaw stepped forward. "This child has no fever, yet she rants as if delirious. She has no ailment at all that I can find."

Young spoke up. "We must do a witch test. It's the only way."

"Avert your eyes, gentlemen." Dr. Shaw stepped up to the bed and lifted the girl's nightshirt.

"What is this indecency?"

Father took my arm and we faced the fireplace, our backs to the girl.

"He is looking for a devil's mark - an unusual mole or brand. This child has been afflicted for three days. Something strange and unnatural is at work here."

After a few moments, the doctor let out a heavy sigh. "There is nothing. Nothing at all to speak of."

Minutes ticked by, turning into hours as the men observed the girl's behavior. At times they would try to talk to her, other times they would cluster together, Father reciting scripture. Her mother kept her tearful vigil near the fire.

I fell to my knees and began to pray. Closing my eyes tight, the words tumbled out of my mouth in earnest for I feared what would happen to the child.

Mercy laid limp as a rag doll, still and unmoving. Breathing labored and heavy, she watched the men as they huddled together to discuss her fate, my father key amongst them. Father nodded at Magistrate Young and the man rushed to the girl's mother, kneeling at her chair. He whispered in her ear and the woman began to howl, a guttural yowling that seemed to come from the very depth of her soul. Her pain-filled screams causing the hair on my neck to stand up.

My father turned to me. "Josiah, there is nothing left to do. Exodus says, 'Thou shalt not suffer a witch to live,' and we must not. The time has come to end this."

I fell to my knees, tears filling my eyes.

"But, Father, there must be—"

"Do not question me, son!"

Heat rose in my cheeks, setting my skin on fire. My heartbeat thudded in my ears as adrenaline rushed to my head. A tingle shuddered down my spine. My teeth shot out longer, sharper, and I growled at the man that gave me life.

Father's jaw dropped and he stared in stunned silence, witnessing my transformation. For the first time in my life, Father had no words. He backed away from me, his mouth turned down in a sneer, and this only kindled my anger.

Dr. Shaw's face, unrecognizable, his features distorted in a menacing grin, moved toward me. He circled me like a lion on the hunt; then lunged. I twisted out of his reach and came around behind him. Grabbing his head, I pushed it to the side and sank my fangs into his neck. His blood pulsed in my veins and I savored the fear trickling out of him. I dropped his lifeless corpse to the ground, and stepping over him, I regarded Magistrate Young cowering in the corner.

"Josiah, p-pl-ease," he cried in fear.

"No, Magistrate. Would you have had mercy on this child?" I bent down and took his bony face in my hands as if to place a kiss on his forehead. Looking him in the eyes, I smiled. He trembled with uncontrollable terror and I relished the sight of it.

"Lord save me from this demon!" he shouted, quivering. "I'm a pious man!"

I threw my head back and laughed. "The Lord is not with you."

His neck snapped easily, bones cracking as his eyes rolled back in his head.

"Josiah!"

I let his body drop to the ground and faced my father.

Shoulders sagging, he peered at me. "What evil beguiles you, son?"

I met his questioning unfazed. "I am no warlock, if that is what you think."

"No, no," he mumbled, shaking his head. "But I do think you sold your soul, wicked child."

I squared my shoulders. "What happened to me was not my choice. But I am still your son and I will not let this innocent child be harmed."

My father seemed to grow two feet. "You do not decide her fate!"

He strode to the table by the hearth, fetching a long-handled knife and holding it high in the air. The girl's mother jumped from her rocking chair, blocking his path. None too gently, he pushed her aside and she fell to the ground. Her whimpering grew deafening as Father strode toward her daughter with renewed purpose.

The girl's bed trembled and shook, bouncing on the dirt floor as if it were a living thing. Mercy shrieked louder and louder and the only glass window in the home pulsed and shattered, shards bursting forth with great force. Specks of red blotted Father's face as the glass sliced him.

As if by their own accord, the straps on the bed loosened and the child pulled free of her restraints. She jumped from the mattress, landing steadily on her feet. Thunder rumbled and a quick burst of light illuminated the tiny shack. The girl's hair stood on end and her eyes glowed yellow like a cat in the dead of night.

I froze where I was standing.

Before he could move, she was on Father; scratching, clawing, digging at his skin and eyes. She bit his head, pulling away bloody chunks of scalp. He tried to shake her off, but it was no use. She snatched the knife away from him and in one solid stroke she sliced his throat. Blood poured from the wound and his body slumped limply to the ground.

I watched, petrified; unable to move, unable to turn away.

She smiled up at me, blood dripping from her open mouth.

Was I her next victim? Would she be mine?

My muscles tensed, preparing to fight, if necessary.

Instead she dropped the knife.

"Thank you," she said. "You saved me—and I saved you. Had it been left to these *men*," she spat the word, "Neither of us would have survived the night." She narrowed her eyes. "It's best we go our separate ways now, wouldn't you agree?"

I swallowed hard, eyeing her, my legs shaking. "I was taught not to make deals with… with demons and witches."

She wiped the blood from her chin. "You were taught not to trust your own kind. In time, you'll see we are the only ones you can trust."

Her cackle echoed throughout the tiny home. Grabbing her mother's hand, she closed her eyes and chanted. Softly at first, then her voice growing stronger. The house vibrated with energy, as if being sucked from the ground into the raging storm. The door swung open and shut, clanking in the wind. I planted myself against the wall to keep from being caught up in the torrent.

Mercy's eyes popped open, her head flung back, still gripping her mother's hand. A blinding light sprung from their chests as they rose high above the dirt floor, levitating in the churning wind. The two figures faded like dwindling smoke or fog on the horizon and, before my eyes, were gone.

The light flickered out and the wind died down. I was alone. A monster in the dark.

DEATH IS ABOUT CHOICES

Roberta Eaton Cheadle
UK

The drought was devastating the land.

"It's terribly dry. The maize kernels are shrivelling on the stalks and the ground is cracked and parched." The messenger shook with fear as he imparted this information to the Sapa Inca. The emperor was known to lash out in rage at the bearers of bad news.

The emperor's main advisor, the High Priest of the capital city of Cusco, addressed the deity. "The mountain gods are angry and need to be appeased before they will send rain and restore life to our crops. A Capacocha ceremony is necessary. You must advise the chiefs to bring their sacrificial offerings to the city at once and I will arrange their distribution throughout the empire. I will lead the ceremony at which the purest and most beautiful children will be offered."

The feathers on the Sapa Inca's golden headdress swayed as he nodded agreement. A single ray of sunlight shot through the room, reflecting off the golden threads of his heavily embroidered clothing and surrounding him with a golden haze.

"The gods approve." The High Priest's face broke into a huge smile.

***

Juanita was not the first child, nor would she be the last, to have made this great journey from Cusco to the base of the high mountain selected by the High Priest, as the most appropriate shrine for his Capacocha ceremony.

The arrival of the ceremonial procession at the site, where the base camp would be established, was met with relief. The location at the foot of the mountain had everything the participants and the builders needed, including water, food, and access to a stone quarry.

Exhaustion was evident in the stiff and pain-filled movements of the older members of the party after travelling for many days. The High Priest had set a moderate pace to accommodate the slower moving among the accompanying priests and worshipers, but it had still fatigued them.

The journey from Cusco to the selected shrine was long and arduous. Tradition dictated that the travellers not follow the easier royal road, but rather take a direct overland route, following a straight 'as the crow flies' path from Cusco to their targeted camp site. The group had forged rivers inhabited by shocking electric eels and flesh-eating piranhas. Low, wet swamps greeted them, infested with the highly toxic poison dart frogs, mosquitoes, and powerful green anacondas. They struggled to pass over high mountainous terrain.

Juanita had enjoyed the monotony of the travelling routine after all the pomp and ceremony of her time in Cusco. As each day blended into the next with dreary regularity, she focused on controlling her fear.

What happens to you after you die? Will I really continue to exist as a deity, achieving divine status as a direct link between my people and the gods? Or will I just stop? Will the universe simply carry on without me as if I never existed at all? If only I knew the answers.

Dying along the journey did not frighten her. Such a death might be better than what lay in store for her and the two other children selected for sacrifice, Anku and Palla, at the end of their journey.

At least the end would be quick. Instead, I am one of the living dead with the stamp of sacrifice upon me.

The glimpses of brightly-coloured birds she caught among the palm trees and her sightings of herds of gentle Alpacas on the highland plateaus soothed her agitated soul.

The birds and animals live such peaceful lives. They don't have to wrestle with the meaning of life and the prospect of an early death. It would be so much easier to be a bird. They can fly away from danger. It must be wonderful to have wings and be so free.

A few weeks before their arrival at the camp, the procession had passed through Juanita's home village where, in accordance with tradition, her family had joined them. The families of Anku and Palla were already among the travellers, the procession having passed through their villages earlier in the journey.

Her father was the chief of her home village. He and her mother were incredibly proud that Juanita had been chosen for sacrifice by the Sapa Inca.

"Your sacrifice to the mountain gods will ensure a tie between your father, as chief of our village, and the Emperor. It will also bestow an elevated status on our family and our descendants. We are greatly honoured by your selection and you will be forever immortalised through your sacrifice." Her mother's expression of exalted wonder didn't have the desired effect on her twelve-year old daughter.

"Your perfect beauty has been recognized." Her mother tried another avenue of persuasion. "You are entirely unblemished and beautiful to look at or you would not have been a viable subject for selection."

Juanita would not be coaxed into expressing gratitude or joy at her situation. She, along with two other children of equal purity, had been chosen to die.

It's easy for her, she's not the one whose been chosen to die. She will continue to enjoy the warmth of the sun on her face and the wind in her hair. I'm the one who is expected to be joyous about giving up everything I love.

41

Two of her brothers were among the worshipers, and she was comforted by their presence—although, being younger than her, she was not as close to them as she had been to her older brothers, Tupaq and Mallku.

Brushing tears from her eyes, she thought of their tragic deaths. Just a few short months before, she'd left the village to travel to Cusco to meet the Sapa Inca and attend the feast held in her honour. The victims of a hunting accident, her brothers' mummified bodies now lay side-by-side in an underground tomb.

I wish they were here to support me through this awful time. Sometimes I think I see their faces among the people in the procession, but when I try to approach them, they disappear.

Three years ago, before she had been selected for child sacrifice, she had overheard Tupaq and Mallku discussing the practice. It was late one evening, when their parents were away attending a ritual where several animals would be sacrificed. Her brothers thought she was asleep.

"I am worried about Juanita. She is too perfect, too beautiful. She is the perfect subject for selection by the bloodthirsty priests," Tupaq said.

"I agree and I am also worried, Tupaq," Mallku's, deep voice rumbled, "but there is nothing we can do to help her if she is chosen."

A few months later, their predication had come true and Juanita had been chosen. During the months between her selection and her journey to Cusco, she had been fed an elite diet of maize and meat.

Fattening me up for the kill, she'd thought miserably. *They wouldn't want to insult the gods by sacrificing an inferior product.*

Nothing could stand between her and her destiny. Following the deaths of her beloved brothers, she grew unable to eat. She became thin and pale. Her frailty had attracted the attention of the local priest who had told her to start eating again or he would order the arrest of her family and younger brothers. Juanita had obeyed.

***

Two long, slow months passed in the base camp, and Juanita wished for an end to the waiting. Permanent structures of stone had been built to accommodate her and the other child sacrifices, as well as the priests. Her life was comfortable, but it was difficult to take pleasure in the natural beauty around her when the day of her death grew ever closer.

Every night she awoke sweating and gasping with fear, knowing that high above the camp, in the bosom of the mountain, the sacrificial platform where she and the other children would meet their ending was being constructed. Several sealed tombs from previous ceremonies already existed at the mountain's peak.

At least I'll have company, she thought bitterly.

Wherever she went in the camp, people treated her as a spectacle, gawking at her and observing her every movement. Most of the observers demonstrated no common courtesy but stared at her in open-mouthed wonder as they took in her extraordinary beauty.

I never thought I would wish for death, but I want it over now.

The two other children attracted nearly as much attention as she did. They were both younger than her. Anku, a boy, was seven years old, and Palla, a six-year-old girl, was his sacrificial mate. They would be sacrificed together in a symbolic marriage.

The calmness with which Palla had accepted her destiny helped to sooth Juanita's own fears, but Anku was a different matter, vacillating between angry tantrums and sobbing fits at the thought of his impending doom.

***

Finally, the sacrificial platforms were ready.

"Tomorrow at dawn we'll start our ascent of the mountain," the High Priest announced during breakfast one cool and cloudy morning. "The air at the top of the mountain is thin and frigid. Make sure you have appropriate clothing to keep yourselves and your families warm. Rest stops have been built along the path for us to stop and refresh ourselves during the journey. The thinner air will make you feel tired and breathless but regular stops will help you acclimatise as we move higher into the mountain."

Piercing wails pierced the silence that followed the High Priests short speech and Juanita watched as Anku's father dragged him, struggling, and kicking, away from the gathering.

Her own breath came in short gasps as fear gripped her heart. Closing her eyes briefly, she heard a voice.

It was Tupaq. "Do not fear, fair sister, Mallku and I are here by your side. We have a plan."

That night, her brothers visited her in her dreams. Tupaq stroked her brow and told her not to worry. "We are here, Juanita, looking out for you. We are going to stop that bloodthirsty High Priest once and for all."

They both kissed her lightly on the forehead and Juanita fell into the healing embrace of deep sleep.

The following morning, she awoke still wrapped in a warm blanket of comfort following her brothers' visit. The places where they had kissed her burned slightly, giving her the strength and forbearance to undertake the strenuous hike up the mountain.

***

On the day selected for the ceremony, the sun slipped above the ice-covered peaks of the Andes Mountains, pouring its cold rays through the flap of the fur-lined tent where Juanita, Anku and Palla lay sleeping, cuddled deep within their thick wraps.

Shivering, Juanita slipped from beneath the coverings, thrust her cold feet into warm boots and went outside to relieve herself. The intense cold shocked her as she gazed about at the dazzling plain of ice and snow.

Today's the day.

Two faint and wavering shadows extended on either side of her, protectively encircling her. "Fear not, sweet sister, we are here by your side."

The morning passed quickly as the children were prepared for the sacrificial ceremony which would commence in the mid-afternoon.

Juanita sat patiently on her bed while her long hair was braided into an elaborate style. The coca leaves she was given to chew made her feel happy and relaxed. In between chewing on the leaves, she took large gulps of maize beer. Her fear of death gave way to a mild euphoria.

A quick glance in the direction of Anku and Palla reassured her that they had also partaken of the mild narcotic. Anku sat quietly in the patch of sunlight near the tent flap, his beautiful face relaxed and peaceful.

The women had been up since dawn preparing for the feast that would follow the sacrificial ceremony and the rich smells of cooking food wafted intermittently to Juanita, making her feel slightly nauseous.

The happy shouts and cries of the unaffected children caused her to smile gently as she imagined them getting under the feet of their busy mothers and driving them to distraction. As the morning wore on, her occasional glimpses of groups of boys, men or priests walking past their tent, increased in frequency. After the great fires had been lit and the kindling piled high in readiness for the celebration, there was nothing for the men to do until later in the day. They were full of restless energy as they prowled around the site.

The excited anticipation had risen to a fever pitch by the time Juanita stepped up onto the platform, dressed in her fine clothes and with an elaborate headdress of feathers resting on top of her head. The coca leaves and maize beer had done their job and she slid into a seated position on the rough stone floor from where she watched the actions of the High Priest and other priests through a gauzy film of unreality.

Next to her, Anku and Palla sat back to back, their eyes closed. Palla was dressed in a traditional light brown acsu dress and, immediately on her right, Anku wore a gray tunic, a silver bracelet, and leather shoes. They were surrounded by a collection of useful and decorative objects which they would take with them into the afterlife.

The ritual music of drums, bells, flutes, trumpets, and tambourines swirled around Juanita like fine mist. Through her drooping eyelids, she observed bright spears of light from the setting sun showering down on the frozen plain. The rays stained sections of the snow blood-red and glinted and sparkled off other sections like bright stars.

Relaxed and happy, with a lump of half chewed coca still in her mouth, she half smiled at the shadowy spectral shapes, with no discernible faces, moving around in front of the platform. She could hear their voices, indistinct and rumbling like distant thunder, but she couldn't understand what they were saying. It didn't occur to her to try and speak to them, and even if it had, she could not have forced her cold lips to form the necessary words.

The sun went down with astonishing rapidness, plunging the world into darkness except for the flickering dancing flames of the fires and the twinkling of the bright stars. The stars moved forward and then back, shrouded in shimmering light, that brightened and darkened in rhythm with the movement of wild dancers in front of the fires and the pounding of the throbbing music.

Neither the icy wetness of her fine clothing, the result of her bladder letting go earlier during the ritual, nor the uncomfortable tightness of her tightly braided hair, permeated her dreamlike state. The blood in her limbs was slowing down and her eyes were fluttering closed from time to time as hypothermia started to set in.

Forcing her eyes open, she watched as two of the faceless silhouettes around the biggest fire metamorphosised into the forms of her long-dead brothers. She smiled at them, sure that her drug induced dream was ending, and they had come to escort her into the great darkness of death. A horrible, croaking giggle forced its way out of her slack throat.

The forms of her brothers grew larger and larger curling upwards like white smoke. Their hands disappeared into the dark clouds that hung over the top of the mountain and reappeared holding several lightning bolts which jerked and writhed.

A small gasp of fascinated horror squeezed past Juanita's blue tinged lips as the hands drew back, preparing to throw. The mind-altering coca leaves and maize beer combined with the effects of hypothermia had pushed her mind to the brink of a great void of emptiness.

Enormous cracks accompanied the bolts as they streaked earthwards, hitting several of the dancing figures. The dancers exploded into showers of sparks in front of Juanita's dazed eyes.

The sight of the High Priest and other priests dissolving instantly into black ash, was nearly too much. Her mind teetered desperately on the edge of the dark void.

"Let the children go! We do not want these sacrifices of human lives. Let them go or suffer our wrath."

The words drove her into the endless abyss of blackness.

***

"Juanita," the voice called. "Juanita, come back."

Mumbling, Juanita eyes fluttered open and then closed again as she curled up into a fetal position.

"Juanita," the voice called again, pulling her out of the blank mindlessness of her death-like sleep.

Juanita stirred. "Tupaq?" The word was slurred.

"You don't need to speak with your mouth, Juanita. Just think your answer."

Her eyes flickered with shock. *He's inside my head. I can feel his emotions and feelings and hear his thoughts.*

"Oh, Tupaq, what happened? Did I dream it all? Did I dream the ceremony and my own death? Is it still coming?" She dropped the words into her mind, like pebbles into a pond.

"No, my sister, you did not dream it. Mallku and I intervened to destroy the evil High Priest and his henchmen. You are still alive, but you have a choice to make."

"A choice? What is the choice I must make?"

"I will show you."

Juanita saw herself in Cusco. She was kneeling in front of the Sapa Inca, telling the story of what happened to the High Priest and other priests on the mountain. The mouth of the emperor opened, and his lips moved soundlessly as he passed sentence over her. She couldn't hear what he said.

Then her mind cleared, and awareness of her half-frozen body, curled up on the hard-stone floor of the platform, filtered into her semi-conscious brain. Her younger brother was standing over her, shaking her roughly as he desperately tried to wake her.

"What's the other choice?" She moaned thickly and her eyes fluttered as the shaking grew harder.

"You can come with Mallku and me. We will escort you into the afterlife. Our task is done and the evilest of the High Priests has been destroyed, along with his vile minions. There are others who will try to take over. They will want retribution for what has happened here on the mountain. We cannot know what the Sapa Inca will decide about you. You may be free to return home, or you may be killed like a common criminal. The choice to return to life or come with us is yours alone to make."

"What about the other children, Anku and Palla?" Overwhelming fear rippled through her.

"They are gone, Juanita. It is too late to save them, but you still have a choice."

"Noooooooo," the mental scream reached a crescendo and then started to fade. "I'm coming with you. Take my hand, Tupaq, hold it tight."

The warmth of Tupaq's grasp gave her courage. She inhaled a gasping breath. Her soul attached itself to her final exhale and exited her body, still clutching Tupaq's hand.

THE
MOST VALUABLE SKILL

Christine Valentor

Chicago, Illinois, U.S.A.

witchlike.wordpress.com

My brother, Simon, extended his arm and placed a hand upon my shoulder.

"Consult her, I beg you."

"It is forbidden."

I watched as his arm changed into a wing, large as an angel's, black as onyx. The other followed, and he transformed into a grotesque thing, unnatural and twofold. Half man, half swan.

"Do it!" he commanded. "Do it or we shall be forever condemned, to this – this _dual_ life. Which is no life at all."

His throat became covered with feathers, a long, graceful neck. His lips, once pink and fleshy, now pointed into a sharp yellow beak. Feet flattened to rubbery bisected triangles. And then his human body was gone entirely. He was no longer with me, not in thought or comprehension or awareness. The swan flapped its wings and was off, quickly as the sun rose and daylight broke over the land.

I clenched my fists, nails digging into my palms. Father, if he were still alive, would never abide such a thing. I had always known Grizelda was demented, but I hadn't realized the depth of her wickedness. At least she had not tampered with *me*. Not yet. I was the only one left to find a cure, and I had but one choice.

When the clock struck midnight, I donned my hooded cloak. I'd risk this journey only in the dark of night when none could see me. The witch lived far in the Daemonskov, a vile and treacherous forest where decent folk dare not tread. The path to her house was not a path at all, but an overgrown mass of brambles. I walked carefully, sidestepping weeds that grasped like claws at my ankles. Animals howled in the distance. Every rustle in the thicket set my nerves ajar. Fog rose from the ground, a foul-smelling haze that grew denser as I came nearer to her dwelling place. I covered my nose in disgust.

The witch's cottage was a crumbling shack where spiders spun webs like geometrical lace in the railings. Bats swooped through the trees. I tapped on the door, which almost fell off its hinges.

"Who *dares* ask entrance to my abode?" The voice was a nasty screech.

"It is I, Eliza Skildenburg. I've come to ask a favor."

"And what favor could *you*, a crowned princess, ask of *me*, a mere forest witch? Be gone!"

"Please, Madame, hear my request." I clutched the gold coins in my pocket. I had stolen them from Grizelda, the only remnants of the fortune I once had. "There is a reward, if only you'll cooperate," I added.

The witch cracked open the door. She held a lone candle which illuminated her greenish face. She surveyed me, cocked her head, and arched an eyebrow. "What *sort* of reward?"

"Gold, Madame." I held up one sovereign, bright in the darkness. At the sight of the coin the witch became more hospitable. She invited me in and motioned me to sit at her table. A kettle boiled on the fire and she offered me a cup of tea, which I declined.

"Suit yourself," the witch said tartly.

On the shelves above the fire were stored all sorts of peculiar things – skeletons of small animals, fur pelts, a tiny heart floating in a jar, human fingernails, snips of hair, and a vial of red liquid that looked like blood. It was anyone's guess what she put in her tea. The witch sat across from me and clasped her hands.

"I have eleven brothers," I began.

"Of course you do. Simon, Samwise, Gideon, Godfrey, Thomas, Timon, Aleric, Nathanial, Eldore, Lancelot and Bard. I know of the royal family." She stared at me hard, yellow eyes challenging. "Now *what,* pray tell, is your business?"

"All eleven have been cursed by our stepmother, Grizelda. A most hideous curse it is. By night they live as men. Walk upon two legs, touch with two hands, think and reason, wish and yearn, love and scorn. But come daybreak it is over. Their bodies change to black swans and they fly, with the brains of birds, condemned to endless skies, deprived of their humanity." My throat tightened as I blurted the words. Saying it aloud made it so much more real.

"When our father, the king, died," I continued, "Simon, the eldest, should have taken the throne, as rightful heir. Unfortunately, Grizelda prevented that."

Prevented was an understatement. We knew no one would accept a swan as king. It was absurd! Fearful of ridicule, we fled the castle. Grizelda took our lands, our titles, and our livelihood. She now ruled the kingdom of Larkspur like a troll on a throne, predatory, destructive, and hateful. Anyone who questioned her authority was put to death.

"She is a tyrant," I said, my sadness now turning to anger. "An evil, seething tyrant! Can you help me or not?"

The witch paused and narrowed her eyes. "I have one such remedy, but it will be impossible for you to carry it out."

"How so?"

"It involves nettles. And patience. And pain. Sharp nettles, mind you! So sharp they will prick your manicured fingers."

"I will withstand any pain," I said coolly.

"Will you?" The witch smiled a near toothless grin. "First you must gather nettles from the cemetery. *Urtica dioica,* they are called. Nature's needles. The poisonous variety. They shall stab and shred your pretty, pristine hands." The witch let out a bawdy laugh. "I suspect a spoiled princess such as yourself will quit before the first batch is plucked!"

"I will endure any task, Madame," I said, even more coolly. I was royalty, and therefore, ultimately invincible.

"Hmph!" She sneered and eyed me from head to toe as if I were a peculiar insect. "You must pick enough nettles to make eleven shirts, one for each of your brothers. You will crush the nettles into flax and spin them. Your hands will bleed and smart. The pain will seem unbearable. You will long to cry out in anguish. But you may not! As a matter of fact, you must keep perfect silence, from the time you gather the nettles, until you place the woven shirts upon the backs of the swans."

"I can do that."

"Can you? Many will question your activities. Secret deeds preformed in secret places. You will be given no chance to explain yourself. If you utter but *one word* before the task is completed, your brothers will all be struck dead."

"I'll do it." I had intended determination in my voice, but much to my shame, it cracked with uncertainty. The witch was right. I had led a pampered life of luxury and ease. What did I know of pain and suffering, let alone silence? I had never picked an herb in my life and the thought of poisonous nettles agitating my hands was not a comforting one. "I'll... I'll do all in my power to complete this mission," I added, wanting to at least sound believable.

"As you say. Once you place the shirts upon each of your brothers' backs, they will become human once again and Grizelda's curse will be broken."

I gave her the money and left the cottage. The next night, I crept in stealth to the cemetery. Nettles grew in abundance around the gravestones. The first stem I picked caused my fingers to burn as if they had been stung by a hundred wasps. My hands bled profusely, yet I kept on. I would need a large batch to complete eleven shirts.

I worked until my basket was full. I then made my way back to the flea-infested hovel where I now lived. It was a shack worse than the witch's, a desolate hole with a dirt floor, a scant hearth, and only straw pallets for beds. But at least I dwelled in peace, far from the threats of my stepmother. There I could crush my flax, undisturbed. I had a spinning wheel and silently I would work.

Hannagal, my maidservant, who had stubbornly come with me when I fled the castle, looked at me in shock. "Princess Eliza!"

she cried. "What has happened to your hands? And why are you carrying those noxious nettles?"

Alas, I could not answer. Hannagal hurried to bandage my hands, but I shooed her away.

"Why do you not speak, my lady? What is this torture of which you partake?"

Silently I began my spinning. "Such sorrow!" Hannagal wailed. "First your brothers have been cursed and now you." Hannagal was a slow-witted girl. She couldn't begin to understand the complexity of the situation. Servants were dull creatures. Finally, she left me alone with my wheel.

For days I toiled diligently. From sunrise to sunset I did nothing but spin. Hannagal brought my meals, bread and cheese on a cutting board which she nearly forced down my throat. "You must eat, my lady. I'll not have you drop of hunger."

When I had completed five of the eleven shirts there was a knock upon our door. My breath stopped in my chest. We never had visitors. Few knew of our whereabouts and I wanted it that way. Outsiders were trouble.

Hannagal opened the door to find Fencington, the local sheriff, standing like a soldier called to duty. He held a scroll in his hand.

"What's your business here?" Hannagal asked.

"I have a warrant for the arrest of the disgraced princess Eliza Skildenburg. Let me in."

"She is *hardly* disgraced, my lord," Hannagal replied. "What has been done to her family is most unjust – the work of a malevolent, diabolical woman who now claims the queenship with no right to do so! And *furthermore…*"

"Silence, you ignorant wench!" Fencington pushed past her.

He crossed the room to find me at my spinning. "Eliza Skildenburg, you are charged with witchcraft. You were seen in the Daemonskov, consulting with that loathsome, midnight hag, an act *forbidden* by law. What's more, you have visited the cemetery in the dark of night, summoning spirits and dancing upon graves."

I had not danced upon graves! How dare he accuse me when my own father was barely cold in his tomb? But I could say nothing, offer no explanation. Fencington grabbed me by the arm and slapped iron shackles across my wrists.

In a dank and gray inquisitor's chamber, where the air was stale as dust, I was questioned by the committee, four men in wigs. I uttered not a word. To them, my silence proved my guilt. Three midwives then entered. They stripped me of my clothes and shaved my head, dull blades making endless cuts and gouges to my scalp. I winced as my long black tresses fell to the ground, dark as squids' ink upon the straw rushes. The midwives then clothed me in a dress of burlap that itched like the scabies.

Fencington, holding a pistol to my head, marched me down a corridor which led to a stone staircase. At the bottom was the dungeon, an abyss of concrete and iron that opened its dark mouth to me.

"Here you shall await trial. And may the Devil take you."

I stared at him coldly. My spinning was gone, my task uncompleted. Yet I would not speak, for fear my brothers would be struck dead, as the witch had warned.

All was hopeless. A botched undertaking for which I blamed myself. I had been careless, had underestimated the far-reaching tentacles of the nosy sheriff.

The dungeon was perpetually cold and damp. Rats, the size of small dogs, lurked in corners, their sharp teeth ever threatening plague and rabies. Daily I was given a bowlful of gruel, my only meal. Its look and taste were like decomposed maggots, a blob of yellow decay that I stirred with a spoon, barely eating. My fingers still throbbed from the nettles. Yet I longed for my spinning, my only chance at completing my task.

On the third day of my imprisonment a miracle occurred. Hannagal came to visit. The leather clad guard unlocked the bars of my cell to let her in. "Ten minutes, girly," he told her. "Tho' ya won't be needing it. This witch speaks not. She is a mute idiot!"

When the guard walked away, Hannagal reached beneath her corset. She pulled out a bag filled with my five completed shirts, plus a bale of flax and needles. I wanted to sing in appreciation! But instead I embraced her, so hard I almost snapped her rib cage.

"I know not why you need this, my lady," she said. "But I trust you have reason."

By the day of my trial the eleven shirts were completed. I took them with me, hiding them under my skirt as the guard led me to the courthouse. A crowd of townspeople had gathered, eager to witness my debasement as I faced my fate – the hangman's noose.

Inside the courthouse Judge Phillip Maplethorne, a tall man with kind eyes, pounded his gavel. "Hear ye, hear ye! We are gathered here today to determine the guilt or innocence of Eliza Skildenburg, disgraced princess of the kingdom of Larkspur, accused of consorting with a witch, summoning spirits and dancing upon the graves of our dearly departed."

Sheriff Fencington paraded before the crowd. He described my crimes, stating with conviction that I was a dangerous criminal. Before he could finish, the doors of the courthouse flung open. Fencington stopped mid-speech. The townspeople turned to see who had entered. There, at the door, stood eleven black swans. They flapped their huge wings and swooped all around me.

I wasted not a single moment. Reaching beneath my dress, I pulled out the shirts. One by one, I flung each over the backs of the swans. I watched with relief as they morphed slowly from birds to men. First Simon, then Samwise, then Gideon and Godfrey (together, for they were twins) then Thomas and Timon, all standing upon sturdy legs. Then Aleric, Nathanial and Eldore. Lancelot followed, strutting proudly, his head held high and his mane of black hair streaming (for Lancelot was the most handsome). Lastly, transformed was my youngest brother Bard, who ran in front of the magistrate and, in both excitement and frustration, began his tale.

"Your Honor," he said, "my brothers and I have been victims of the most heinous crime, a curse from our stepmother Grizelda, a plot to rob us of our lands…"

Before he could finish, Fencington raced across the room, pleading to the jury. "We have at this moment been presented the most *resolute evidence* that this woman is a *witch!*" he proclaimed gleefully. "For who else but a devil's maid could perform such a task as to turn birds into human beings?"

The men of the jury glanced at one another. "It is true," one said. "It is definitely true," another agreed. "This work – it is demonic. The girl is *indeed* a witch! And the men are surely warlocks!"

Soon all twelve were in accord, pointing fingers, declaring our guilt.

"But no!" I shouted. "You misunderstand!"

Judge Maplethorne pounded his gavel. "Order! Order! In consideration of these new and… unusual circumstances… I rule the proceedings stop for today and reconvene tomorrow."

The townspeople cheered and jeered, depending which side they took, some in favor of me and my brothers, others set upon our destruction. My brothers were shackled and taken back to the dungeon with me.

"Take heart, sister," Thomas consoled me. "Surely our good name will prevail. The jury tomorrow will see we are innocent."

I wanted to believe him.

"If only we could seize Grizelda," Timon added. "Make her testify and face her crimes."

"No chance of that," Aleric said. "She is secluded, safely inside the palace walls. None can touch her there."

It was true. There was no way to question Grizelda, and no one would believe our story.

"It is so unfair," Bard said, sinking his chin into his palms. He was the purest one, the vast depravity of humankind still inconceivable to him.

"Shut yer gobs, ye nattering knaves!" the guard bellowed through the rusted bars. "Now get some shut eye."

That night I dreamed of the gallows, where I stood with a noose around my neck. I screamed as the stool beneath me was kicked from my feet and I fell, the rope tightening like a snake on my throat.

But I never died. It was impossible to die in a dream.

I awoke the next morning to find my brothers in distress. Samwise picked at his bowl of gruel. Nathanial vomited at the sight of it. Eldore removed fleas from his shirt and Aleric tended a rat's bite, inflicted in the night.

"What will happen next?" Bard asked, his eyes wide as coal stones. "I am scared."

"The guard will take us back to the courtroom and the jury shall decide our fate."

"I don't like that jury."

"Have faith, little one." I turned a brave face to him, never revealing my own fear.

The guard clanked his key in the lock. "Ye wretched minions of Satan," he growled, voice coarse as granite. "Happy I'll be when yer necks snap."

We climbed the stairs to daylight. The yellow sun shone bright as citrine. I looked up and noticed a flock of seagulls flying low, forming a V through the air. This was unusual. We were miles from the ocean and gulls never flew so far inland.

"The verdict fer witches is always guilty," the guard continued. "Ye ain't got a chance, not the slightest!" He chuckled, as if our lives were a joke. "By this time tomorrow ye'll be dead. Dead as stuck pigs, thrown to the field, never to be laid in a marked grave…"

The guard stopped mid-sentence as one of the seagulls lunged for his head.

"Mother's BLOOD!" he wailed. The bird pecked his scalp. He swatted it away, large hands like two cleavers. But as soon as that gull had flown, two more followed, digging claws to his head, covering his eyes with their hard-pressed wings. The guard tilted, lost his balance and fell to the pavement.

"Scavenging beasts!" he shouted, but that only seemed to attract more birds. They pecked at his shoulders, pointy beaks boring holes in his leather tunic. The gulls then ascended and disappeared like figments into the sky. The guard staggered to his feet. He eyed us suspiciously.

At the courthouse the same crowd had gathered, shouting insults as we entered.

"The imps of Beelzebub have returned!"

"Hang 'em high!"

"Justice shall be served!"

Judge Maplethorne pounded his gavel. Fencington once again began his monologue. "Ladies and gentlemen, good men of the jury, I will prove here today that the accused are foul witches who deserve to swing by the *neck* until they are *dead*!"

Applause thundered. It amazed me that anyone would be so eager to see us die. I looked up toward the ceiling.

And there, like a necklace of black pearls, they sat.

A murder of crows. Still as statues, so quiet no one noticed them, their entrance seemingly invisible. They perched in the rafters, a little army. Observing. Listening. Judging.

"These repugnant *monsters*," Fencington continued, "who can not by any stretch of the imagination be considered *human...*" He was cut short as one of the crows dove for his head. "Infernal thing!" He swatted the bird away. Another followed, then another. Soon the entire flock was upon him.

The birds pecked. Fencington hid his face and doubled over. But it did no good. The birds overtook him, biting like snapping turtles. Within seconds blood trickled from his head.

"It is the work of those witches," someone shouted.

Judge Maplethorne ran to Fencington, losing all composure, flailing his arms, trying to ward off the birds. A few of the townspeople joined him but it was no use. The crows, like hungry vampires, nipped and gnawed, gouging their beaks into Fencinton's flesh. They did not stop until the sheriff lay in a bloody heap.

"He is dead!" a woman yelled. "The witches have killed him!"

The townspeople, now panicked, tried to exit the courthouse, so many heading for the door they made a bottleneck of traffic. Women sobbed and men cursed. "Let us out! In the name of all things holy, let us OUT!"

I watched as their bodies piled, a hill of human flesh. With my hands shackled I could not help. Where had they come from, these nightmarish birds?

I had no time to ponder, for now the swarm of crows had doubled in size. They began attacking the twelve men of the jury. Like a thick net, they descended. There was a ruckus of caws and screams, a rustling of black wings and black robes. Wigs rolled off heads and the birds pecked at bald scalps. I shivered, remembering that I, too, had been shaved bald beneath my headscarf. But the crows attacked only the jury, paying no attention to me.

In a few moments it was finished.

All twelve men slumped in their chairs. Pulseless, lifeless slabs, blood still trickling from their wounds. Their eyes were purple sockets.

"Are they all – dead?" I asked carefully, incredulously.

"Dead as a slaughtered cow," a man muttered. "Serves 'em right. Pompous lot. Think they have the power to judge. To condemn people to death."

"You're a fine one to talk," a woman hissed back at him. "Yesterday you, your *very self*, judged her guilty as Judas."

"Did not!"

"Did so!"

"Stop this arguing," Judge Maplethorne ordered. He looked at us despairingly, a man struggling between law and reason and superstition. "Considering the situation," he said, "I think it fair you all are proclaimed innocent. Mistress, you are free to leave the courthouse. And the gentlemen as well."

"Best we undo those shackles, my lady." It was Hannagal who spoke. I had not even known she was there. She grabbed the keys from the prison guard, who stood numb, gulls' feathers still strewn across his tunic. Quickly, Hannagal unlocked our shackles.

Freedom. It was a sweet and welcome thing.

We hailed a carriage and rode back to the palace. There was one last battle to be fought. The defeat of my stepmother would not be easy. She was a woman of malice, and I could only guess what tricks she held up her evil sleeve. We entered the palace doors, pushed past the servants, and went straight to the throne room.

Ah, but Grizelda. She was not quite herself.

My stepmother lay like a pile of rotting meat on the dais. Her elegant gown had been shredded and her skin was a polka-dot of peck marks, her fingers decayed with gangrene. Her eye sockets were deep craters, now filled with black blood. A tiny, grasping 'O' formed on her withered lips, as if she had died trying to get in the last word. The crown she had stolen lay strewn on the floor.

"She had it coming," Aleric said.

"She deserved it," Godfrey agreed.

Simon picked up the crown.

"Evermore, you shall be King of Larkspur," I declared as he placed the crown upon his head. "We trust you shall rule fairly."

Simon took his seat on the throne. He smiled. But in that instant his expression revealed more than victory. A combination of pride and arrogance. A greed I had not seen in him before.

We descended to our knees. "Long live the king," we all chanted. All except Bard.

My youngest brother stood off to the side. He was contemplative, almost morose. "Absolute power corrupts absolutely," he said.

"What, little one? Why would you say such a thing?"

"That's what father always told us."

"And your father was a wise man," Hannagal added.

Just then there was a fluttering of wings at the windows. With a cacophony of squeals, they flew inside.

Would we never be free of these dreadful creatures?

The crows swooped around the room, then settled themselves on Simon's throne. Some perched on its velvet arms, some on its ornate back. A few sat upon Simon's shoulders, causing him to squirm. One landed on the glistening peak of his crown. I counted four and twenty in all, stern little sentinels, watching with beady eyes.

"Get rid of these malignant things!" Simon cried. "Where are the servants? Call the servants!"

But it was too late.

The top crow squawked, took a peck at Simon's head. He brushed it away, causing the crown to fall. Hannagal laughed, a high-pitched guffaw not unlike the caw of the crow.

How *dare* she?

"Do you find it so amusing?" I asked coldly.

"Oh, my lady." She shook her head. "You don't understand. And how could you? A pampered *princess* who never in life so much as dirtied her hands… until now."

"Understand what?"

"You think a poor servant girl could have no skills beyond washing, mending and emptying slop pails? I too have visited the witch."

"You? Whatever for?"

"Is it so hard to imagine? While you were in the dungeon, I made use of my time." Hannagal stared at me boldly, a stare beyond her status. Had the girl forgotten her place?

A knot began to form in my stomach.

"The witch taught Grizelda to transform men into birds," Hannagal said. "She taught you to transform birds into men. And me?" The maidservant lifted her chin and smiled a triumphant smile. "The witch taught *me* the most valuable skill of all. To *command* birds! I knew one day I'd get my chance."

"Chance for what?" Simon demanded, his face reddening in anger.

"Why my lord, have you not guessed?" Hannagal popped her eyes in feigned innocence. Her voice was syrup. "A chance to usurp your throne."

Four and twenty blackbirds. Enough to bring down a jury of twelve.

Or an evil queen.

Or a family.

One crow descended upon me and pecked at my bald head.

Spellbound

GLASS MOUNTAIN

Roberta Eaton Cheadle
UK

robertawrites235681907.wordpress.com

The wavering line of boys marches steadily towards the distant hump of the mountain. They'd caught their first sight of it a few hours before, when they'd finally stumbled out of the deep gloom of the forest. It reared up out of the frozen wasteland, its icy slopes steep and forbidding in the constant grey twilight.

The line had faltered briefly at the impressive sight. Boys stopped and stared in awe and wonder at the subject of the stories and speculation that had resulted in the 'Polar Bear Challenge' and the formation of this climbing expedition.

"Wow! Look at that! Just seeing it makes that march through the forest worth it," a voice cried.

Even the prefects had forgotten their roles as stern co-ordinators and disciplinarians, slowing down briefly in their fascination. They recovered quickly and shouts of "Move along, boys," soon ended the moment.

For Jack there was no magic in that first sighting of the mountain. It took his breath away, but not in a good way.

He's reminded of the time he and his younger brother, Brett, had found a plastic bag lying in a gutter near their house.

"What do you think's inside it, Jack?" Brett had asked.

"I don't know. Let's open it and see." Jack had broken a stick off a nearby tree and used it to rip open the bag.

The two boys had staggered backwards in shock. The stench was overwhelming. The bag was filled with raw meat. Jack had never forgotten the look of that meat, heaving with maggots and a putrid greyish colour, like human brains.

He'd run over to the nearby ditch and vomited. Brett hadn't puked. He'd wanted to poke the meat with the stick, but Jack had forcibly dragged him away.

Somehow, the mountain reminded him of that meat. There was something very wrong about it.

Sighing deeply, he returns to the present. Despite his thick, fur-lined jacket and hood, thermal trousers, gloves, waterproof cloak and snow boots, he is cold. He can't feel his toes and his calf muscles ache from trudging through the thick snow.

It's colder here on the open plain than in the forest which had offered some protection from the piercing wind. Squinting through his snow goggles, he tries to gauge how far away the mountain is, but his vision is too impaired by the continuously falling snow.

The boy ahead of him in the line drops back. Thrusting his hands into his pockets, he gets into step with Jack, matching him in stride and speed. "How're you doing?" he asks, giving Jack a sideways glance.

"I'm okay, still feeling strong, and you?" Jack flexes first one knee and then the other. The joints pop loudly.

"I'm a bit tired. I'll be glad when we make camp for the night."

"It's Peter, right?"

"Yeah, I'm Peter Harrison. It's hard to know who's who with all this gear on, isn't it?"

Jack nods, "Why'd you accept this challenge, Peter?"

Peter slows, reflecting deeply.

"No slacking," shouts a loud voice from behind them.

"Stupid git," mutters Jack resentfully. He is not enjoying the pompous and dictatorial attitude of the school prefects who have accompanied the junior boys on this trip.

We know the rules, Jack thinks.

The head prefect had laid out the rules before the selection process for this challenge had started.

"Boys who are fortunate enough to make it through all six qualifying rounds for this challenge are expected to be fit enough and strong enough to keep the pace set by the prefects. If you hold the group up by slowing down or getting injured, you are forced to drop out of the challenge. You get left behind with your tent, your gear and enough food and water to last a week. No exceptions will be made to this rule."

"I don't really know," Jack's thoughts are interrupted by Peter's response to his question. "I guess I thought it would be awesome to be part of the first ever team of boys to climb Glass Mountain. The prize for the survivors isn't bad either. I wouldn't mind being able to ask for anything I want for the rest of my life. What about you?"

"Same," he says shortly.

No way I'm going to tell this guy what I want. My mother's cancer and the biotechnological treatment I hope to get for her if I'm among the survivors, is not for sharing.

"I've heard it's impossible. To climb Glass Mountain, I mean. It gets its name from its sheer ice-covered cliffs that provide no traction or hand and foot holds for climbers. A few professional climbers have tried but have never reached higher than the third coil."

Peter reaches up and swipes at his googles, brushing off the accumulation of snow. "Is that so? How the hell are we supposed to climb it if the professionals can't? What stops them from reaching the top anyway?"

"My dad said there are frequent avalanches and earth tremors on the mountain. Also, there's some superstition that climbers shouldn't use ice picks or other tools to help them scale the mountain. All the climbing expeditions to date have used non-invasive methods that don't damage the surface of the cliffs."

Jack looks again at the mountain. Its strange, sharp angles and jagged peaks are not yet visible, but he knows they're there. His dad had shown him aerial pictures which indisputably indicate their existence, even though the pictures are indistinct due to the thick cloud that hangs over the top of the mountain. "Some of the climbing parties never made it back. Their bodies are still up there somewhere, buried under the snow."

Peter looks at Jack thoughtfully, "Maybe we're just lambs to the slaughter, then? Destined to fail before we start."

Jack looks at their target, its highest peak hidden in grim-looking cloud. "Well, based on the three ice picks we were all asked to bring with us, I assume they've changed the rules for this challenge. The challenge organisers must think we have a chance of making it to the top or they wouldn't have selected it for this year's challenge."

"We just have to be sure we don't fall by the wayside and get left behind." Jack shifts his gaze back to the boy walking by his side. He can't gauge Peter's reaction to his bland acknowledgement of the situation as his eyes and face are completely covered by his face mask and goggles.

"Definitely," says Peter. "In this environment, that's a death sentence."

"Yeah, it's intended to be a death sentence. The authorities don't want to have to give forty boys everything they ask for, do they? There were only fifteen survivors of last year's 'Anaconda Challenge'. That's what we signed up for, isn't it?" Jack is surprised at how calm his voice sounds, even to his own ears.

Am I calm? I suppose I am. I can't imagine ending and no longer existing, but I'd rather die than stand by and watch my mother die, little by little over months and months. Will the prefects really leave boys behind if they get into trouble? I can't imagine it.

Peter didn't answer. There was nothing to say.

***

The next morning, two of the boys elect to stay behind. The news travels down the line of boys, ready to start their forward march, like a weird grapevine. A boy named Colin joins up with Jack and Peter and gives them the details.

"They're twins. One twisted his ankle yesterday and can't walk on it. His brother chose to stay and take care of him until he can walk again," he says.

"I guess I'd do the same if it was my brother," says Jack.

I wonder what will happen to them, all alone in this icy wasteland. We've at least got dogs and sledges accompanying us and carrying our tents and food supplies.

Jack shifts his heavy rucksack on his back. It only contains his personal items and climbing equipment, but it is dragging on his shoulders and his back aches from carrying it for four continuous days.

Could I carry my tent and food as well if I ditched my climbing equipment?

He has no answer to his question.

The line of boys moves forward. The day has started. Jack, and a few of the other boys, turn and walk backwards, watching the small, lonely tent. Neither twin emerges. After a short while, Jack turns around and looks straight ahead.

The day passes extraordinarily slowly. There is less conversation among the boys today. Exhaustion is their new best friend and they conserve their energy by keeping quiet and concentrating on their goal of reaching the mountain. The snow falls relentlessly, effectively covering up their trail.

Our passage through this wilderness makes no difference at all. We pass by and it just goes on.

His complete unimportance in this icy universe makes Jack shudder.

I wonder how the boys we left behind are managing.

After lunch, another of their number falls by the wayside. This time it's a boy called Shahid. He just sits down and refuses to get up regardless of the threats from the prefects.

They leave him sitting there with his tent, backpack, and supplies. When Jack looks back, Shahid has not moved, has not started unpacking his tent for shelter. His immobile figure becomes whiter and whiter as the snow settles on him. He doesn't seem to have the energy to swat the flakes away. Jack looks forward again and keeps moving.

Later, he asks Colin, who seems to be an all-knowing oracle, why Shahid had stayed behind. "Was it because of exhaustion? He looked like a strong kid and he passed the physical assessment, so it seems a bit strange to me that he chose to stay behind."

"Nope," Colin says, "He didn't like the look of the mountain. He said he had a bad feeling about it and would rather risk the elements than climb it. Weird huh?"

The boys are even quieter during the afternoon. The most talkative among their ranks have finally fallen silent.

Is it merely exhaustion? Jack wonders. *Or are they considering their own mortality and wondering if they can keep going and what will happen to them if they don't? Or is it the mountain?*

Jack's own muscles feel weird, loose, and stretchy as if they don't belong to his body and his feet are distant lumps of frozen meat. In his own head he knows that there is more to his trepidation than this journey, there is something dreadful about the mountain.

He pushes these pointless thoughts away and focuses on the end of the journey, staring at the mountain, sizing it up.

I'll get to you, no matter what. I'm going to at least try to climb you, he silently tells his mountain nemesis.

It is much closer now. The shape of the mountain is weird, like a triangle, but from about halfway up, it has thick coils wrapped around it which ultimately rear up into a massive flat plateau. He can see the strange ridges that run across the top of the coiling part of the mountain.

To his mind, the intervals at which the ridges appear are too even to be natural. They looked almost like the spines of some great animal. Fear laps around the edges of his mind, chipping away at his determined focus and trying to make inroads.

Jack imagines himself plugging the little holes made by the fear. He visualises himself slapping cement over them to seal them closed.

I'm like the Dutch boy in the story. The one who plugs the leaking dike using his finger and saves his country.

The following morning, two more boys drop out of the challenge. They elect to stay together and take their chances alone in the wilderness rather than attempt to climb the mountain.

This time, Jack does not look back. He no longer cares about those who are left behind. Keeping himself moving forward, one step at a time, engulfs his every thought.

It's going to be fine. I'm going to be among the winner's and get my mother her treatment.

"We'll arrive at the foot of the mountain tomorrow," the word travels along the grapevine.

Tomorrow. We'll be there tomorrow and then the adventure really begins. Until then, I'll just keep moving forward, one step at a time.

***

The shining hulk of the mountain looms above him. Jack drops his head back on his neck and gazes upwards. It didn't look like a mountain at all, but more like an enormous cut diamond. The sides are sheer and smooth, unblemished by any protrusions or holes.

How can we possibly climb it? There is nothing to hold onto, nothing to pull ourselves up with.

Overwhelmed at the enormity of the task ahead, unexpected tears of rage and frustration overflow his eyes. They slide down his eye sockets and catch in the bottom of his goggles.

There's no escape for my tears either. They're trapped, just like me.

The burning and itching in his hands and feet is an unpleasant reminder of his frost bite. He flexes his fingers and the joints pop, like a string of firecrackers going off.

I hope I'm going to be able to handle my ice picks okay. It looks like I'll be relying on them, and only them, to hold my body weight when I climb.

Jack walks over to the other boys grouped around the huge fire they've built. The fire crackles and pops, striving to heat the frozen air around it. The wind howls and rips around them, tugging harshly at their clothing. Through his earmuffs, Jack imagines he can hear mocking laughter.

***

Jack stares at the wall of ice in front of him, focused and waiting. The sun is shining brilliantly but it holds no warmth.

More snow's coming, Jack sighs.

The head prefect gives the signal and the boys rush forward, each determined to start up the cliff face as quickly as they can. Jack is swept along by the crowd.

69

There's no turning back now, so I must just do my best to climb.

Jack smashes two of his ice picks into the smooth flawless ice, about half a metre apart. It requires force to sink them in sufficiently deeply to hold his weight. Pulling himself up, his arms feeling the strain, he stands on the jutting handle of the lower ice pick. He pulls a third ice pick from his belt and pitches it into the ice wall, at his shoulder height. He repeats the process, again and again and again.

The first coil is just above his head. Muscles trembling so much he must repeat his throw, Jack sinks his ice pick deeply into the coil. Mustering his last reserves of energy, energised by the thought of the short break he can take once he breaches the ledge, he hauls himself over the hump and lies on his back in the snow, panting.

Eyes closed; he feels the tremble. It ripples along the top of the coil. Jerking upright, he looks around. Further along the coil, several other boys, lie or sit. A few are eating energy bars.

Everything looks normal.

Did they feel the tremble? Is it a warning of an avalanche or snow slide?

The other boys look unperturbed.

So why do I feel as if something is about to happen?

His flesh has formed into goosebumps beneath his thick clothing and the hair at the back of his head is standing to attention.

He squints up at the coils above but sees nothing. There is no sign that anything is wrong. Glancing down, over the edge of the coil, he sees boys below, struggling up the slopes below him, and the puffy cloud of smoke from the prefect's fire at the base camp.

You're such a scaredy cat. Best act normal or the boys will rag you to death when this is over.

Unwrapping an energy bar, he takes a big bite, chewing slowly, trying to enjoy the cloyingly sweet, chocolatey taste that floods his mouth. The earth beneath him shifts again. Bile rises in his throat. Tiny bits of snow, like pebbles, fall on him from above.

Standing, he decides to climb again.

Spellbound

That's what I'm here for; to climb this mountain. It's best to get going. More snow is coming, and I should try to get this mountain climbed before it arrives.

His hands are sweaty inside his gloves. Leaning back, he gathers his strength, and launches his pickaxe into the coil above him. It sinks in deeply.

The scream is inhuman and unearthly.

Good God, what's that?

As one, the coils begin to twitch and move. Jack sways drunkenly.

Oh no! No way can this be happening.

The coils heave and twist.

No! No! This can't be happening.

He clutches at the ice pick with both gloved hands, trying to save himself from falling. His weight drags it free and he falls backwards, landing with a thump on his back on the pulsating coil below.

A bright coppery jet of fluid spurts from the hole. "It's alive! The mountain is alive!" Jack's screams are lost in the cacophony of shrieks and yells as the boys evacuate the mountain.

The ground beneath Jack ripples, as unused muscles test their strength.

Next, it's going to rise up and eat me.

For a moment Jack's brain freezes in utter panic. He can't think. Then, frantically, he pulls himself over the lip of the coil and slides down the sheer wall of the mountain. Great chunks of ice and snow rain down like mini avalanches.

With an enormous shudder, the coils start to separate and stretch out above him.

Looking down, the ground rushes towards him and Jack hits the deep snow in a soft billow, sinking deeply into its stifling embrace. It pushes under his face mask and over the tops of his boots, biting into his warm flesh like a horde of army ants. He flounders to the top of it and then lies, momentarily, on his back, gazing upwards and catching his breath.

The head of the enormous serpent looms above the mountain. It huffs and hisses out plumes of boiling hot steam from its gaping mouth. Its anger at being wrenched from its icy sleep is palpable.

Terror steals through his veins, it makes him almost drowsy.

I've got to move – run – this creature is going to attack.

Jack staggers to his swollen feet and runs.

There is nowhere to run to. The frozen wasteland extends on all sides, barren and free of a single tree or rocky outcrop. Jack slows and turns, walking backwards. He is reminded of his early actions when they left Shahid behind in the snow.

The head of the monster bobs down, towards its own body. A triumphant scream pierces the frigid air as it opens its gaping jaw.

Escaping steam billows onto the ice that has held the creature captive for thousands of years. Rivulets of boiling water flow down sides of the mountain, burning furrows into its glassy smoothness, marring them forever.

Plumes of fetid steam roll off the mountain, the stench of searing flesh from those boys who had not made it off the mountain brings churning bile up into Jack's throat.

Its body free, it rears up again. Seconds later, its head rushes down towards the boys to the right of Jack. Bright flames gush from its mouth. Jack watches his friend, Peter, turn into a moving pillar of fire and, almost instantaneously, into ash.

Jack sees the head turn in his direction. A blast of warm air pushes him, and he's thrown backwards.

Look at me, I'm a superhero.

And then all thoughts stop as his body crumbles to ash. The challenge is over.

BE CAREFUL WHAT YOU WISH FOR

Geoff Le Pard
South London, UK

geofflepard.com

Albert Albion stood back and smiled. It was as perfect as he thought it would be. He stepped forward and, shivering with anticipation, ran a finger over the rolling hills, imagining the perfect moment when Adam Able-Cain, the Genius, committed his soul to this canvas. It was such a visceral thing, this communing with an original Adam.

So powerful was his response to that touch, he staggered back slightly and lowered himself into a chair, exhausted. He must be the luckiest man alive; otherwise how did you explain it was him who had found the final piece? He shivered. If it had been someone else, someone without his knowledge of the history of the three Adam Masterpieces, who had been called to value that estate, the picture would have remained lost. He smiled to himself. He should feel a little guilty, he knew, for having persuaded the grieving relative to part with what was clearly an unloved watercolour. But if he hadn't, what then? The third masterpiece, for so long thought lost, or even destroyed, would have remained hidden. When you considered the alternatives, no one would really criticise him or think his actions unethical. The ends, in this instance, clearly justified the means.

He sat forward. It was barely credible that the keystone to this artistic miracle was in his den. He closed his eyes, visualising the moment when he revealed he had that last piece of the Genius' final work. He would be the one to bring the last third to its rightful place. He would be hailed a hero amongst the art establishment, a visionary. When he revealed the existence of his find, the world would be at his feet. It was no exaggeration to say that modern civilisation had waited for this moment, the reuniting of Adam Able-Cain's three History paintings.

He knew by heart Able-Cain's words, spoken when the paintings were first displayed to a fascinated public:

All the world, all the history of before, and the history to come, is within its frame, everything that was, is, and will be, is captured inside these works

One moment, Able-Cain's words filled the auditorium, the next he had gone, vanished in front of an astonished audience.

Then there were the rumours. The incessant whispers about a Faustian pact, of how Able-Cain had sold his soul to create these magic marvels. The insidious speculation had spread, "gone viral" as they say. The pictures had gone, too. One minute they were there, on that stage, the next the frames were empty, as absent as the artist himself. A clever trick, the cynics said it was a way of pushing up their value.

When the first painting reappeared - *Air* - in a skip outside a refurbished condominium in Seoul, there seemed to be some basis in those views. Its journey from its discovery to its current owner, a Belarusian billionaire, Oleg Distaninov was reputed to comprise a trail of deceit and blood. It now hung in the Metropolitan Museum, on long term loan. Many had wanted to know about the find, the price paid by Distaninov and how he had persuaded those who found it to part with this masterpiece. From the moment his PR people announced its acquisition by Distaninov, and the loan deal with the Met, Distaninov had disappeared from view; a paranoid germaphobe, it was said that he had become a complete recluse and spent his days circling the globe on his yacht.

Then -*Sea*- turned up in a crate of bananas in Costa Rica. Desmond Minnelli, Professor of ancient mysticism now owned the second work. How it left Costa Rica and ended up in Oxford was not known; suggestions of voodoo and black magic piqued the media's interest, but all that could be said for certain was it was displayed on the walls of the main hall of Minnelli's Oxford college while the professor himself never ventured from his suite of rooms, apparently researching the inspiration for Able-Cain's work.

And now he, Albert Albion, auctioneer and art lover had found -*Land*-. He wasn't like those other two. No way was he hiding. They might be paranoid about their privacy, but he was going to make the most of this opportunity. He was going to let the world know what he had and do all he could to bring about a reunion of the three paintings.

Oh yes.

He squeezed his eyes shut before forcing them open, as wide as he could, intent on saturating his vision with every little detail of his new love. He blinked. The painting had gone. Not only that, the room, his chair, his house had all gone. In their place was the landscape of the painting, but this was a real landscape. There was the river running fast to his left, the boggy ground beneath his feet, the chilled air as the mist rolled from between the hills, making him shiver.

He shook his head, certain this must be some sort of daydream, brought on by his heightened emotional state, a result of his extraordinary success. He shut his eyes again. This time, he heard, in the distance the unmistakable sound of his phone's ringtone.

Feeling relieved he opened them and recoiled in horror. While he remained standing on the wet, boggy ground with the mist moving ever closer, he could now see a painting; but this painting was of his room, of the chair he had been sitting in, with the table where he had left his phone positioned to the chair's left. As he gawped at the phone, painted in the same idiosyncratic style used by Able-Cain in his works, the ringing stopped and his own voice cut in, asking the caller to leave a message.

A movement to his left distracted him. Two men, each holding paintings the same size as the one in front of Albert were approaching as fast as the boggy ground allowed. Even though he had never met them, he recognised Oleg Distaninov and Desmond Minnelli. Each man had aged well beyond what should have been their current ages and each had the same expression: they were terrified. As they approached, they kept glancing towards the ever, encroaching mist.

It was then that Albert noticed the small, squat figure that walked at an even pace a few feet in front of the roiling mist: Adam Able-Cain RA, laughing.

As Distaninov and Minnelli rushed to his side, the sound of his brother's voice brought him back to the painting in front of him.

"Is it true? Have you really got Land? Amazing. I'm on my way."

Hands tugged at his sleeves.

"We need to go."

"Now."

The two art collectors were frantic.

"Why?"

They didn't answer. They were already running past the painting of Albert's den. As they did so they began to smudge against the landscape. He turned to look at the mist, at Able-Cain. This time he could see what they were running from. It wasn't the near-hysterical artist but what he led towards Albert.

The mist was changing, finding definition as it neared. The smoky front had become a face, rolling inexorably forward; an eyeless face with gaping, gasping mouth and gnarled tongue, its prongs lacerating the sides of the mouth as it spread across the plain and soaked the marsh water like blood, colouring the translucent flesh. The eye sockets filled with fire as the cragged teeth scoured and scarred the slopes and valley floor, devouring all in its path.

Albert did what nature had hardwired into him long before art and civilisation veneered his life, hiding so many, awful, instinctually understood, fundamental truths.

He picked up his picture and ran.

MONTAGUE LAST AND THE CRYSTAL SLIPPER

Geoff Le Pard

South London, UK

geofflepard.com

In his dreams, Montague Last found freedom. Sometimes he would sail away on the silver waters of the crystal river. At others, the waters called him to their peaceful embrace, guaranteeing an end to pain, humiliation, and despair. On each occasion, his guardian angel, his fairy godmother beckoned him to accept this gift and be free. The waters were calm, their gestures said. Accept them.

In those dreams, all Montague Last needed to do was take that first step.

"Monty, wake up. Please." The familiar voice pulled him back, the step forgotten. "You must wake up. Monty, please." Once more his head was filled with fear. "They're back already."

Montague didn't open his eyes. He knew the scene too well. He stood and knocked the bench where he had fallen asleep. His eyes popped open, in time to see the pool of silvery liquid spreading quickly from the flask, mocking his dream.

He watched as Cindy tried desperately to scrape the residue back into the flask. He wanted to stop her, tell her not to bother because it was defective, and they'd know soon enough. But he let her continue. At least it stopped her crying for a while. He held his head in his hands. All *they* cared about was the product. He'd have to make more. He couldn't be worrying about her, about the girls.

Her snivels made his flesh creep. He snatched the flask from her and poured a beaker, pushing it to her. They both knew it was what she wanted, what she craved. They also knew it was madness for him to offer it and her to take it if they were back as she'd said.

He squeezed his eyes shut, trying to empty his mind of what they'd do this time. When he looked up, Cindy had limped back to the door, peering out of the crack, her bruised bony shoulders unnaturally twisted. He poured the beaker's contents back in the flask, not that it would stop their anger. He considered the emaciated girl again; even though he couldn't stop being indifferent to her condition, part of him wished he could do something for her. They were both victims here, even if they both knew they would kill the other if it meant their freedom.

Slowly he stood, knowing he needed to be ready to do what *they* demanded. As he steadied himself against the table, he realised he no longer cared. Once he had believed he would be let go, as they promised. *When you've paid your debts, Monty.* He'd forgotten what it was he owed, but now he knew he would never repay it.

As he studied the familiar twitches of the girl, he knew neither of them would leave. Whatever they'd done, whatever promises they'd been made, their fates, his to make product and hers to sell it to whatever gullible punter wanted it, were inextricably linked. They'd remain in this sweltering hellhole of a prison forever, or until one of them finally, gratefully accepted whatever end was granted them.

And while he accepted the reality, he also knew he couldn't take it anymore. This time would be different. As his head filled with this new power, she turned as if she, too had be suffused with the same thought. Her gaze was slow to meet his but as it did, hope expired. She nodded towards the corner of the room and mouthed "Ella."

Of course, there was now another. Ella-May. The new Cindy. He could see her now, rocking metronomically, her face never raised, her whimpers constant. She didn't move unless dragged out; she ate nothing, pissed herself where she sat and never spoke. Once, he thought, he might have felt sorry for her, but he no longer knew how.

But Cindy did. That was what was different. Now Cindy had another to care for, to whom she could be fairy godmother.

The sound of the locks sliding back brought him into the present. In moments he was blinking as sunlight streamed in, fracturing the Stygian gloom with a parody of freedom. Two guards, bemuscled unsmiling brutes stepped inside and framed the door. There was a pause before the tall man's silhouette filled the gap. Martin Charmant, their very own Prince of Darkness.

"Doctor Last, I hear you've been sampling your own product. Is that wise?" The laugh was both cruel and knowing. "You don't think I'd let my chemist, my very own magician take such an easy way out, do you?" His voice changed, a businesslike brusqueness entering it. "I have some new recruits to help distribute your products. They're such loyal customers, too. You should be gratified to know how popular you are."

Charmant stepped back and three more women, girls really, stumbled forward; two looked terrified as their eyes darted wildly around the room, while the third did her best to maintain a semblance of poise. Montague recognised the attempt at resilience knowing it wouldn't last.

Charmant swiftly crossed the room, digging out a set of keys as he moved. Behind him, the guards closed the gap left by the open door, forestalling any ideas of escape. "Ladies, this is where the magic happens." He fiddled with the padlock and pulled open the door. Stepping inside he switched on the stark overhead light, revealing a complicated set of glass refraction jars, pipes, and tubes. "There," he opened his arms wide as he showed the laboratory to the three women. "Didn't I promise you the earth? Our good doctor takes the very humblest of materials and with a wave of his wand, produces the magic that will turn you from paupers to princesses. It's everyone's very own fairytale."

Two long, manicured fingers picked up a small transparent tube with a funnel at one end and a globe at the other. "All you do is drink from this, your very own "crystal" slipper and the good Doctor's meths will turn each of you from drab non-entities to princesses in your own magical realm."

He spun and stared towards Cindy and Ella-May who were watching. "Ask Cindy and Ella. They both know of the joys that can be bestowed by embracing the crystal slipper. It fits everyone perfectly."

Montague shrank back. The guards hustled the three newcomers forward, while the other two women, both broken yet desperate for product slid towards the door to the laboratory, their desperation for another fix overriding their fears of the guards. For them, escaping reality couldn't come soon enough.

Montague understood that bone deep craving, wanted that oblivion for himself. Yet he knew with a gnawing certainty that his dream of escape was futile; no savior would ride up and save them. Nothing would change now. There was no going back to the dull delicious mundanity of his previous existence; for him midnight would never come to set him free.

THE TWISTED SISTERS

M J Mallon
UK

mjmallon.com

Luna kept an abandoned shopping trolley in the far corner of her garden where the wild mushrooms grew. Within which lay a discarded face mask, surgical gloves, and a replica of a precious stock item. Nestled towards the back of the trolley there was a burnt cover of an ancient book. Legend stated that the book had belonged to a long line of descendants, witches of great renown. Many feared the book, believing that the chosen could read the spells within if the book spoke to them. Luna and her coven of witches revered its demise. Its old pages had become yellow and torn and its spells strangled by the white trumpeted bind weed which overpowered everything in its path.

"Words and books written in the past have little meaning in 2020," Luna muttered. "It's all about us. My Twisted sisters," her hands opened in a gesture of welcome as she smiled at each sister in turn.

The Twisted Sisters sat bathing in a circle of splendid moonlight which immersed Luna's back garden in a strange light.

"Thank you for your welcome, Luna. We sisters have much to discuss, so many important matters, your plans for your latest venture?" asked Aradia, leaning forward, her green eyes gleaming with curiosity.

"There are ten Team members Aradia. Five of each sex who adopt various personas based on fairy tale legends..."

"And what is the purpose of this nonsense?" Minerva the eldest witch, butted in, her voice rising a notch. She gritted her teeth, her forehead revealed deep burrows of unease.

"2020 has weakened the world, Minerva. After Coronavirus the economies are in tatters. Shops are closing everywhere. People are tired. They *want* excitement," replied Luna.

"I see. You're bored!" laughed Rhiamon, giggling, she feigned a yawn.

"No! It's not that, Rhiamon. Boredom doesn't drive this. Ambition does."

"Ambition to do what exactly?" asked Minerva, ignoring the youngest witch's previous comment.

"To take control. With a franchise of successful shops beginning in the capital and then spreading throughout the world we sisters would be all powerful."

"But Luna a fact remains. You have weakened our coven by allowing a man into your house!" replied Aradia, spitting the words with vehemence.

"You worry for nothing. He won't be any bother, I promise Aradia. Steve and I are in love. He will do as I say. I will make sure that he does."

"It has come to this," replied Minerva, clucking her tongue, and shaking her head. "Non-Wizard lovers. Shops! Bah. Disgraceful!"

"Strange times call for desperate measures. Witches must move with the times. Let's vote," commanded Aradia.

The witches cast their votes to the listening moon. The reluctant moon took some time to speak. When he did his cheery moonlit smile vanished. "Witches, before I depart for another day let me announce the result: Three votes in favour of Twisted Fairytales, one vote against."

Minerva hunched and scowled. "Age is no longer a guarantee that others will listen. My old friend the moon, you disappoint."

The moon sighed as it began its descent. "I'm sorry Minerva. You are of the old school of witches and I value your counsel, but it was not my decision to make."

***

Luna had perfected the Little Miss Red Riding Hood look complete with red cape. Her long, dark tresses fell in curves beyond her shoulders giving her a wholesome, dare to kiss me look. The basket she carried may have looked innocent, but who knows what was lurking in amongst her crisp red apples. There was something sharp, metal and long, a silver object and a flash of long red tresses hidden in her roomy basket.

Luna cracked lewd jokes whilst handing out face masks and gloves. The usual idiots didn't want to wear masks. Excluding, vulnerable adults, children or innocents, the strict protection policy in store meant that they were never permitted in store, *ever*.

Luna didn't fret. She coped with all manner of difficulties with a flash of her special Twisted Fairytale smile, saying, "Sorry Madam, sorry Sir, it's company policy you *must* wear a face mask at all times."

"Ugh," or "Why," or "Do I have to?" would be their standard reply.

Luna's smile would grow wider and more menacing the more they complained. Her smile strained at the edges of her face, pulling her ears apart until her face mask threatened to pop.

That was the sort of smile it was, a smile that threatened to rip off her face. Looking at her in alarm, the complainer's jaws would drop, and they'd snatch a face mask real quick. She'd grin, her face would zip back to normal, her eyes calm, and her mouth still.

Today, Luna had moved away from the meet and greet area and was standing in the middle of the store. The manager had divided the shop into distinct sections: the Grimmer than Grimm Fairytale area, Rapunzel's Ladder of Coiled and Sculpted Hair, Hansel and Gretel's bake your own witch oven, towards the back of the shop there was a new area - Design your personalised Twisted Fairytale, which lured customers with a large glowing neon sign that said: BY STRICT APPOINTMENT - ONLY AVAILABLE AFTER APPROVAL FROM THE STORE MANAGER.

Luna replenished new sanitised stock to the shelves. She picked up a pack of coiled and sculpted hair, which the manufacturers had packaged in sturdy plastic. The kind of plastic which could only be opened with a pair of sharp metal incisors. There was a warning on the pack: DO NOT OPEN - DANGER OF DEATH. Above the display there was a video playing, showing the pack's contents in action. Luna watched the screen, a strange smile playing with her lips. The actress in the video cut through the pack, tearing it apart, the hair piece sprang to life, coiling and lengthening in her hand. She screamed as she swatted it away. It paused for a moment, then crawled up her chest, over her face, and attached itself to her head. She yelled even more loudly as the hair piece coiled around and around her head, the now lengthy piece of rope hair tightened around her scalp and travelled down to squeeze her neck. The actress's eyes bugged out. She clawed at her head, which just made the hair more resolute in its intention. She waved her arms frantically, fell to her knees, blush-coloured skin highlighting her distress. Then, apparently bored the hair grew tired and released her. She tumbled forwards choking, gasping for air.

The video ended and in moments started playing the same hellish scene again.

Some folks will do anything... mused Luna, chuckling, rolling her eyes. She wondered how much they had paid that particular actress to shoot that video. And if sometimes the hair didn't let go…

She patted the pack, caressing it lovingly. She sighed and set it on the shelf with a promotional sign next to it, on special offer it said.

Her colleague Phil appeared. His freckled face twitched as he moved towards her.

She reluctantly stopped her shelf stacking.

"Hi Phil, First Day. *Welcome!*" Her high-pitched welcome rang throughout the shop.

Phil winced as if she'd made the announcement via a loudspeaker. He pulled at his face mask, twisting it this way and that, adjusting it as his nose peaked out.

"Make sure your nose is always within the safe confines of the surgical mask. We have much to run through today, routine stuff to begin with: health and safety training, face masks, gloves, disinfectant. Don't let me see that nose again," Luna growled.

She gave him a playful shove towards the safety area at the front. He almost tripped over his enormous feet. Her bag of apples tipped forward, giving him a glimpse of what lay hidden in her basket.

His eyes widened, and he gulped. He wiped a bead of sweat off his forehead.

"Are you okay Phil? You look as if you've seen a monster lurking in my sweet apple basket. Or perhaps it's too warm for you? Be careful," she laughed, her eyes narrowed as her chest heaved. "This is our health and safety area, gloves, wipes, disinfectant, you name it we've got it covered."

She explained the various areas, and he followed her at a safe distance as if he didn't want to get too close. She purposely didn't mention the change room to him.

"What's that noise?" Phil asked, pointing. His large adam's apple wobbled, sinking down into his neck.

"It's one of our regular customers trying on our new item: the sculpted hair. Lush, what a lucky lady. I wish it was me!" she flashed him a gleaming smile that showed her white teeth.

"Oh," he replied, wiping a bead of sweat from his forehead, he gulped. "Do you think she's okay?"

"I'm sure she *will be*," Luna replied. Her gaze followed his eyes to the changing room cubicle. The blue curtain twitched back and forth. A disembodied leg kicked at the curtain, cracking it open to reveal a glimpse of a person struggling within. There was a loud crash as the shopper tumbled backwards and one leg pushed the curtain aside before the curtain promptly fell back in place.

Phil rushed towards the outstretched leg.

"I *wouldn't* if I were you," Luna growled. Grabbing his arm, her sharp nail extensions dug deep into his skin.

Phil hovered, "But…"

"Don't but me, Phil!" Luna's nails broke the skin of Phil's arm. "Our customers hate it when we intervene. They prefer to enjoy their near death experience in peace, believe me."

The leg moved a bit, and a whimper came from inside the cubicle.

"See, I told you. That's a jovial sound, isn't it?" Luna flashed Phil a grin, and her basket of apples shone even more brightly than normal.

Phil nursed his wounded arm. His eyes looked lovingly at the exit, but Luna knew he couldn't leave. He had a family to feed, two young kids, and a pregnant wife.

Luna moved away from the changing room and paused near to the BSA Appointment only area. Phil took a few moments to follow her this time.

She turned and glared at him, her eyes piercing his with irritation. "You are coming aren't you? And stop bleeding on the shop floor!" she passed him a plaster which she drew out of the basket, giving him another glimpse of what lay inside.

His eyes widened, and his skin blanched. He didn't dare to ask her about the contents of her basket, so instead he pointed a trembling finger at the BSA Appointment area. "What's that?"

"It's only for senior team members," she replied as she pointed at her badge. Her eyes widened. "Nothing for a new member of staff to worry about."

He nodded, but his eyes fixated on the sign.

The leg within the changing cubicle reappeared and then retreated backwards. The customer chair tumbled out of the changing area and flew back in. Hangers ricocheted like boomerangs, whizzing out, threatening to hit the other shoppers who were perusing nearby. Loud crashes and bangs filled the air. At last a silence ensued as the unfortunate female shopper struggled out, revealing the damage done: torn clothes, tights ripped and tattered. She clutched the coiled hair in two divided segments between each hand, her arms outstretched, as she tried to make her way to the till. None of the shop assistants dared come near her. The other customers stopped to watch her movements with a mixture of fascination and fear.

Whispers echoed in the store as the shoppers grouped at a safe social distance, strangers commenting on what they could see.

"Oh, I wish I had the guts to try that!"

"Poor soul, she looks half dead."

"She's taking it home!"

"I prefer baking my own witch, that coiled hair is a darn nuisance. Look at the damage it has done to her hair and scalp!"

Only a few strands of hair remained on her head. Red scratches, rope like burns marked her neck and her blood-red eyes were rimmed in red too. She stopped to try to stuff the coiled hair back into the plastic, but it kept on reappearing and threatening to do more damage. The well-trained cash register assistant grabbed the hair from her. She threw it to the floor and stamped on it with special metal shoes before repackaging it for safe transportation home.

The customer smiled. She swept a solitary piece of hair away from her eyes. "Thanks for the lesson. I'll do that from now on. Do you sell the metal shoes too?"

"Yes, they are £29.99."

"I'll have them too! That'll teach coiled hair to behave badly!"

Luna smiled, she'd seen it all before. She stroked her Senior Team Member badge, recollecting the day she'd received her promotion. How proud she'd been and how glad to receive the huge rise in her salary. That very night she'd celebrated with her partner Steve by opening several bottles of booze. They'd drunk themselves silly. Steve didn't seem to care what she'd have to do to receive such an enormous increase in pay. He didn't ask those searching questions. After COVID19 had messed with their lives, nothing seemed worth worrying about. At least nothing worried Steve...

The next morning Steve wasn't smiling so much. He had a terrible hangover, the worst he'd ever experienced. He couldn't get out of bed, he couldn't move his limbs. So Luna, being the caring type, left a tray of food, drinks and her special vitamin tablets beside his bed. She kissed him on his forehead and promised that he'd feel better soon. She packed her lunch in tubs for her long shift ahead. On her way out, she lingered by the hallway and heard the reassuring sound of Steve gurgling and snoring. She'd call his work later and tell them he wasn't feeling well.

That first day as a senior team member was long and boring. Perhaps it was the hangover. As the day progressed, she felt more and more dehydrated. During her breaks she tried to rehydrate with lots of water, but that just prompted her to go to the toilet.

Towards the end of her shift, her manager Ruby approached her. She was a short woman, with a severe fringe, black hair and even blacker eyes. She asked her if she was free that evening to take an Appointment Only Session.

She just smiled and said yes. What else could she do?

Her boss's ears moved, suggesting a hidden smile, but the smile didn't touch her eyes. She handed her an envelope with the client's wishes, which she said Luna mustn't read until five minutes before the appointment time.

Luna held the envelope in her hands. It felt heavy and yet it was just a thin envelope with perhaps one or two sheets inside.

She nodded. Ruby's eyes were black and brooding above the red face mask. "Don't forget you mustn't sneak a peak at the envelope until it is the time to do so."

Ruby instructed her how to lock up the shop but left her with no further information.

Luna watched Ruby's back as it trailed away, leaving her alone in the shop. She picked up her basket of apples and found a tissue to give an apple a shine. By ten minutes to the appointment time she had polished all of the apples. A mixture of curiosity and excitement worked their way through her mind. She looked at the clock; it was now eight minutes to the hour. She decided to peer inside the envelope and reseal it again.

The envelope opened easily, as if her boss had purposely left it that way.

Inside, the first line said:
Don't be afraid.
"A witch afraid?" she said aloud.
There was nothing else on the page.

Behind that was another sheet which lay folded into tight squares.

She could see two words on the front of the first square:
He's coming.

She heard a knock, a rat, tat, tat on the basement door. She was still on the shop floor. It was a long way down to the basement, past all the stockrooms, which were full of so many dangerous Twisted Fairytale toys. It was dark down there. She looked at her watch. It was now five minutes to the hour.

She took a huge bite of the apple and opened the rest of the message.

It said: *He's Coming. Meet him in the basement.*

She let out a gasp, dropping the half-eaten apple, it fell to the ground and rolled away.

Steve…

Running down the stairs, she made her way to the dark, grimy basement. Her foot caught on a rag which moved of its own volition. She lost her balance for a moment but stopped herself from falling. The lights flickered overhead, threatening to switch off. She peered down, screwing her eyes tight as she discerned that the rag was moving. She gave it a ferocious kick; it yelped and cowered.

"An ancient piece of coiled hair. Pathetic old thing. You couldn't harm a flea," she mused out loud as she continued on her way to the bottom of the steps.

On the basement floor, she rushed past the toilet, her bladder complaining. She prayed that a member of staff had locked all the stock rooms. If any new toys escaped, they would slow her down. She had known it to happen. The keys dangled on her thighs. She stopped for a moment, checking each of the doors in turn. They were all secured. On route to the large double stock doors, she blindly ran to the loading bay.

Her mind raced as she ran.

Steve would be there.

When she opened the door, the area looked deserted. But she heard sounds, a low steady moaning, grinding and clicking. She bit her bottom lip, drawing specks of blood. It was so dark down here that she had trouble distinguishing anything. The eeriness of the setting made her mind play tricks on her. She imagined a man coming towards her with a long, sharp knife. Listening more carefully, she realised that the sound was a metal shopping trolley moving towards her. As the trolley came closer, she could see a hazy figure pushing it. It was difficult to make out what it was, but it had the most startling, long red hair.

The pulse on her neck forced her skin to protrude. She stood deathly still as her feet pressed hard into the ground. As she drew the long knife from her basket, she inadvertently pulled out the hidden zipper.

The trolley whirled around and around, doing a strange dance. It came closer and closer until it stopped in front of the loading doors. Then she saw the shadow that propelled the trolley. It was a man dressed as a grotesque sea world character: red lips, long red hair, aqua blue eyes, an oversized multi-coloured seashell bra, with a sea green fish-like tail. She smiled, her creation had been approved, a Twisted Mermaid.. .

As he moved towards her, she moved with intent, raising her arm. He flinched, awakening from his drugged state, his eyes widened with shock.

The sound that erupted from his mouth was inhuman. She set to work with the zipper. Time to use it.

***

Afterwards, she patted his face mask in place. Fresh specks of blood covered the mask. He lay at her feet. She picked him up, glad that she used to weight-lift as a hobby, she folded his shocked body into the oversized packaging section of the trolley.

Before she sealed him up with fresh plastic, she peeled his face mask back. She smiled as she surveyed her handiwork and the silver patchwork zipper embellished with the words "Open me."

She wiped the bloodied knife with a clean Twisted Fairytale tissue and returned it to her much-loved basket.

She patted Steve on the head and touched her badge. "You understand, don't you darling? The coven and I decided that you'd make a wonderful Twisted Mermaid. You've always enjoyed dressing up. Remember all those times when you wore my lingerie secretly? I pretended I didn't realise, but I've always known. What an honour! You're about to become our most popular stock item. I'm so proud. I had to come up with a fresh promo idea. Coiled hair is so last year."

Luna brushed a tear away. She touched the zipper on his mouth and slowly eased it apart.

Steve's eyes filled with tears. "Don't cry, my dearest darling. Everyone will love you. I love you." She reached out and caught one of his tears.

She removed her face mask. Touching her face, she moved her fingertips down to her mouth. She felt the stitches, his mouth on her face. "See, I kept a keepsake. I always loved your beautiful smile."

She held the knife and it gleamed, its sharp edge poking out, tempting her to play later.

Steve never spoke again. Luna had wielded that knife swiftly to remove his voice box.

She removed her old badge and pinned her new one to her chest. It said, Twisted Sister. She smiled as she wheeled the trolley past the stockroom. She heard the old manager within; making a muffled sound. She'd deal with her later.

She had work to do!

Spellbound

RED

Adele Marie Park

UK

Copyright © 2020 by Adele Marie Park. All rights reserved.

firefly465.wordpress.com

Just how long can you hold a piece of toasted bread, fresh from the toaster, between your fingers before it hurts? I must be a wimp. Two seconds and I drop the toast, in the sink.

"Really! Welcome to another day, Red."

I suck my fingers and ignore the toast. The sound of laughter coming from the television grates in my ears and pounds inside my head.

I stride through the kitchen my bright red hair flopping into my eyes, it's how I got stuck with this nickname, and stand in the doorway of the lounge.

"Emily." My little sister is four going on fifty and she can ignore better than even I could. Oh my God, it's that stupid show again, the one with the piper dude. He's obscene. They really shouldn't let kids watch this shit.

"Emily!"

Nope still no response. I spy the remote lying on the chair and go for it. A moments pressure and silence.

I expect Emily to be pissed but she turns around and hell, I don't recognise my sister. Her face is twisted into a raging mask of terror and she comes at me before I can back away.

Pain registers and I glance down in horror to see Emily chomping on my hand, the one holding the remote which I let go. Pain reflex, and I scream.

"What the? Seriously, Emily?" I cradle my throbbing hand and watch goggle eyed as she turns the television back on and sits in front of it again.

I'm still frozen when the damn programme finishes; she only had around a minute left. She gets up from the floor and smiles at me. She smiles at me!

"Ready for kindergarten now," she says and flounces past me, her blonde curls bouncing as she skips. I scowl at her back still holding onto my throbbing hand. "I'm so telling Mom," I shout but I hear the back door open and know she won't have heard me. I won't tell Mom, she has enough to worry about working shifts at the local hospital and Dad; well he barely keeps his job as a fisherman. There is only me and Emily and as soon as I graduated high school, I got a job too.

Now I must find the keys to my car, drive with an injured hand and act as if all this is normal. The chaotic start to the morning is usual, Emily acting as if she's the child of Satan, not so much.

I mumble a lot, under my breath, it helps but after I lock the door and turn around, I don't see Emily.

"Really! We're having this situation now?" I throw my bag over my shoulder and it immediately slides down again but I charge ahead huffing and puffing like a hippo in the water. I catch sight of her red boots as I round the corner to the forest road and get ready to haul her into the car. I stop. She's talking to someone and as I start walking towards her again, I recognise Dodge the old graveyard digger. Gross. I'm sure he's a perv because he makes my skin crawl, always has.

"Emily come on or else we'll be late," I use my best control voice without having to look at Dodge, but something pulls my head up and I find he's looking at me.

"Holy stars!" His face changed, it morphed, folded, or melted into a long-nosed thing with green eyes. I feel my empty tummy flip over.

"Morning, miss Red. We were just talking," he says, and I realise I've reached Emily without knowing and I grab her arm.

"She's got school. Bye," Emily goes with me easily, but I can feel his eyes follow us. Once at the car I turn and, yep, he's still staring. Emily is in the passenger seat already, so I push away the feeling I'm in a horror movie and get in the car.

***

Downtown traffic flows this morning which is a good thing for me as I'm on auto pilot. Emily's behaviour, Dodge's weird transformation has made my mind float away more than usual.

Just in time I remember not to pass the kindergarten and stop with a squeal of brakes. With the engine turned off I lay my head on the steering wheel for a second then I hear Emily get out of the car. Sniffing back tears I gaze at her and smile.

"Bye, Red. I'm sorry I bit you," she says then scampers off to join the line for class while I'm still vibrating from how hard she shut the door.

"Get a grip. I need coffee, that's all," this mantra calms me until a loud knock on the window makes me scream.

I turn around and I can feel the hairs on my head stand up, I don't want to imagine the expression on my face.

"You fudging idiot! Get in here!" I'm in pain again, this time from speaking through clenched teeth at my idiot boyfriend.

"Hey, Red. What's up?" he says as he slides his long legs under the dashboard and grins. Now, normally that grin is enough to make me as sweet and as trembly as jelly candy, but today?

"You just scared the bejeebers outta me!" He just gets the door shut as I roar the engine and focus on the road ahead.

***

By the time we reach our destination, the only art workshop in town, where we both work, I've told him everything.

"She bit you!"

As he says those words the whole thing crashes down on me and I start to cry, not pretty, little, movie star tears either, huge galumphing sobs which come with free-flowing snot.

He holds out an arm and I'm in his embrace. I wail and cover his shirt with snot and tears while he, sweet guy, strokes the top of my head.

I look up at him, his wavy thick hair flops over one blue eye, the other one is brown which earned him the nickname, Wolf. Yep, Red and the Wolf partners in love for nearly five years now.

"I don't want to worry you," he says then stops. I hate when people do that, as it's always a downer that follows.

"But?" I ask taking a deep breath in with a noisy snort.

"Well, my neighbours' kid is the same. Won't stop watching the damn show and screams like a demon if anyone tries to take him away from the box."

I don't realise I've been holding my breath until I take a gulp of air and start coughing. Wriggling out of his embrace I stop retching and sit staring ahead at what was my normal life fleeing out of town, suitcase in either hand.

***

Okay, so there's something going on.

There is a small café attached to the art studio and I draw waitress duty. The café is extremely popular with ladies who have the time and the money to waste on cakes and coffee. You know the type? They smile at you but then proceed to ignore you as if you don't exist on their radar, but that can be useful.

They gossip mostly about each other but today it's about their kids and how since that kid's show has started their little darlings have turned into monsters. Normally, I'd say they were monsters already, but, the first chance I get for a break I tell Wolf.

My stomach gurgles but I throw the bread roll into the bin, I can't eat when I'm twisted inside with nerves. I don't want there to be anything wrong, I want life to remain simple, but Wolf notices something's not right as well.

We part at the end of the day with the promise to meet at my house and go through the internet. There's got to be something on the web which will explain this.

***

With Emily in bed, Mom at the hospital and Dad still at sea the house feels comfortable, warm, and safe. Wolf is here too, so he might have something to do with the whole atmosphere.

I take a break from staring at my lap top screen and leave Wolf to the search. The bedroom window is open a smidgen allowing a trickle of air to caress my face as I stand beside it. I look down at our back yard, Mom's done her best to make it pretty with flowers and shrubs. The smile on my face is wiped off the moment I change my gaze to the woods that back onto our property.

"Wolf. Come here and look at the trees."

"Why what's wrong with them. Oh."

He sees it too, good. That means I'm not crazy. Something weaves its way in and out of the trees. A glowing figure which seems to be dancing. My heart pounds loudly in my ears as the blood rushes around inside me like an ocean. The hairs on the back of my neck bristle because of the wrongness of what we're seeing. The figure continues it's dance oblivious to us but now music of a sort is added to the strangeness.

I frown and purse my lips. "That sounds familiar." Then it hits me with a sucker punch. "It's the theme tune to the kid's programme."

Wolf stares at me then I see recognition flare in his expression.

My tongue goes dry and all I can do is stare at Wolf with my jaw sagging as inside me a growing dread causes me to hyperventilate.

He keeps staring at me his brow furrowed, and I want to shake him, but I can't seem to move. I must. "Emily!" I manage to blurt out and then he curses which lifts my paralyses and together we run from my room, along the corridor to Emily's room.

The door is slightly open as I left it, but Emily is not in her bed and a frantic search of cupboards and under the bed are futile.

Panic makes me clumsy and on the way down the stairs I tumble, slipping down the last few steps. The pain in my back kicks in but adrenaline gives me a boost and I burst out of the back door. Nothing.

I run around the corner to the front, Wolf following.

"Jesus!" He breathes the word in my ear as we stare at the scene in front of us. Half the neighbourhood has congregated in the middle of the road. Women shout children's names and father's mill around like drugged zombies.

"No." I whisper and grab the wooden fence with both hands.

***

I turn around as I hear a familiar sound which penetrates through all the others.

"Mom!"

I run towards the crappy car she drives, the noises it makes have always brought me comfort.

As I reach her, she is standing beside the car gripping onto the keys and staring at the scene of the once peaceful neighbourhood resembling a war zone.

Seeing Mom reduces me to tears. "I'm sorry, Mom. I'm sorry."

Finally, she focuses on me and I watch as her chest heaves with a deep breath. "Red? What's going on? I heard children were missing. Where's Emily?"

She has a kind of confused expression as if she doesn't know where she is. I guess it's because she was in the middle of a fourteen-hour shift.

"She's gone," I say through bubbles of tears. Nice one, Red, real nice.

***

So, the local cops. Yeah, they're out of their depth. It's a small town. Mass child disappearances are not a normal occurrence. They've radioed the next county for help, and they are trying to keep the media out of the situation, so everyone has been asked not to use social media.

Wolf stays with me and Mom as the reality sets in that Emily is gone. I pop painkillers to ease the pain gripping my head and I cross over to the window to open it and let some night air inside. My nose is blocked from all the crying and the cops who were here left their own scent of coffee, stale smoke, and shoe polish.

The catch on the window is tricky and as I sigh a flick of movement catches my gaze and I frown. There is a faint light bobbing between the trees. My eyes go wide as I recognise Dodge the creepy old gravedigger. I should have known. He was talking to Emily just today.

A strange taste fills my mouth and I swallow but it's still there. Fear and anger rolled into one bile-filled knot has come rushing upwards from my stomach. If he's harmed Emily, I will kill him.

Getting Wolf to the kitchen without blurting out exactly what I saw will be difficult. Mom is gripping onto his hand so tightly he's grimacing.

I rake my fingers through my hair and tap the side of my head with a fingernail. We must follow Dodge, times running out. I feel it by the twisting in my guts.

I'm saved by Mrs White from two houses down. She arrives as if she is a guardian angel and takes control.

Mom is held in her arms and allowed to pour out her grief in huge bursts of sobs and unintelligible words.

I grab Wolf's arm and pull him through to the kitchen. "I just saw Dodge in the woods. It's him! I know it! We have to follow him."

Any words of caution from Wolf don't register as I still have a grip on his arm and pull him through the back door into the quiet of the woods.

"Red this is madness. We don't even have a torch."

"I've played in these woods since I was a sprout. I know where I'm going."

***

I should have added that I knew these woods in the daylight. Darkness changes everything. A friendly branch in daytime turns into a monster that grips your hair and won't let go. A pounding heart hampers your hearing and every sound is ominous.

Dodge's light flickered and moved around until I was confused enough to stumble into holes in the ground and bump into trees. Behind me I kept hearing Wolf's muttering and curses. God bless him, he followed me without question. I hope I'm not leading us into the valley of death. I'm nervous, shoot me, I quote things when I'm afraid.

I stop as Dodge's torch vanishes. My breath wheezes out of me and I take deep lungsful of loamy air. A cough builds up and I place my hand on a tree trunk willing the irritation to go away, concentrating, and trying to stop rising fear from paralysing me. The shadows are darker than black ahead of me but as I focus on not coughing my awareness sharpens and I notice black shadows in front of me are in a rough circle shape.

The cough is forgotten as I realise, I'm looking at the mouth of a cave and without waiting to say to Wolf I trust he will be behind me and take off, sure of my direction now.

At the entrance to the cave I halt, one hand on the rough cold stone. The hairs on my arms stand up and shivers play a polka up and down my spine. I do not want to go into that blackness. A giant mouth which will swallow us, bones, and all.

The palm of my hand scrapes across the rough stone and a sharp pain makes me exhale loud enough to break the terror. I breathe so heavily my shoulders rise and fall but I push through the barrier and I am inside.

The scent of mould, dead things and long forgotten nightmares strangles me as I force myself to take each step. The darkness is not complete the stone walls of the cave are lighter the further in we go and underfoot I crunch on small pebbles.

Just as it seems to go on in a straight line we come to a ledge. I hear voices and recognise Dodge's drawl of an accent but it's sharper. Something answers him, I think it's a voice, but it sounds garbled, full of growls and hisses.

I hunker down and gaze downward. I cock my head to one side and listen as the sound of music drifts upward.

"That's the song from the show," Wolf says.

I grunt a reply my voice harsh with the fear that twists in my gut and makes me want to run away from this place and forget all about it. I can't. Emily is down there; I just know it, I can't explain my sense, but I cannot leave.

When a cry from Dodge shatters the air around us, I move, scrabbling down the gritty slope, Wolf's warning cries echoing as he follows.

I reach level ground, totter, and then fall on my ass. The thump jolts my bones and as I stare at the light filled cavern, I've landed in I want to be back in bed tucked up and asleep.

Dodge is not Dodge. He's that creature I saw when he was talking to Emily. A tall, thin, hunched over in pain creature. His face is long, his nose longer and he is staring at me, his green eyes screwed up and liquid drips down the side of his face.

I might have stayed on my ass if it hadn't of been for that scream and the sound of scuttling across the floor.

Oh no, Miss Wilson the kindergarten teacher is a prisoner here too. Except…

I scream, a primal sound torn from deep inside my gut.

A huge spider, a massive insectoid body with eight gigantic legs that wears Miss Wilson's head except she has a mouthful of sharp teeth and her eyes… Oh God help me, she has eight eyes each of them whirling orbs of red.

She's coming straight towards me and fear has taken my senses away because I can't move. My brain is refusing to believe this monster exists and it's having such a hard time it's going to get me killed.

There's a sweeping movement behind the monster and Dodge is on her back yelling something which I don't hear but Wolf does because he drags me away to the side as the monster's attention is now on Dodge.

A thin thread of luminous white stretches from the gigantic body of the spider and is attached to a figure straight out of fairy tales.

A character dressed in reds and greens, a peaked cap on his head, is playing a flute from which the sickening song emerges. He's tied to the spider bitch queen and in front of him sit the children, all of them.

"Emily!" I struggle in Wolf's grip as the adrenaline of seeing my sister kicks in and I kick and scream until he has no choice but to let me go.

"Break the connection!" My head swivels to where the voice came from.

Dodge is holding onto the spider, but he is covered in bites and scratches. A moment of calm washes over me and I know he is telling me to break the chain between the spider and the piper.

I must stop my gaze roaming everywhere and concentrate on the bond between the spider and the piper. It reminds me of a worm, white and pulsing with obscene life. Yuk. If I don't do something now it's all over.

I close my eyes for a moment then open them and rush towards where the piper holds the children hostage to his music. As I stop my feet slide on the floor of the cave, and I knock the piper over. His flute skitters away from him and we lock gazes. His expression is full of horror as if he's woken from a nightmare, but he turns over and I see where the spider has spun her web. Gritting my teeth, I grab the threads with both hands, ignoring the nausea which rises as I touch something so unfamiliar and alien. I tug but it's like getting the glue off those cut price stickers.

The piper moves onto his knees and as I pull, he crawls. There is a moment when fear replaces action and I think we're going to fail, but with a final tug on my end the threads release with a squelchy popping sound. I fall back and the damned threads flop on my face.

"Get them off me!"

Wolf is there beside me and he grabs them. He holds onto them and I watch as he takes his lighter and holds the flame to the ends.

The spider screams and rears back from Dodge who, taking a chance, smashes his fist into her face and he keeps on hitting until I can't watch anymore and turn away.

There is a different sound but one that I recognise which makes me burst into tears. The children: they are all aware now that the piper is not playing.

Wolf is trying to calm them down, but I grab Emily and hold her against me in a tight embrace. I guess I'm trying to hide the horrible battle between Dodge and the spider, who was her teacher. Jeez, what a mess.

I forgot about the piper, but I catch a glimpse of red and watch as he takes a knife out of his coat and buries it deep into the spider's body.

She screeches and the cave shudders before she slumps, a few of her legs twitching. Dodge kicks the body, but his foot comes away covered in green slime. As we watch, the spider body dissolves into a gloopy, green, and red puddle.

The children are crying while Dodge and the piper stare at the putrefied corpse. Then, as quick as his name, Dodge gazes at me. "Get the children out of here. We'll clean this up."

Between us, Wolf and I herd the missing children out of the cave and into the forest. The tops of the trees are piercing the sky and we can see daylight stretching over them. How long were we down there?

Spellbound

There are still people outside on the street and two police cars so when we appear everything goes crazy.

Adults scream, children bawl as they are re-united with parents and siblings. I cuddle Emily and with Wolf following us we slip away and into my house.

I know we'll be asked questions. What the hell do we say?

"Yes, sir, officer it was a giant spider bitch what done it?" I shake my head and tiredness brushes me. I have no idea what just happened or why. As I take a gulp of air inside me, ready to cry, there is a timid knock on the back door.

I open the door and find Dodge standing there, in his real form and as I stare into his eyes, I get the sense I'm the only one who can see him like this.

"It's all taken care of Miss Red," he says and there is so much I want to ask him but not now. Now, I stand watch over those I love because once seen never forgotten. There is another world out there and it's a nasty piece of work.

Spellbound

HIGH, HIGH, AND ONWARD

Dan Alatorre

Tampa, Florida, USA

geni.us/DanAlatorreAuthor

The sea was rough that day in June
When Swanson said we'd sail.
He swore as in a battle cry,
"The Marksman will prevail."

"High, high, and onward!"
The Captain cursed the sky.
"I'll let no gale wind cower me.
My crew would rather die!"

The ship was tossed and waves a-crashed
Upon its wooden decks.
And as we gathered down below
We feared the ship would wreck.

"Now, Ma," said I, "let's worry not.
These sailors know their craft."
But in the lantern's swaying glow
Her look said I was daft.

Spellbound

She held a worry in her lips
Her eyes were wide with dread.
"'Tis not the storm, nor crew's resolve,
"That ice my heart. Instead,

"Our days at sea now worry me.
"June days are surely marked
"With pain and death and agony.
"'Twas known when we embarked."

The words were right that my wife said.
July was our best bet.
But dark times came to London, so
We took what we could get.

Each year, June days bring horrors deep.
Dark times without a warning.
Crews like *The Marksman's* could be lost
Upon a June day's morning.

July was safe; we knew this well
We'd sail without a worry
But troubled times to London came
And hastened our long journey.

"Fear not," the Captain called to us
As lightning lit the sea.
"We'll land upon Bermuda's shores
"As safely as you please.

"Then to Virginia, your new home."
He'd keep us safe, he said.
"We'll steer around this devil storm.
"Now, off with you. To bed!"

"High, high and onward!"
He shouted to his men.

Spellbound

Then thunder split the sky in two
And lightning flashed again.

That night we did not sleep at all;
We huddled close for praying
Until at last with dawn's first light
The Marksman stopped its swaying.

Although the sea was calm and flat
No captain did we find
Nor any of the officers
Just crew were left behind.
The others, taken by the storm,
Washed o'er *The Marksman's* sides,
According to the Bosun's Mate
Who I could tell had lied.

"High, high and onward!"
The Bosun told his mates
And they did follow, ev'ry one,
Aligning all our fates.
"The Marksman's listing bad," he said.
"We'll sink, but don't despair.
"I'll plot a course for closest land
"And there we'll make repairs."

They steered into a strong crosswind
And as we headed south
I wondered what had happened in
The teeth of the storm's mouth.

The next day found us on the sand
Of some forgotten cay.
The men were nervous, that I saw
When told the island's name.

It was decided some should go
to search the island's wares.

Spellbound

"Be back before the sun sets, lads.
"No telling what's in there."

So, six young crew departed and
They vanished 'mongst the brush.
That night, the air was filled with screams
and none returned to us.

Again, the morning light did come.
Again, some crew went forth
into the island's inner lands.
Again, night brought remorse.

Three days we sat upon that sand
and listened while men died.
Not one returned to tell us what
any had found inside.

"I'm done," the Bosun said at last.
"This place is cursed!" he wailed.
"No treasure's worth my life, you lot!
"Untie the lines. Let's sail!"

"High, high and onward!"
He shouted to his men
They raised *The Marksman's* anchor high
And set to sea again.

But now *The Marksman* had no list.
Its path was straight and true.
Whatever had been done to it
The island did undo.

And then,
Upon the midnight call,
A scream came from the decks.
The night watch hurried down below
Fearing what might come next.

Spellbound

"The island gave to us a curse!"
"The Captain, from the grave,
"Has come to take revenge on us!"
The tales were vast and vague.

"High, high and onward!"
The Bosun, trembling, said
To murdering London mutineers
Now cowering in bed.

That night, the last scream from the crew
Echoed across the sea.
The curse these men had feared so much
Had come for them indeed.

"High, high, and onward!"
June's fangs were there to see
And bathed in each man's blood because
The curse on board was me.

Spellbound

THE COMEUPPANCE OF ROB KEARNEY

Ellen Best
UK

ellenbest24.wordpress.com

Mary crouched low and arched her back, her face twisted, every sinew screamed in pain. The night shadows moved, as the wind howled through trees and leaves. Snatches of light between the moving clouds made the blood pulse on her tongue.

"Mary, Mary," Rob called, his voice screeched against the wind.

He clutched at twigs and brambles, renting the flesh on his face and forearms, but he kept searching. Rain hit in jabs that stung his exposed skin, fired into his eyeballs and warped his vision. The crack of limbs made him duck. Bark smashed into the earth distorting his view, spinning him in a new direction. Fists clenched he bellowed against the roar of the wind.

Mary was close enough to stroke his creased brow. She could hear the terror in his voice and notice his cries falter. Like a fox, she would stay hidden, but afraid to let him out of her sight. Mary watched his frantic hunt. Hours passed, and the rain eased, as thunder rolled deep overhead. Afraid that lightening would expose her pressed into the bark of a tree, Mary took a chance and moved in the opposite direction; the sound of her escape covered by lightning hitting a huge fir tree, smashing it into the undergrowth.

The debris-strewn forest floor was hard to manoeuvre. Strands of ivy crisscrossed the earth in readiness to trip her. Roots tangled and the lack of light obscured any chance of moving swiftly. Not knowing where he was, made the fear worse, but on she ploughed. Near the rolling river was a long since fallen trunk, unlike most of the trees it was fat and held a coat of moss and lichen. With her raw hands, she hollowed a space beneath the middle, where she squeezed in. Mary clawed the wet earth, with bloodied fingers, dragged in leaf mulch, twigs, and pine-needles to mask her hiding place. She wished her breath were quieter and her tears didn't plop so loud. Without a doubt, she was sure if near, he'd hear her. Frozen, wet, bleeding with her senses on high alert she remained hidden.

Rob crouched at the river and gulped at the violently rushing water, desperate to soothe his throat. He whipped his head towards a creak or snap. Eyes bulbous, as he searched the dark for a clue, a sign of her whereabouts. A bolt of lightning lit the forest, followed by a clap of thunder. Rob used its intermittent light to search the area moving between flashes, covering ground safely but slowly. On the second crack, the light hung for a few seconds and he caught sight of a scrap of khaki cloth snagged on a bramble; torn from Mary's coat as she ran.

Fired with a new enthusiasm he shouted between claps of thunder; in hope that she'd hear. "Mary, please! Don't be scared, Mary, I promise."

Four or five minutes between the quiet and the roar told him the storm was moving. He ploughed on, the louder he called the more frantic he became.

Her gut churned, and legs burned with cramp, she felt a clawing at her feet. Instinctively she knew there was more to be feared in the open than under the fallen tree. She heard what she thought was him, her teeth began to uncontrollably chatter, Mary gagged as she stuffed her fist into her mouth. She heard his pleading voice, saw the soles of his boots as he climbed on the trunk above her.

Mary's body had somehow found a way to separate from her feelings, the pains and cramps were less than her fear. She could hear a tirade of swearing and stomping in the undergrowth; she heard his temper flare. Mary became warm as terror opened her bladder. Barely ten feet from her, ranting and spitting was her hunter. One more streak of light illuminated the clearing showing his barred teeth, curled lip and bulging eyes. Her fist still pressed tight between swollen lips. Some creature crawled near her nostrils. Tears washed her cheeks and stopped the clawing for a while. How could she have got Rob so wrong? Now wasn't the time to dissect events that landed her in the position she was in.

Mary must have slept because she opened her eyes to shards of daylight, through undergrowth that so-far camouflaged her. She had to pry her fingers from her mouth to gulp air. Dust and debris, filled her, choking each breath.

Exhausted and filthy Rob stretched, combed his flop of curls back with his fingers and winced. Strands of hair slid like cheese wire between scab and flesh, where nails once were. As if just realizing what he had done. He shook his head and dropped it into his hands as he rocked on his haunches. What would he do? How would he get out of this? His thoughts were ramshackle at best. Muscle and bone ached as if he'd ran a marathon.

"Where are you? He cursed … Where are you?" he bellowed, with his face facing the once turbulent skies.

Mary thought she heard him call and trembled.

"Mary! Please, don't be scared, Mary, … Mary." This time she knew he had returned, his sounds were distinguishable, less frantic, not broken or distant.

Mary was long past having feeling in any of her limbs, knowing herself incapable of quiet movement or the ability to run all she could do was freeze.

Rob found the clearing where he lost any trail the night before, he recognized the place where he drank. The water was only knee-deep and trickled across boulders on the riverbed, a vast change from last night's torrent. He washed his face and hair, drank a cool mouthful of water from cupped hands; slumped where he squatted.

He decided he'd head for the tent to give one last search, then remove all traces of their visit. A couple of hours passed before he found it; pitched, amongst a group of pine trees. You couldn't tell there had been a tussle, other than piles of newly strewn pine needles and fresh debris on the ground. Another camper wouldn't know anything more than an island storm had occurred.

In five minutes, gear was thrust into two rucksacks: except the sleeping bag. The bloodstained fabric had scabbed. Between the teeth of the zip meaty strips of gouged flesh dried. A stickiness filled the fibres that were supposed to keep warmth in their bodies. In his rush, he failed to spot the splashes on the inside flap of the double-skinned tent. The baseball bat that was meant to provide fun; sat next to the bag waiting.

Looking at the items brought back the begging, and the ugliness of her. Face puffy and distorted with fear. He felt a stir in his loins as he remembered wiping her face with the flat of his hand, as he shushed her. His lip curled and he salivated while recalling her exposed body, tight and ripe for the picking. Rob tried not to think about the way the bat rammed, how excited it made him. He put it from his mind with a shake of his head, her electrifying scream. With her unconscious, he had stepped outside, needing to clear his head; work out a plan. Fear had taken over his thoughts. His thoughts had turned to sheer anger when he returned to finish her off. The shock was physical; she was gone.

Rob's mind slapped back to the now. He gathered the rucksacks and threw them in the boat. He had buried the bag and bat along with his blood-stained clothes. All he could do now was to cover his tracks. He must get back in time; continue as normal. He pulled the outboard motor to life, circled the Island one last time. With binoculars pressed to his eyes, he searched the dense pine forest for movement, from the vantage point of the river. Sneering when the only movement was a grizzly with her cubs, on the bank.

With any luck they will eat her remains, he thought as he swept an arc with his rudder and turned for the mainland.

Mary couldn't believe her ears. She crawled forward, just enough to see the vessel head off. Forty minutes passed before she saw him again; a snatch of light glinting from the water as the sun hit his binoculars. A fawn hopped over her, followed by two more sets of hooves. She'd seen no sign of the boat since late morning. Not trusting herself to move, she lay in her wet stinking hiding place.

She must have slept because the sun had made the stench intensify; defecation never smelt good.

Hungry, dirty, scared and in pain Mary began to stretch. Gently she rubbed her hands together; trying to circulate the blood. The pain was hot and dull but eventually, she had control over her fingers. Enough feeling in her upper body to pull herself free. Mary slid in and out of consciousness on the bank alongside the river. When the sky darkened, and thunder rolled back it was dusk. She had lost precious time, it was the time she needed to get clean, make herself safe.

Dragging her body to the water's edge she drank greedily, retching as the ice-cold fluid hit her empty gut. Smoothing it over her arms and face with her hands, she numbed some of the pain and washed dried blood away. It took what seemed a lifetime to remove her jeans, she submerged her lower body into the rush of the water. It was with dock leaves and ferns she cleaned herself. The freezing water and shock made her teeth chatter and skin turn blue. Eventually, she was able to release her underwear, clogged with dried blood and faeces, took patience and tears.

Mary tugged on her jeans, they bit hard on her tender skin. The seams were sharp and made her wince. Pulling on the still wet sweater over her head took strength. It was the strength that she desperately needed to conserve. Rain returned beating the earth like a drum. The wind swirled and threw muck and pine needles around; to make her task harder.

Automatically she trudged the curve of the river. Her keen eyes spotted an old wooden structure, built between two trees; shoddily raised by a hunter as a hide. Crawling into the gap she pushed hunks of fallen limbs and wood to conceal the entrance. With no way of knowing how long she slept, or even if she slept, between the nightmares and the storms; Mary fought to stay awake. Her temperature rose and fell like the wind, her damp clothes barely gave any warmth. Mary would relieve herself as far from the hut as she dared. She would wash and drink at the murky water's edge then fall once more into a restless sleep.

Mary lost count of time. Foraging only in her immediate area, as her discomfort was too great to move more than a few feet in any direction. She took her chances by eating raw golden mushrooms snuggled at the base of a great Ash. A small patch of fiddlehead ferns sustained her weak body. Mostly she drifted in and out of her sweat induced nightmares.

One morning she woke to heavy crashing and groaning, it was as if something was forcing its way through the forest. Frozen with shock, her eyes dilated. Less than ten yards from her, with paws like dinner plates a huge grizzly lumbered her way. The wind was strong, and she prayed it wasn't taking her scent towards the huge beast. Mary summoned all her strength and began to mutter under her breath. Mary wobbled as she stretched her hand between the branches, … but even magic won't work when you're that broken. Unperturbed the creature passed within feet of her. She twitched at yet another near miss, another one out of her control. The events made her more determined than ever to find her way back to civilisation.

Rob listened for something on the news, the radio broadcasted traffic offences and misdemeanours, drunk or drug-fuelled fights, but no missing persons. This meant he had time, time to think. The weekend would take him back to the island, Rob hoped the storms would lessen enough so a search would be possible, but not enough to allow the ferry and bridge to open. Until then he would hide in full sight, at work.

The warehouse was busy, its vicinity to the airport brought contracts aplenty, more than most firms, so Rob was left alone as he liked it. He lived in Delta, it felt like a village, everyone knew each other's business. Townsfolk used the same schools and shops, stayed in the same house for a lifetime. People fell in and out of each other's kitchens and lives, a community of gossips.

All but the vagrants fell to their knees each Sunday, and Rob sneered at them. Holy Joes he called them, or hypocritical, small-minded people. He scowled at the collections for the homeless, frowned at the good works in church groups to raise funds for veterans, and the mindless. All the people that he thought didn't deserve a life.

His mother, Dara, at eighty-six years old, baked cookies and sold them in the hospital foyer. She visited the first nations with an open mind, food, and conversation. Knitted for the bedridden. He said she came home stinking of death from the dregs of life she met in nursing homes. People who were dissolving in their beds; he hated what she did, he despised her.

He showed up for work, grunted a greeting and left at the end of a shift. Not knowing or caring about anyone but himself. He walked the backstreets at dead of night, smoked his roll-ups and kept out of sight. Rob used the thrifts to get any clothes or gear, keeping his spending to a minimum; his look shabby and himself easily forgettable.

Once a week he took his mother to get her provisions, this week with him being wired and on edge, he had less patience with what he called her constant verbal diarrhea, moans and wittering on about crap he couldn't stand. Rob unloaded the truck of the brown bags, with his head bowed, his hands clenched, and he ground his teeth into his lip.

Dara spoke softly as he stacked bags on the worktop. "I'll put the pot on Rob, coffee and some soup, ... would you like some soup? I've a nice loaf, bread baked by Karen, you remember, the old girl with veins at number two."

Banging about the kitchen she continued. "What do you think Rob? Stay a while with me? Brigid's daughter Zena will be coming for a visit ... we could have dinner, such a nice girl, you couldn't do better; time you had someone."

He dropped the last bag on the worktop with a thump. She prepared the oven to warm his bread and heated the hob for the soup.

Rob grabbed her wrist from behind. "Shut your big mouth."

Slamming her palm on the hotplate he pressed down. His hand slapped over her mouth forcing her head back into his shoulder. Four maybe five seconds passed before he leapt back with his hands thrown up in submission, he watched her struggle to the sink and hold the blistered hand under the faucet. Her legs could barely hold her as she slumped, all her weight on the edge of the sink. She mewed through tight lips as bubbles of saliva slipped out the cracks, falling in strands to pool in the sink.

His face twisted in revulsion, "You asked for that! How many times? I tell you over and over, shut your mouth." Scraping stiff fingers through his hair he ranted through barred teeth, spitting as he spoke, "You never learn."

He paced the floor and slapped his hands against the table, as a pulse flicked at his jaw. She didn't beg or turn to look in the face of her son; she knew better. Rob tugged the bottom of his jacket, rolled, and snatched his head, straightened his back, and marched to the truck.

***

Gretta dropped her keys on the hall table and shouted. "I hope there is wine on the menu Mary." Frowning she opened each door, looking for her best pal and flatmate. Everything was as expected except for Mary's absence.

Gretta's return had been planned for weeks … there was no way Mary would miss it. The friends shared everything, the flat, food, clothes, and secrets. Gretta pressed her smartphone; it went straight to voicemail. Next, she searched Facebook for clues. The last post was a photo of Mary's feet dangling over the side of a small boat, toes rippling the water, and #IslandCamping underneath it. That post was Friday afternoon, today was Monday.

Gretta opened their shared desk and fired up the laptop, she searched history and followed a trail to Instagram. Mary had posted a picture taken over her shoulder, a boat being secured by a man, dressed in fatigues, his body side-on, the photo all artsy as Mary liked to do. #CampingOnVI Dated Friday.

She called the gallery where Mary worked, only to be told what she feared, Mary hadn't been seen since Friday. Concerned, her colleague asked if Gretta would call her back when there was any information. Mary had been given exhibition space for her photography in return for work in the gallery. A brilliant opportunity for her. It was her dream. Gretta knew it was out of character to not go in or send a message.

Grabbing her keys, she jumped into her car. Delta being small and village-like was a godsend when it came to getting help. Within the hour she had an officer at the flat. He said others were working on the case. At least she knew her statement was being taken seriously. It was not long before the vessel was traced, and a call to apprehend Rob for questioning was put out. The Ladner Police were following up all family contacts. All Gretta could do now was wait.

The local news ran a call for information on the whereabouts of Robert Kearney. The report was regarding a missing woman from Ladner. Footage, of a very distressed elderly Mrs Dara Kearney; with a heavily bandaged arm, was shown. She was being rushed through St Paul's Hospital on a gurney. Reporters interviewed a reluctant woman of about thirty, Zena it seems found the injured octogenarian. It was confusing, Gretta sat open-mouthed in front of the screen. Afraid to move, waiting for news.

The area the vessel was moored in had been identified by search and rescue. A team of experts were combing the area throughout the night. Eventually, they found a buried sleeping bag and a baseball bat which was sped off for forensic testing. At about the same time detectives recovered two rucksacks and a tent at Kearney's home. Splashes of blood were soon identified as Mary Holder's and the D.N.A. matched the gruesome find on the sleeping bag on the island.

It was five in the morning when Gretta received the call to say Mary was safe. She was dehydrated and in a poor state, but alive. Other than that, Mary was in Hospital and under close guard. She couldn't be told any more. Mary's recovery was both long and hard, she had been moved to protect her while the search for Rob continued. Gretta packed Mary a bag and an officer collected it. Contact could not be made between the girls.

Rob listened to the police radio when he heard a call for his arrest. With connections, to a survival group, he met in Spokane years earlier, he thought he had found a way out. The group had taken him in, taught him the skills of the wild, he was encouraged to explore his needs for pleasure. He had kept in touch with Merl, one of the group. He remembered him as a weak, distasteful bloke. Rob remembered Merl boasting that he had looked in the face of Satan, more than once, when he was on a mission. With his help and a little cajoling, he could escape the mess.

The police traced a call Kearney made to a burn phone, and in that one call, the group was compromised. The cult-like group had been infiltrated and now a covert operation could proceed, furthermore it was linked to Kearney. Unbeknown to him he had put centuries of secrets at risk.

Rob teetered on the fringe of the group for months, excluded from meetings but given tasks to complete alone. Cloaked and under cover of night he stalked towns, grabbed targets, left them tied and gagged in an underground bunker deep in the forest. Neither caring nor wondering why. Fed up with the secrecy, Rob formed a plan. He hid beneath bracken and watched. When he had evidence of sorcery and witchcraft, he knew he had leverage.

Rob met Merl at the clearing as planned. A package with food and money was thrust into his hands along with a phone; he would get fresh instructions tonight. Merl scuttled off, his weasely face twitched, his head snatched back and forth as he went. He hated the stench of Merl … oozing fear from every pore. Rob waited in the musty bunker, only the flicker of a lantern to see by. He rubbed his palms together staring at the phone, his knee juddered like a piston, his eye twitched.

Each second felt like an hour.

Tonight, he thought. *Tonight, I will make them pay.*

The beep made him jump. He dropped the handset, it bounced from the floor bursting in two.

Scrabbling in the half-light to reach it lost valuable time. The sim card, he couldn't find it. His scratching of the soil hampered the task and escalated his fury. Fat dirty fingers struggled to push it home. Now all he could do was wait.

That night, he sat, hunched in the hole, not knowing if the handset would work or not. Two A.M. it beeped, waking him from a trance. The instructions were clipped, no room for discussion. Dropping a hooded cloak over his clothes he began the trek. He had two days to collect a potion from a derelict store, the woman would be tall, blond with pink tips to her hair. She would answer to the name Chanteclaire. With her would be an adolescent, she must be taken with care, cover her eyes carefully whatever you do-… do not look into them, do not harm the child. On completion of this last task, we will give you a new identity and enough money to start over in another country. With that in his mind, he pressed on. Pleased he would not need to use his plan after all. Completion of this last task would set him free.

Rob reached for the charred door handle unsure if it would work due to the damage. Just as his fingers neared the door, it squealed open on rusted hinges. He bobbed his head round to look behind the door, wide-eyed, mouth open ... staring at the space. For a moment he was unnerved.

In a doorway to the room beyond he could just make out a figure. A fire sprang to life in the hearth behind her. The hood dropped to her shoulders revealing her hair. Shocked, he stepped forward, He mumbled, "Mary?" He was flustered at what was in front of him, "What's going on?"

A curdling scream filled the air, as the woman's hooded eyes sparkled, a beam of light shot from her eyes. Flames engulfed his body. The woman stood and silently watched, as his body writhed in pain; until he lay cremated in front of her. She picked up a book from the shelf next to the now cold embers of the fireplace. And took one last look at the dust and cinders on the floor. Lifting her hands, she carefully pulled on the hood, covering her hair, disguising her face. She gently positioned her scarlet stiletto heels on the ground, her eyes flashed amber as she elegantly stepped over the smouldering corpse and disappeared.

A ring of the doorbell woke Gretta, she lifted her smartphone, clicked the app to see who rang her door. Mary stood on the doorstep waiting, her bag dropped at her feet. With no thought for slippers or a wrap, Gretta ran towards the door. Mary frowned at the sound of feet slapping the wooden floors. Seconds later and it was flung wide.

They threw arms around each other. Locked in tears and sobs, together the friends clung on. For endless minutes they held each other.

"How, why, I don't understand? Have they got him? Is he dead?"

"... I can't say I understand either, but I am safe now. Believe you me, he got his comeuppance. That is all I can tell you, trust me, Gretta."

Over Gretta's shoulder, Mary's eyes flickered to amber, and back.

Spellbound

THE GLOWING

Nick Vossen
Sittard, The Netherlands
www.goodreads.com/nickvossenauthor

It is said the glowing folk of Heksen Hill only come down and show themselves after tragedy has occurred. More often than not, death. It was no surprise then, that in the rain swept night of the last day in October, when five men filling their lungs with soot and dust for meager pay lost their lives in the mines, that the lights appeared on the hill's broad side overlooking the village. In the darkness of the storm they flickered menacingly, all the way from the border post of old farmer Ferguson's land, down towards the peat bogs and marshes where the air is cool and stifling, and where devils will whisk you away for trespassing.

It was not long after the mourning bells tolled in the middle of the village square, at this most unusual of times, that my initial anxiety turned into sorrow and regret. Towns clerk Peters, holding a big black umbrella that could narrowly withstand the sweeping winds, came over and told me of the unfortunate fate that had befallen my father. He told me that he was sorry for my loss, and that he would stop by soon to make proper arrangements. He avoided the topic of the obvious omen that lit its way along the town, just past the backyard of Mr. and Mrs. Dekkers' home. He wished me a good night, all things considered, and left me there standing in front of my door. Sodden and alone, unclear how to move on from the fact my father had been buried alive, his bones crushed beneath debris and rock, his life slowly fading away from his body and off to kingdom come.

I never really have been a pious man. Oh, I went to church yes, and Lord knows I believe. But I never asked much from religion. Not unlike him, not unlike father. But that night I prayed. My knees had gone red from kneeling on the broken wooden floor panels besides my bed, and I felt sickly and weak due to the lack of sleep. But prayed I did. Prayed that my father would find his way towards forgiveness, would be allowed to enter the gates of Heaven and reunite with my mother, whom I also missed so dearly. The rest of the night felt like a fever dream. I had constantly been drifting in and out of sleep. Often, I would be awoken suddenly by such mundane occurrences like the rapping of the tree branches by the wind against the roof of my house. Other times I woke due to more unsettling events. Bad dreams had been a constant for me ever since I was a young lad. Now after all those years, they had started to turn into some sort of waking nightmare.

I opened my eyes only to feel a presence in the room with me and a growing pressure surmounting on my chest. Through the cracks of the walls in my humble abode I swore I could see feint lights blinking. Blinking they did, in and out of existence until ever closer they came. That is, until they blinked no more and I felt free as to breathe easy again. Nothing evil lurked in the dark here, I thought. Just mice and the dreary rains of autumn.

Rap tap tap, the branches went again, now against the stained-glass window above my front door. Just as I sank back into that turbulent uneasy sleep once again, a little voice inside my head reminded me that there were no trees near my front porch.

The great mining tragedy of 1891, they had called it. It was only the next day, and the paper boy had shouted it all across the market square as if the entire ordeal had only been a terrible distant dream, instead of the grim reality that I, and many other good townsfolk, had faced only hours before.

As I had suspected, the day had mostly consisted of neighbors and distant family gathering out in front of my house all day, waiting for tea and biscuits in order to chat me up for five minutes to tell me how sorry they were for my loss and how my father was such a good man. I was having none of it, to be fair. I did not even get time to properly mourn, for no funeral arrangements could me be made yet until the next shift of miners went down nearly two-and-a-half thousand feet into that black abyss in order to attempt to free the remains of my father and his fallen comrades. I let the chattering of my well-wishers continue as their meaningless words, preached only to keep their own prestige and petty reputations in town intact, flew in and out of my head within seconds. My mind wandered off as they cackled on.

For in the clear light of the sun, so rarely seen in the orange haze of this October country, I saw something shine down from the half-way point of the hill. It had been so bright it had blinded me temporarily. Only due to the incessant inquiries of my visitors, who had seen my face turn white and the beads of sweat drip down my forehead so unusually for the time of year, I managed to snap out of whatever spell had taken me in its grasp that sudden moment. I waved away their faux concerns for my wellbeing and requested to be left alone to my own devices and sorrows for the rest of the day. And alone I was, save for a brief visit by Peters informing me that the attempt to uncover my father's remains had, as of yet, proven unsuccessful. Alone I was, until night fell, and I once again made a feeble attempt at comfortable sleep.

In my dreams I was wading through the back bogs and fens that stretched out across the northern side of Heksen Hill. It was night, but somehow, I could see clearly and very far into the distance. I remember standing on the edge of the reeds, staring in disbelief as I saw the golden shimmering apparitions wandering along the outskirts of the wood. It was right near the border towards the next county over and several of the glowing ones seemingly loitered around a particular border post beneath a large willow tree. It was the largest in the region in fact, I somehow knew, and its ancient bark was still revered today long after the last ritual fires of the hill had extinguished so many years ago. I remember my feet being planted deep into the soil, yet somehow my body floated closer and closer towards the frightening manifestations. Upon the moment they spotted me, they all turned around in unison and the cold, shadowy hand of fear grasped around my neck as I saw each of the glowing men wearing the face of my late father.

"'Tis a damned shame. An injustice!" I heard one of them wail. The words were like acid splashing in my eyes and ears. Gurgling and hot. "No rest, no rest until all rights have been wronged," another howled.

I tried to reason with them. I'd ask what they wanted, why they had chosen me. But it was to no avail. I witnessed in silent horror as one by one the golden apparitions opened their mouths wide in agony and despair, letting out painful shrieks and mournful moans. One by one I saw them floating towards the heavens and witnessed their lights fading in the night sky until it was only myself and my own horror-stricken thoughts left shivering in the swamp.

I awoke again to the rapping and knocking on my walls and front door. Listening carefully for the wind as to find any evidence of another seasonal storm, I could not find any. Once again, I felt that strange presence creeping about in my quarters. Once again, I felt the pressure on my eyes and ears as my body and senses wanted to tell me that there was something not right in my house. Something that was looming just outside my peripheral vision, or perhaps simply just on the other side of the wall, outside. And again, as quick as it came, so it also disappeared. But something was different this time. It was only after I had flung off my covers and got ready to get up for a glass of water, that I stared down at my feet and saw the traces of fresh mud glistening between my toes and the dried sand curling around my ankles.

That morning I hurried across the town square. I tried my hardest to avoid Town Clerk Peters, even though I had gathered he was actively searching for me. I knew the only news he'd bring me was the kind that made me spiral further into depression and anguish.

Instead, I opted to pay my good friend Pierre a visit. A historian of sorts, Pierre knew the county like no other, and so he might shed some light on fearful things that had been happening to me. What Pierre told me was astounding. My still smoldering pipe nearly fell from my lips, almost scattering the ashes and embers onto the priceless Persian rug Pierre had procured, when he told me of the The Glowing.

These spirits, men made of fire with unsolved business or who met an unjustified end, would often been seen in the wake of tragedy, or simply on certain very dark nights when the conditions were just right for them to manifest. All this I knew, but it wasn't until he had told me of a specific tale of a man turned into one of the Glowing after illegally moving a border post, that I felt shivers going down my spine. The Glowing had been cursed to wander aimlessly with the border post in hand, and would only be relieved and granted final death if he had set right what he had done, and place the post back in its rightful place. But the Glowing had forgotten where this place was, and so he wandered still to this day, every night.

It was this, Pierre reassured me, that would make the Glowing appear most often. The fact that wrongs had to be righted. If the Glowing descended Heksen Hill in the wake of tragedy, then there was no question about it, Pierre stated, someone among the deceased had been wronged. Pierre further inquired if there I needed any help pertaining to my father's last wishes or anything of the sorts. He expressed concern over the paleness suddenly stricken across my visage. I assured him that I simply hadn't had the best night's sleep and made my leave.

Outside, I strode immediately home, ignored Peters' jabbering about papers to sign and approve. There I closed the door behind me and waited until it was dark. This time, however, I did not lay down in my bed silently praying for dreamless sleep. Rather, after some preparations, I put on my best hiking boots and left for the slope of Heksen Hill about an hour or two after sundown.

It was a brief but treacherous venture into total darkness as I followed the steep path up the hill where, years ago, the witches that gave the hill their name held their intricate and ominous rituals and danced long into the black night. Perhaps the Glowing were also the result of some dastardly magic spell that had once been cast in one of the many stone circles that littered the hill. Then again, tales of woodland spirits, men of fire and will-o-wisps reached as far as the Peel lands way up north, so the truth can only be that the haunts are numerous and universal.

I arrived at the top of the hill. Almost immediately I noticed the now familiar feeling of dread and anxiety I had come to familiarize myself with over these past couple of nights. Beneath me, many boys and men toiled with blackened coal faces in the narrow shafts of the mine. The work never stopped. I knew, for I am one of them, normally. I had been granted a few days leave to deal with my grief, but in a few days' time I too, would return to the mines. But it would've been too late for me. As expected, there in the middle of the night high atop Heksen Hill I came face to face with the Glowing, the Glowing that had taken my father's face as my own.

It was silent throughout, but it's eyes, pleading and sorrowful, pierced my soul nonetheless and right then I broke down crying. I told my father how sorry I was for the hurt I had caused him. I told him how it was my fault. I told him I had faked being ill so I wouldn't have to go into the mines that night. I told him I never meant for him to take over my shift.

The shimmering apparition stared at me. It bent its head slightly to the right and for a split second my father's face was gone, and there was nothing more than a blank, featureless sheet of skin where a face should normally be. I told the Glowing that I understood. I understood why they had come to me in my home at night. I told him that I came to right the wrongs I had wrought. The Glowing nodded and the face of my father disappeared. Behind it, several others appeared from behind the trunks of trees and jagged rocks. None of them had faces, yet from all of them I could sense that foreboding feeling of dread, of which I now knew was immense guilt, emanating.

I then screamed as my hands burned like hellfire. I looked down to see them engulfed in yellow and orange flame. I felt my flesh slowly melting away from my bones, yet my hands never blackened, nor did they even turn red or blistered. My whole body was swallowed by fire. But my eyes never turned away from those eerie glowing men that surrounded me. They reached out and I nodded again. I knew.

Beneath me, the ground rumbled. It was ready to relieve my body and soul of its mortal coil. To see justice done, and to see wrongs being righted.

KING OF THE UNDERWORLD

Betty Valentine
UK Channel Islands

www.amazon.co.uk/-/e/B07JH68N23

I fell, not very, far, only about fifteen feet, enough to break my ankle but not enough to kill me.

I lay stunned looking up at the moon through broken planks.

My feet went right through a hatch, the sort they always have outside pubs. It's the place where the beer goes in, or used to. This pub hadn't seen any beer for a very long time.

It was part of a huge redevelopment. Out with the old and in with the new. As a photographer, I was keen to record it all before it went. The interior was pre-war, all dark wood with a yellowing nicotine stained ceiling that some joker had given the colour "Fagnolia" instead of the usual Magnolia!

I wanted a few quiet shots at night because it had a reputation and a vaguely, creepy air about it. Like time had stopped. This wasn't helped by the Victorian graveyard next door. Now I had a broken phone and a broken camera to add to my broken ankle.

Anyway, as I said, I fell through rotten wood and lay on the stone floor. Then, to add a little more joy to my evening, it began to rain. I remember thinking to myself "Brilliant, at least I won't die of thirst!" The cellar was so damp I could have picked mushrooms to keep me going!

I reasoned that there was little point in shouting when nobody was going to hear me. Better to save my strength for a really, good yell on Monday morning when the workmen turned up.

With more than a fair amount of cursing, but not a lot of pain, I managed to drag myself off the floor and into a disgusting, old armchair. It was surprisingly comfortable if a bit smelly. With my foot propped up on a crate, I was a king sitting on my throne and lord of all I surveyed.

At some point I must have dropped off or passed out. I came to with the burning desire for a pee. My ankle was the size of a basketball. Thank the Lord I had the good sense to take my shoe off when it happened, or I would have been in real trouble.

I saw an old fire bucket just within reach and, suitably relieved, I pushed it away again. I might have been brought down to the level of peeing in a bucket, but I didn't have to look at it.

That was when the scratching began. Tiny noises, somewhere on the other side of the cellar. It is funny, big noises are not really a bother, but little ones get right on your nerves.

"Mice or rats?" I thought, as something scampered across the floor. I felt a whiskery face brush my exposed foot and I kicked out with the other one because it still had a boot on it.

The noises in the dark continued, only there were more of them. Occasionally, when the moon shone in from above, I could see their shiny, black eyes looking back at me. I armed myself with a bit of plank in case of further invasion and hoped that I could stay awake until the morning. I did not want my tombstone to read:

Here lies Martin Wainberg
He made a charming supper
2016

Around two A.M., cold and more than a little bit nervy, I looked out of the broken hatch to see the full moon shining down on me. It was absolutely still. The kind of stillness that makes you ache for something to happen. My Granny used to say the dead will walk abroad on a night such as this, but she was nuts!

I heard a noise which shattered the silence like glass. At first, I thought it was the rats again, but it wasn't. This noise was coming from above. Someone was moving about in the empty pub.

"Maybe junkies or a down and out looking for a place to sleep," I reasoned. Either one could have helped me out and called an ambulance.

I called out, but the noise continued pacing backward and forward on the boards above me. I called again, but there was no answer.

I swore in sheer frustration that whoever it was hadn't heard me.

The pacing stopped right above my head.

I found that I was holding my breath, not out of fear, more in anticipation.

The footsteps went silent and I breathed out again.

I relaxed a bit and prepared to sit it out until the morning. Just me and the rats for company.

The stories about this place used to creep us out when we were kids. Dark tales about Edgar Johnson, the landlord, who hanged himself from a beam in the bar. We used to dare each other to run in and listen for him swinging on his rope. I could hear squeaking but that was just the pub sign swinging in the wind - I hoped!

My grandmother said she had known Johnson when she was a little girl and that he was a solitary man with few friends.

I sincerely hoped old Edgar was busy washing his hair tonight.

So, there I was, in Edgar Johnson's cellar, on my chair with the moon shining down on me. I felt a little edgy, like you do when you are waiting for a taxi to turn up. I hoped that the builders would at least check before they trashed the place and me with it.

I knew that they called last orders on the pub sometime in the Sixties. It was certainly boarded up when I was a child. We used to sneak in under a loose board and sneak out again five minutes later when courage failed us.

I surveyed my kingdom in the moonlight. Not much really, just a few bits and bobs scattered here and there. Most of it was mouldy, rubbish left from its former glory days.

The scratching began again. It was louder this time, more urgent somehow. I realised that the rats were listening, too. The shadowy little shapes had frozen on their shelf, ears pricked up and listening intently. One by one they started to move, disappearing into the walls through cracks and behind the pipe work.

"Thanks for leaving the sinking ship," I thought, as all the hairs stood up on the back of my neck.

Then I realised that the footsteps had started their pacing again, louder, almost stamping on the floor above.

The scratching was getting louder too. I felt a tremor and I knew for certain that the noise was coming from below me under the cellar floor.

I sat trapped as the sounds crept a little closer, then the tapping began. It sounded like someone, very, angry, was drumming their fingers in extreme annoyance. Tapping became a ceaseless pounding of fists, so loud that I had to put my hands over my ears. It was bouncing off the walls removing little gobs of damp plaster. Like a child, I shut my eyes to keep the fear from getting in.

Then it went. A sudden and unexpected silence that cut through me like a knife. When I opened my eyes, it took a second to adjust to the gloom before I saw her.

A young girl stood in the corner of the room. She was staring at me with an expression so intense that I was almost sure she could read my thoughts. She was glowing an unearthly, green colour and I could see the wall behind her body. I could also see that she was very, very dead. Her head lolled to one side a little and there was something around her neck, a patterned scarf pulled so tight that it had bitten into her.

There was no creeping horror about her. She didn't lurch toward me like a zombie, she just stood and stared.

I stared back for a moment, unsure of what to do.

Then she smiled. It was horrible. Her tongue was black and swollen where she had been strangled. She looked up and then she pointed down to the floor. The gesture was plain, she was showing me her grave.

The fear left me, replaced by profound sadness. She stamped her foot in temper and it was obvious that she had waited a long time to tell someone where she had been buried. She stamped again much harder this time and I realised that she was trying to tell me something else.

The shaking started up again and I watched as other hands began to appear through the floor, a waving forest of fingers.

Then I got the message. She wasn't the only one down there.

As I watched, the women began to rise from their graves. Most of them were young, some perhaps a little bit older. They were in a sorry state. All had been strangled and they were staring hard, staring at me.

I was powerless to help, stuck in my stinking armchair. If nobody checked the cellar on Monday morning, I might well have been joining them.

In the end I said, "Ok I get it ladies, you want me to help. I will do all I can if I ever get out of here."

A heavy footstep in the room above us made everyone freeze.

"Is that him?" I asked. "The one who did this to you, Edgar Johnson?"

But they were fading back into the floor.

I noticed that there were marks where they had been standing – well, hovering to be exact.

It made you want to cry. There were names written in the dust. Names written for someone to remember these long-lost souls, eleven of them in all.

Emma, Caroline, Margaret, Maggie, Jane, Charlotte, Louisa, Kate, Mary, Emily, and Mary Ann.

I slumped back in my chair exhausted, eyes closed, profoundly moved by what I had seen. When I opened them again a big, angry face was taunting me. He was so close we were almost smooching. The eyes were hideous, just black craters above a wicked, lustful mouth, which drooled.

Edgar Johnson swirled himself around the cellar wiping out the names in the dust before he disappeared up the stairs that led to the pub and slammed the hatch, leaving only the echo of a word which bounced off the walls and burned into my brain, "MINE!"

Shaken and petrified, I sat clutching the sides of the chair. It crossed my thoughts that I may have hit my head when I fell, that plus the eerie cellar, and an old legend equalled hallucination central. I couldn't quite convince myself it hadn't happened though.

Things seemed quiet enough and I will admit that I dozed off for a while. I didn't want to, but I guess it had all gotten a bit much for me and I zonked out.

I woke up to the sound of machinery. The builders had arrived for an early start.

"Thank God," I thought.

Someone opened the hatch to the cellar and looked in. "All clear here," he shouted and shut the hatch again.

"What about me?" I yelled, but nobody could hear me above the bulldozers. I could hear them getting nearer and nearer, the walls began to crumble above us. If old Edgar Johnson was creeping about up there, I bet he had a headache, because I knew I did!

I could do nothing but listen to the crash of steel and metal as the machines tore through the building. Bits of broken wood rained down like spears all around me.

I looked around for shelter, somewhere I could crawl to until it was over. I made a flying leap off the chair and into the shadowy darkness, thankfully landing on something soft. Then I realised the "something soft" was, what used to be, me.

It took me a moment to understand that we were all in it together. There was mad, old Edgar Johnson and Emma, Caroline, Margaret, Maggie, Jane, Charlotte, Louisa, Kate, Mary, Emily and Mary Ann, all in the cellar with me, every single one of us had a broken neck and of course we were all dead.

It turns out a drop of fifteen feet is more than enough to kill you - you just don't know it at the time!

HOLLY AND GEORGE

MD Walker
Breckenridge, Texas, USA
Plotmonster.wordpress.com

I woke to the sound of my own shrill screaming. The same nightmare, the one that constantly haunted my dreams when the climate control was out, now entrenched strange images in my head. I was staring out a window, unable to breathe, as my parents' bodies drifted through cold, dark space.

Opening the hatch, heart pounding and gasping for air, I rolled out of bed. Huge drops of sweat ran down my back. I slumped to my knees before tiptoeing over to where George was sleeping. I always felt safe with him, even if he was only a minute older and had the maturity of a plucked-too-soon lima bean.

Seeing his breath on the glass, I realized that the climate control function in his compartment was on the fritz, too. If both units were out, it meant Janet hadn't paid the fuel bill this month.

Muttering obscenities to myself, I climbed back into bed instead of waking George. A second before the hatch clicked shut, strange noises drifted from downstairs, arousing my curiosity.

What was that?

I slunk from my bed, clutching my faded pink housecoat. Images of human-eating Creepers flooded my brain. Inching the bedroom door open, I slipped down the hall to peer over the banister, careful not to make a sound.

Janet was sitting on the couch, talking to a strange man in a black suit.

I breathed a sigh of relief.

Janet was attractive—as far as gold diggers go—and she had gone all out tonight. She had her hair down, framing her still youthful face, and she was wearing a light blue kimono that accentuated her baby blues. The stranger was devastatingly handsome, lounging comfortably against the thick cushions of my father's favorite chair, and holding a cocktail.

"So, you will have them at the meeting place tomorrow at 9 o'clock?" The man's voice was deep and husky, with a slight accent.

Janet giggled, staring up at him with wide doe eyes. Moving closer to her prey, she ensured that the top of her silky kimono gaped open. The man's gaze drifted downward, then jumped back up to meet her eyes. "Oh," she said. "They'll be there. Right on time. But, when do I get paid?"

He placed his glass on the table and stood. "You get paid when they are delivered and not a minute sooner."

Her lips turned downward in a fake pout. "But I was hoping to get a little up front."

The man scowled, looking her over. "I can see that." He shook his head and walked to the door.

Janet followed him, but they stood just out of earshot to finish their conversation.

Sneaking back to my room, I crawled into bed. The chill of the air was not the only thing that would keep me up tonight. Lost in thought, I snuggled into my quilt, trying to warm myself as best I could.

Who is that man? What is Janet up to?

As my mind raced with questions that had no answers, I closed my eyes and tried to go back to sleep.

***

In the kitchen, George was already seated, plowing his way through eggs and waffles.

Janet shoved a plate into my hands, stacked high with the round, golden carbohydrates. "Good morning, Holly! You're such a sleepy head." Her tone was overly enthusiastic. Usually, she ignored me whenever possible.

Spellbound

Eyeing her with suspicion, I sat down at the breakfast table. The woman rarely cooked in the morning. When she did, it was burnt toast, pop tarts, or some other pre-fab food item that could technically qualify as "breakfast."

She's planning something.

"I have a surprise for you two today. We're going to the capitol." She filled our glasses with orange juice.

"Why?" George blinked. Going to the capitol was always fun, but we had never been without Dad. Not once. Ever.

"Well, we need to get supplies."

I sipped my orange juice, watching as Janet played up her Stepford Wife routine. "Shouldn't we wait for Dad?"

Janet frowned; her mouth drawn tight before forcing an artificial smile. "Your father won't be back for at least another week. We need supplies now. So, eat up and go get dressed." She grabbed the flour and sugar from the countertop, marching briskly into the pantry.

I leaned close to George, lowering my voice. "She's up to something."

"So, what?" George stuffed his mouth full of waffles.

"I heard her talking to some man last night. He told her she would not get paid until 'they' were delivered. What do you think that means?"

He shrugged, gulping down his last bite. "I don't know."

Our stepmother walked back into the room and snatched the plates. "All done?" Not waiting for an answer, she dumped them unceremoniously in the sink. "Now, run along. Scoot." She flipped a hand towel at us and pointed to the door.

We raced to our room to get dressed. George grabbed his clothes and headed for the bathroom down the hall. I threw on my favorite pair of jeans and then pulled a faded hoodie over my tee shirt. George came back to the room, sat down on the floor, and laced up his worn-out boots.

As he stood, Janet knocked on the door. "Are you ready?"

"Yes," we chimed in unison, walking out to meet her. She was dressed in a hot pink kimono, with her hair up in curls. I raised my eyebrows, but George just shrugged.

Janet pointed at my electro retriever. "What's that thing still doing here? I thought your father told you to vent that a week ago. Get rid of it."

I looked at the holographic dog. He barely functioned anymore.

George bounced his head back and forth, reciting Dad's phrase. "If it's useless and no good, vent it like we should!"

I carried it to the venting chamber. I'd had it as long as I could remember, but times had changed. I'd grown up. Things that used to mean a lot can somehow change to where they don't mean anything.

Sad, but true.

I dropped the holographic toy into the venting chamber and pressed the button.

"Let's go!" Janet shouted.

***

We climbed into the worn leather seats of the family cruiser and clicked our safety belts. Janet turned on the navigation system and pointed the nose of the craft toward the capitol before lifting off.

After what seemed like an eternity, we docked at the port authority and waited in silence as the soldiers checked our passports.

"What's your business?" a short stocky guard demanded.

Janet smiled a sickeningly sweet smile and winked. "We need supplies."

Nodding, the sentinel handed the passports back. He signaled to the other officer and the airlock clicked with a loud popping sound. The huge gate creaked open to allow us access. He made a grand sweeping gesture with his arms. "Welcome to the capitol."

Overhead, elevator music was blasting through unseen speakers as electronic ads flashed across enormous billboards. Spacecrafts of all shapes and sizes were weaving in and out of traffic. After searching for just the right spot, Janet finally parked the cruiser at the mall.

"Now, come along, you two. Let's be on our way." She hurried into the crowded building without looking back.

We fell into step behind her, ever the dutiful stepchildren, until we came to a jewelry kiosk. The man I had seen the night before was standing beside the counter, eagerly looking us over, the way a wolf might survey his next meal.

"Mr. Blackwell, here are the children—as promised." Janet pushed us forward, not so gently.

"What?" George shrugged out of our stepmother's grasp. "What is going on?"

"Oh, shut up already!" The false smile she had been wearing all morning faded away and there was no longer any attempt to hide her intentions. "You'll stay here with him and work in the mines. We can't afford to feed you, so this is best for all of us." Smiling up at Blackwell, Janet looped her arm through his. "Of course, there's also the money. I just could not refuse."

My spine stiffened. "You sold us? Really? That is a little sinister, even for you."

Janet's eyes flashed, her face turning a garish shade of red. A wicked smile spread across her face. "You're someone else's problem now. Good luck in the mines."

We'd heard stories about the mines and the Creepers that lived within them. Giant, slug-like creatures that devoured miners by sucking their insides out and leaving the remnants to rot. Death from exhaustion or death by Creepers, there was no returning from the mines.

Grasping my brother by the arm, I turned to walk away, and ran into a solid wall of testosterone. Two colossal men, also dressed in black suits, blocked our path back to the food court.

Blackwell smirked. "We can do this the easy way or the hard way. It's up to you." He turned to Janet and handed her a wad of cash.

"Thank you. I'm sure you will be more than happy with your purchase." She walked away as if selling your stepchildren into slavery was an everyday event. Having only taken a few steps, she twirled around and blew a kiss to Blackwell.

To his credit, even he looked disgusted.

***

Working in the mines turned out to be more difficult than I had ever imagined—hard, physical labor that left my mind and body completely numb. Each blow of a slave's pickaxe sent clouds of red dust into the cold, dark workspace. At the end of every grueling shift, we were coated in crimson inside and out—and would usually spend the night coughing it back up.

Besides the difficult environment in which we were forced to mine, Creeper attacks were a daily occurrence.

Kids in the mines knew all about Creepers. Several had been attacked by them; some disappeared, never to be heard from again—only patches of blood and slivers of skin were found at their workstations. The rest were scared to death that they'd encounter Creepers themselves.

The worst scare of my life came just days after being sent to the mines. I worked late to make my quota and was alone as I walked back to the dormitory. Exhausted, I could barely lift my feet, one in front of the other. The only sound in the crisp night air was that of my shoes dragging across the dirt as I trudged on.

Reaching the steps of the dorm building, I lifted my foot to ascend the stairs. Something slimy and cold wrapped around my ankle. There was a tug at my leg and I almost lost my footing. I looked down and my stomach lurched.

A thick, gray tentacle curled around my leg. Like a wet elephant's trunk, the shiny limb oozed and stretched, the smell of sewers filling the air.

A Creeper!

Gasping, I jerked my leg free and stomped the thing. My shoes squished into its gel-like mass. The monster let out a horrifying screech. Rows of dagger-like teeth glowed in the darkness. Its scaly tongue darted out, licking across my face, and leaving a sticky trail of putrid saliva.

I screamed and grabbed for my tools. My pickaxe was within reach. I snatched it up and hacked at the Creeper.

Fight! Kill it!

Tears welling in my eyes, I held my breath and chopped at the creature, thrusting my axe into its body over and over. The creeper let out a mournful wail and its grip on my ankle loosened. I pushed the retched monster off me and ran up the steps, bursting through the entrance.

I slammed the door behind me, leaning against it as I caught my breath.

Spellbound

That was the night I decided I was leaving the mines, one way or the other.

***

The days stretched on with little hope for the future. Still, I planned and plotted each night when I returned to my bunk, at least until I fell asleep from fatigue. The wall of my bedroom was littered with stolen maps, notes, and details about previous escape attempts.

So far, each attempt at contact with my brother had resulted in failure. I was continually being caught and whipped, and the bruises on my legs could not heal before more were applied. But I had a plan that I thought just might work, and I was determined to talk to my brother.

At long last, I was able to slip a note to another slave in the boy's dorm, and he promised to give it to George. On the way home that night, amidst the outpouring of slaves, my brother waved to me and I was sure that he had gotten my note.

The day had finally come. This was the day that we would fight our way out of the mines or die trying. I surveyed the guard standing watch behind me. He was tall but not too muscular. He looked young, hopefully inexperienced. He was not even paying attention to the goings on around him because he was busy flirting with some poor slave girl that would probably be his first conquest later that night.

As soon as the bell rang at the end of the shift, I made my move. Running full force, I leveled myself at the officer. He never saw me coming. The impact knocked him down, bouncing his head off the ground with a nasty thud. The other slaves surrounded him to strip him of his uniform and badge. George hastily put the clothing on and threw his filthy, threadbare gear to the horrified guard. By this time, the officer had realized he would not make it home tonight. Dressed as he was, no one would ever believe he was a guard. As the shock wore off, he began to cry.

We made a break for the halls that would lead to our freedom. The frenzy of the shift change helped get us through tunnel after tunnel. The mine supervisors shuffled reports and joked with each other as we raced through the throng of slaves exiting the building. George flashed the pitiful guard's badge at each checkpoint.

Once we got to the final door, we pushed through and headed for the first cruiser. This was the most dangerous part of the plan. Being caught would ensure a bloody death. We would be used as examples to discourage other escape attempts.

The vehicle had seen better days. George jumped into the pilot's seat with me at his side as navigator. He started up the cruiser and made a smooth lift-off despite his inexperience. No one had even noticed we were gone yet. Everything had gone exactly according to plan.

Outside the protective dome, the navigation system helped guide us back to our home. We had no idea what would be waiting for us or what Janet would do when she saw us but going home was a must. We had to find Dad.

We docked at the landing port on our home station. George stayed behind the wheel as I climbed from the cruiser. Biting a fingernail, he looked at me. "What do we do now? It's not like she is going to welcome us back with open arms."

I grinned. "We go get supplies and find Dad."

George groaned, shaking his head as he reached for his door latch. "What about Janet? What if she's home?"

"Won't matter. There are two of us and only one of her. We'll get what we need and go."

Running, we passed neighbors milling about and children playing in the streets. Finally reaching our home, George threw open the door.

Our father was sitting in his armchair, smoking his pipe.

He looked up and leapt to his feet. "Holly! George! I have been looking all over for you! Where've you been?" With tears glistening in his eyes, he hurried to embrace us.

Unsure of how exactly our father played into Janet's plans, I reluctantly hugged him back.

I could not help but be skeptical. He certainly had not looked the part of the worried father when George opened the door.

I looked around the apartment for any sign of my stepmother. "Dad, where's Janet?"

Janet was nowhere in sight, but I spotted new furniture and a holographic telecommunication screen—ionic plasma, like we'd seen in stores before we'd been sold into slavery.

"I don't know." Dad set down his pipe. "You were all gone when I got home, and I've been looking for you ever since."

I glanced at myself in the reflection imager hanging above the couch. I was still filthy from working in the mines all day. "I need to excuse myself to get cleaned up."

My father nodded. "Of course."

As soon as I turned the corner and was out of sight I headed straight to my father's room. Something was not right, and I needed to get to the bottom of it.

A large wad of half-folded bills sat on his nightstand. Then the smell hit me. My eyes immediately watered, and my stomach heaved in response to the disgusting odor emanating from somewhere in the room.

I looked around Dad and Janet's bed. Nothing.

I walked to the closet and slid open the door.

There was Janet, frozen. A look of horror was etched into her face. Her eyes bulged from their sockets. Bright red marks lined her neck. The body was bloated, and posed in a strange, unnatural way.

Horrified, I clamped my hand over my mouth to resist the urge to scream.

Creepers got to her! I have to tell Dad!

Slowly, I backed out of the room—and barreled into my father standing in the hall.

"Dad! It's Janet. The Creepers …"

He laughed.

"You always were a curious little thing." He grabbed me and pinned my arms behind my back while holding a knife to my throat.

I screamed, and George came running. He stopped abruptly and put his hands in the air.

I squirmed against my father, but his hold was too constricting. "Dad, what are you doing? Why did you do this?"

My father laughed again. "Because I'm tired of hunting up junk to sell. Because I am tired of supporting a family. There are so many reasons."

George stared at Dad, his jaw hanging open. "You knew! You knew what Janet was up to!"

"Knew? I told her to do it! Now, go get my money from the nightstand and bring it to me. I'm leaving."

George did as he was commanded. When he handed the cash to father, I made my move. Months of working in the mines had developed my muscles. I twisted out of his grasp and punched him in the nose.

He winced, backing away. "Holly! How—when—" He looked at me with wide eyes, groaning.

I swept his legs out from under him. Money flew everywhere.

When he fell, he landed on his knife. He pulled his hand away from his shirt and blood was seeping from a wound in his chest. He huffed, his chest collapsing as if all of the oxygen had been pressed from his body.

There were no final words. No final declarations of love or hate; he just died.

He took his final breath and his body went lax.

I dropped to my knees, sobbing. No matter what he had done, he was still my father and I mourned the man he used to be. I gathered his lifeless body in my arms and cradled him. Blood from his wound stained my shirt.

George cleared his throat. "Now what do we do?"

I smiled through my tears. "What would dad do?"

Together we declared, "If it's useless and no good, vent it like we should!"

The bodies were difficult to squeeze into the garbage chute, but eventually George was able to make them fit. Once the bodies were securely inside, I pushed the eject button.

BLOODY FEATHERS

Dabney Farmer

Charlotte, North Carolina, USA

August 1913

Norma Betford was a horrid, despicable old crone, and that's putting it nicely.

She was unpleasant even when she was out of sight, since her shrill voice could be heard complaining loudly from miles around her small, sleepy British village. When she was in sight, the people of the village stayed out of her way.

No one knew for sure what went on in her horrid, despicable mind, but it was always something hurtful and deceitful.

No one dared make Norma Betford mad. As horrid as she was during a good mood—"good" being relevant—when she was truly angry, she would bring the full force of her rage down on you.

When a neighbor's beloved dog dared to so much as sniff at her garden, she ground up broken glass and laced his food with it, rather than simply tell her neighbors to keep the dog off her yard.

When Miss Tuple won first prize in the fair with her chicken pot pie over Norma's broccoli casserole, Norma cut a hole in Miss Tuple's fence so all her chicken could escape.

When the loose chickens attracted the attention of a wandering fox, Norma made sure to shoot the fox in the back.

Now, what you have to understand is, Norma was a mighty fine shot for a woman. Most women in the town didn't take up shooting as a hobby, but as Norma's dad had never had a son, he'd taken to teaching his girls how to use a rifle. So, Norma could have easily shot the fox in the head and given it a swift death, but she didn't.

She enjoyed knowing the poor fox would die a slow and painful death, rather than putting it out of his misery right away.

Whenever someone could muster up the courage to ask how anyone could be so cruel, she would smile and simply say, "It's a selfish world out there, and only the selfish survive."

Most people went out of their way to avoid her. Including her own and only sister Ross, but Ross' only child and son Charlie was another story.

Charlie, being the optimist of the family, would visit his aunt to help her with chores.

Rather than being grateful, Norma Betford loathed and despised him as if he was a wart on her thumb that could not be scraped off.

Charlie had been born a little different and was what the rest of the sleepy village people politely called "a little slow." I say politely, because the majority of the sleepy little town was very kind to him.

With the exception of Norma Betford.

You would think even a shriveled old shrew like Norma Betford would have appreciated free labor, since she wasn't paying him one single cent.

But she hated her nephew for reasons that were not even his fault.

Back then, the fathers of many families tended to favor their sons over their daughters. When it came to land ownership, Norma Betford's father had promised his two daughters that should either one of them have a son, they would inherit his farm. Norma Betford happened to be the oldest of the two sisters (as well as the greediest) so she felt confident the land would be hers.

Surprisingly, Norma, did manage to land herself a husband, but no one was surprised when he left her soon after. Norma Betford wasn't heartbroken at all, seeing as she had no heart to begin with.

She found herself another husband soon after, who also came to his senses and left her.

As time went on, Norma Betford had three more husbands but no children to show for it.

Her sister Ross *did* marry, and had Charlie. But Norma wasn't worried when he was born at all. Charlie was born small, with one withered arm, making it impossible for him to ever shoot a gun.

Something Norma took great pride in.

As time went on and Norma lost five more husbands... Some of which left rather mysteriously. She also lost all the money each husband had left her through her drinking and sheer laziness. So, she ended up having to sell her house and move into a run-down shack that used to be an old barn. It was a small house; there were cracks in the walls, and cracks in the ceiling as well, with old, moldy hay in the attic—which had been used as a hay loft when it was a barn, but had never been cleaned out when it was converted into a house.

Most of all it was cold, but Norma didn't mind that; she was cold enough already, so she barely noticed. As for the moldy hay, she could barely smell it, as she smoked like a chimney. So, she wasn't too worried. Soon, her father would die and she'd move to his big farm, leaving this nasty shack behind her.

Meanwhile, Charlie grew into a strong young man despite his one bad arm. He could do many things with one arm; his mother even taught him to play a little toy drum with his one good hand.

With no other male heirs, Charlie's grandfather's let it be known that the farm would be left to him—much to the rage of Norma, who could only sit and stew in the juice of her own misery. But it would seem there was nothing she could do. She might have been the oldest, but Charlie was the only male heir. She'd only get her father's farm now if she could have a son or if Charlie were to disappear.

But how would she do that? Then, one day in 1914, something changed.

Most people would say for the worst, but for a horrid, deceitful old woman like Norma Betford, it was for the better— since she saw this as an opportunity to finally be rid of her nephew for good.

It was the start of the First World War, and all the men in town were strongly encouraged to join the Army. Those that didn't were often shunned, in the hopes of encouraging them to join out of shame.

But when that wasn't enough, the Order of the White Feather was started. This was an organization whose sole purpose was to shame men into enlisting in the British Army. They did this by having women give out a single white feather if they saw any man in town not wearing a uniform.

Norma Betford had heard of this and waited eagerly for Charlie to get his white feather.

But as Charlie was well known in village, everyone was fully aware he was not capable of shooting a gun—physically or mentally—so, he was ignored. The very idea of trying to shame a man like Charlie, who was now taking care of his elderly mother after his father died, was unheard of.

But Norma Betford did not give up when she wanted something, and wouldn't you know, she always wanted something. She decided to simply shame Charlie herself.

She started by butchering one of Miss Tuples' chickens. Those were easy to catch, since poor Miss Tuple had no one to help her fix the hole in the fence.

Then, Norma plucked every feather off the chicken's body. When she was done, she walked over to Charlie's house—knowing full well his mother would be there—and presented him with a whole basket of white feathers. Then she walked away proudly.

If she'd just done this once, Charlie might've forgotten about it. But Norma Betford was as stubborn as an old mule's butt, and twice as ugly.

She continued to leave white feathers in the mailbox, near his front porch… even in his Bible at church.

Charlie was a simple man; he did not understand a lot of things in his life, but he was fully capable of feeling every emotion known to man. And at that moment, Charlie felt great shame.

Despite his mother's insistence that he was of great help to her on the farm, Charlie signed up to join the war—in another town. One that didn't know about his slowness. They were so desperate, they overlooked his withered arm.

Charlie's mother was devastated when he left.

Now, you would think maybe at this point, just maybe, Norma would be feeling the tiniest, little bit bad by now. But no, she was as proud of herself as a dog who had found a bone.

That is, until her sister knocked on her door. Norma was more surprised than annoyed that someone was knocking at her house. She was even more surprised when she opened her door and saw her sister standing there.

"What do you want?" Norma asked.

Norma's sister Ross said nothing, she just stood there, eyes red and bloodshot, glaring at Norma.

"Well?" demanded Norma. "Out with it!"

At that, Norma's sister Ross thust something white and red at her chest. Norma recognized it right away.

It was a single white feather, covered in blood.

Norma took the feather in her hand and thanked her sister sarcastically, as if she'd been given a bottle of cheap wine, and slammed the door in Ross' face, laughing.

Norma did not laugh much, but when she did, it was always at someone else's expense.

That was the last time Norma saw her sister Ross, who became so miserable with grief she never left her house for the next couple of weeks. But it was not the last time Norma saw bloody white feathers around.

A few days later, Norma found more than bloody feathers at her doorstep. She found a whole dead chicken at her door. Its throat had been cut so savagely it barely had a neck left.

It was a bloody mess. Norma was somewhat surprised her sister would up her game to mangling an animal, but she was not scared or unnerved by this. In fact, she thanked her sister for the free chicken and happily ate it for dinner, telling herself it tasted better than the first one she'd stolen. Which wasn't true, as there wasn't much meat left on it.

But that wasn't the last mangled chicken Norma found, or the last of the bloody feathers.

As days went by, the first thing Norma would see when she woke up in the morning were feathers. Bloody, white feathers. Every morning, the number of feathers would increase.

Sometimes she would find mangled chicken parts with the feathers. Norma was not one to admit she was unnerved, but even she found it unsettling how the chickens had been killed. It was as if they had been mangled by something that wasn't human.

Or a human full of unbridled rage.

Norma couldn't tell for sure, but she wasn't sure she wanted to know. Pretty soon there wasn't a spot around or in her house where she wasn't seeing bloody feathers.

Norma had no idea how her sister was pulling this off, but she refused to ask. She screamed and yelled when she saw blood on her floor. The town folks had noticed that she was ranting louder—even for her—but since Norma had always been so unpleasant, they didn't dare ask her why.

Norma got paranoid. She stopped leaving her house. She stayed inside and looked out her window, staring at her sister's house a few hills down. Her trusty gun in hand, she waited for Ross to come out.

I'll teach you to spread mutilated chickens and bloody feathers around my house.

But Ross never came out of her house. She was beyond depressed, since Charlie hadn't written her back in two weeks, and she feared the worst.

Norma stayed up three days straight, rocking in her chair, rubbing her gun, waiting for Ross to come out of her house with a basket of bloody feathers. When she did, she'd show her. But Ross never did.

Norma started to see something red and orange run by. It wasn't running fast, but her eyesight was poor and she couldn't see exactly what it was. But she had her suspicions.

It's the devil! You're trying to take me to hell. Well, I won't go without a fight.

She fired her gun at the red and orange thing, but out of fear and lack of sleep, her aim wasn't as good, and she blasted several holes in her house.

As time went on, she eventually ran out of bullets and decided to go to bed. She crawled in her small bed and for once wished just one of her many ex-husbands was with her. Demons tend to take men to hell first, over women. At least that's what her father used to say.

Pretty soon she was in a deep sleep, until she felt the rain on her head. She intended to ignore it, but there was something different about this rain. It didn't feel like water. It felt stickier. Thicker. And it didn't smell like water.

She felt something light and fluffy on her cheek. A feather. She opened her eyes and screamed. Her whole bed was covered in blood, dripping from her ceiling, and bloody white feathers falling like snow around her.

She looked up at her ceiling and saw it was soaked in blood. Through the cracks of the ceiling, she could see red, beady eyes staring at her, with razor-sharp teeth.

She let out a bone chilling scream.

Charlie came home three days later. He hadn't written to his mother because his other hand had been injured. He'd been given the easy job as the drummer—when they saw he couldn't work with two hands injured—and had been sent home early.

His mother was overjoyed. Neither thought to tell Norma the good news. They didn't go check on Norma until another three days had passed.

By then, Norma had been dead for four of the six days she'd been inside her house.

A post-mortem was performed, although it wasn't necessary. Everyone knew what had killed her right away. It was her own stubborn rage.

Or, that's what the villagers thought. If anyone had bothered to ask the doctor, he'd say it looked like rabies.

Rabies that she'd contracted by eating the chicken killed by the rabid fox. The very fox she had shot in the back, who had not only survived, but managed to crawl into her shack house, since the cracks were big enough for it to fit through. Eventually, it had dragged itself to the hay loft, where it mangled many of the loose chickens still roaming free from Miss Tuple's yard. That chicken Norma had thought was from her sister had really been the fox's handiwork.

The whole thing was rather odd, as rabies was very, very, *very* rarely found in England. The doctor only knew what it was since he used to work in America.

Maybe it was even what little shreds of conscience she had in her dark, black heart that drove her mad thinking about what she'd done. Or maybe it was her fear that the fox was the devil come to take her home.

Who knows for sure? He wasn't the best doctor, and Norma was not the best person, anyway.

Whatever the reason, Norma's fate had been sealed the moment she ate that mangled, bloody chicken.

Only five people came to Norma's funeral. Charlie, his mother Ross, their grandfather and two ex-husbands of Norma, who had only wanted to be sure she was dead.

After the funeral, Charlie wasn't sure what to do with Norma's old shack of a house, which he'd inherited, as Norma hadn't left a will.

Until his mother gave him advice. So, he decided to raise white chickens in it.

(It's a selfish world out there, and the selfish get what's coming to them.)

THE KILLER WOLF

Alana Turner

Florida, USA

facebook.com/AuthorAlanaTurner

Today was the day. In all technicality, it would be tonight, but that didn't matter. It had been a month since the last time. The Beast was clawing at the walls to be free once more. It would get its way tonight. It would only have to be patient twelve more hours. I would bide our time until then.

I clicked the news on while I made breakfast. The talking heads were babbling on about the weather, or something else unimportant. I was listening for one thing. While waiting for them to get to the good stuff I went ahead and took out a ham steak to slice up.

Using the closest steak knife, I cut it up into small bits. The Beast was pent up. The simple action made it so I had to take a breath to steady myself. Gripping the counter, I closed my eyes. I hoped I could make it for twelve hours. I would have to.

"… In more grim news, tonight is the night of the full moon. Police advise everyone to stay indoors after nightfall. There are still no suspects in the string of murders known as the 'Big Bad Wolf Killings.'" My eyes snapped open to stare at the screen. "More at eleven." The Beast growled low in my throat and I went back to cooking. Of course, they wouldn't talk about it until later. No matter. We would give them something to talk about.

I finished up my breakfast eager to get on with the rest of my day. I scarfed down the ham and eggs while imagining it as The Beast's next victim. Glancing at the clock I saw I was way ahead of schedule. I always moved faster when I was eager for the night's events.

Methodically, I put together what I would need for tonight. The work stuff I didn't care about, so I put it by the door and moved on to the more important things. My shift went later than I'd like tonight. I knew I wouldn't have time to come home before the sun went down.

Fortunately, I knew how to stash everything in my truck. The mundane stuff no one cared about. A garbage bag or a dark hoodie wouldn't raise suspicions in my old beater, but the fun equipment would.

I eased the box out from under my bed. Nothing in here was delicate. No, it was sacred. It was holy. It was a reminder of my gift-curse-gift. I entered the date into the lock and snapped it open. My claws, the Beast's claws, were nestled there, sharp, and shiny. I went through great pains to clean them, perfect them after every hunt. This was my best work yet. It was almost a shame I'd get them dirty again. Almost.

There was still time before I had to leave.

I fit the mechanism over my hand. The Beast rumbled in euphoria, tail swaying. Flexing my hand made the claws extend and retract. We were one. Man and Beast. The claws were more part of me than any natural part of my body.

The temptation to hunt now was excruciating, but the time wasn't right. The moon was not yet out, not yet full. If it's not done right, it's not worth doing. As insatiable as the Beast is, I knew senseless murder would only anger him. The hunt had to be done properly, even if that meant I suffered in the meantime.

Gingerly, I removed the claws from my hand. I still hadn't transformed fully yet. The Beast was testing me, had been testing me, for quite some time. These claws I crafted would have to do until he fully accepted me. I knew if I pleased him, if I found the right prey, he would merge with me. We would be truly bonded. An apex predator. A wolfman.

If I worked a white-collar job the scars from my initial attempts at forging them would raise alarms. I didn't mind. They were reminders of The Beast, my devotion to him, and what would happen if I disobeyed. Putting the claws back into their nest, I glanced up at the clock and cursed. I had taken more time than I meant. If I were only a couple minutes late, I'd be lucky. I rushed out of the door, equipment in hand. I hid the claws under the seat of my truck and started it up. Work first, play later.

***

The sun was beginning its descent when I finished my shift. I would have just enough time to get to a good hunting spot before The Beast took over.

Hanging my hardhat up, I clocked out. The weight of work was shed off, making room for more enjoyable ventures. Getting back into my truck, I took a settling breath. Almost time. This would be the most important hunt. Everything was aligned. The time was right. I had to find the perfect prey to make it all right.

I flipped the visor down and the newspaper clipping fluttered towards me. I snatched it out of the air.

"Jericho!" *My boss.* "Glad I caught you." Quickly, I stuffed the clipping back under the visor.

I didn't get out of my truck or even undo the seatbelt, just rolled down my window. He needed to catch a hint. "Yes, sir?" The Beast growled inside me. Deferring dominance was not something The Beast liked to let slide, but appearances had to be kept. We both knew The Beast was the true alpha.

"Listen, you're acting a bit off. I don't know what's wrong, but you can't come in late again. I don't want to let you go. You do great work, but you snap at the guys, you come in late at least once a month…" He tilted his head back and forth, no doubt trying to figure out his words. I wasn't dumb enough to go off on him. Taking care of The Beast wasn't cheap. My boss had witnessed several of my attacks though. Some people didn't know not to poke an angry animal.

"I get my work done. I haven't physically harmed anyone. Unless there is a complaint in there I *have* to go." I started my truck, barely holding back a growl. He was testing my patience.

He sighed, resigned, "Just be on time Monday, alright?"

"Yep." I rolled my window up. That was the final hint he needed to walk away. *Nuisance.*

Again, I took the clipping down. My parent's faces stared back at me in black and white. Seven years ago, today. A winter solstice just like today. The obituary praised their good character but glossed over the details concerning their killer. A wolf. A wolf woman. She had killed them but gifted me. I had lived while they died, and now I served The Beast. I would never be a victim again as long as I served him. *A small price to pay.*

A pinkish hue washed over the picture and the rest of the world. I had to get moving before night fell. The longest night of the year, and this would be the perfect hunt.

I drove off, leaving the work site behind.

The spot wasn't far, on the outskirts of downtown. It was where all newcomers passed through town. Bus stops and taxis were more common than individual cars. Still, my truck would go unnoticed. Especially in the parking lot across from the busiest stop.

I had the perfect vantage point. Every passenger would be visible as they got off. The streetlights, which came on early in this part of the city, would give me a clear view of each one. The Beast would have his pick of the litter.

The first bus of the night pulled up. The very first passenger to get off was a young woman wearing a red hoodie. She kept her head up, hands in her pockets. Her curly, black hair kept the hoodie from obscuring her face. Mahogany flesh paired with soft, round features made her ethereal under the glow of the streetlamp. Under any lighting, she would be familiar. I knew I would never find anyone more perfect.

She looked just like the she-wolf from all those years ago. Golden eyes locked onto my truck for half a second, before she started down the street. Apparently, I went unnoticed. She would never be ignorable. Perfect opportunities didn't just fall into my lap often. Tonight, would be a tribute to the she-wolf, to my gift-curse-gift.

The Beast rustled in anticipation.

Quickly, I put my claws on, and let him take over. We exited the truck, following her, but keeping enough distance so as not to alert her. We kept our hands in our pockets, careful to conceal the claws. The sun's last rays were still present, and any stray glint would give us away. Stealth was key in these instances.

She paid us no mind. Clearly, she had no idea what was to befall her. It would be painful, yes, but a noble death, one serving those greater than herself. Beauty feeding The Beast. If only she would stop glancing at her watch.

Her gaze switched constantly between her watch and the sky, all the while muttering curses under her breath. We growled low in our throat. She was distracting from the hunt. As the prey she needed to be still, be flighty, be scared, but not agitated. She was going to be a tribute -- a *perfect* tribute.

In our own impatient state, we got closer. There were no people out. We needed to be careful not to alarm her. We needed her. The people would know that the Big Bad Wolf was alive and well, out for the hunt. They would know and be scared, but only if we could kill her first.

Her curses got louder as the sky got darker. If she noticed us, she gave no indication. A blessing, but annoying. Perhaps she knew it was a bad idea to be out after dark. We would be happy to prove her right.

Her hurried walk turned into a sprint. We followed close behind. We did not run just yet. We were stalking, not chasing. If she got away however, the hunt would be ruined. The kill had to happen as soon as the moon rose, full, into the sky. The gift-curse-gift was most powerful then. Kills were most satisfying then. It was the anniversary and *had* to be perfect. This little girl would not screw that up. As it happened, she scurried off to the best possible location. We stayed on top of her without the slightest shortness of breath all the way to the park. Most visitors had filtered out by now. Even in the middle of a city, people were afraid of the woods at night, no matter how out of place the trees were. Down a hill and under a bridge she ran, while I tailed quietly after.

Pounding her fists on the concrete underpass, she checked her watch and the sky once more. "Not now, please not *now*." The little doe's distress had reached a breaking point. *We would be happy to break her beyond that point.*

Careful to keep our claws hidden-it wasn't time yet- we stepped out of the shadows into view. "You lost?"

She whipped her head around to look at us, her mouth making a little "O". We were right, she hadn't noticed us before. Perfect. Pushing her surprise down, she had the audacity to growl. "Look dude, this isn't the time." She bared her surprisingly sharp teeth at us. *We liked a fighter. They're fun to break.*

"Just want to help you, little miss-?" We let the question hang.

"I don't need or want your help. Just get out of here." She whirled around again, intent on leaving. The last rays of sunlight disappeared from view.

We grabbed her arm, claws digging into soft flesh. Her yelp of surprise made my mouth water.

She turned her head to glare at me. "I'm telling you, you don't want to do this."

"I assure you, we have no choice." We grinned at her, barring our teeth. Soon we would taste her flesh. The Beast would be satisfied.

The cycle complete.

The anniversary honored.

We dragged her closer. She yanked her arm out, swinging with her free fist. We barked out a laugh.

"Don't say I didn't warn you." Her empty threat bounced off the concrete overpass, only encouraging us further. We pounced on her, pinning her arms to her sides. She squirmed under me, thrashing, and screaming. That wouldn't be a problem when we ripped her throat out with my teeth.

First though, we looked up to the moon. It filled the sky, bright and beautiful. We howled at it, honoring her before our feast.

Underneath us we felt her shift and squirm, her screams harmonizing with our howl. *Glorious.* We raised our claws, ready to rip her chest open. She caught them. She must have managed to get a hand free. We looked down. The girl was no longer there.

Instead a wolf, with golden eyes and sleek black fur was under us. It knocked us to the ground, growling. We were territorial, we would win our hunting ground back, and find the girl again.

Before we got a chance to attack, it was on us. We were pinned to the ground now. Growling, we kicked and spat, trying to get the intruder off. A shriek ripped out of my throat as it tore into my chest. Something warm splattered my face. Copper filled my mouth.

I looked at the beautiful, full moon and tried to howl again. My Beast had left me. It had gone back to the moon. It had abandoned me. I begged The Beast to come back, as the wolf bit into my leg. We could still get our territory back if he returned.

My hopes of a victory were dashed as it ripped my chest open. I could no longer scream, only meekly whimper. Sticky liquid hit my face. Blood. My blood. Its claws, its perfect *real* claws, unzipped something inside me. Its muzzle disappeared into my chest. Over the pounding of my heart, I heard it chewing.

There was no pain. Or, if there was, it was so intense my mind blocked it out. Only the sounds of chewing and ripping and breaking. I had to focus on something else, anything else. In the sky, the moon glowed brilliantly.

The Beast watched from the moon, leaving me to be dinner.

The anniversary was complete.

Spellbound

NOT MAGICAL ENOUGH

Dan Alatorre

Tampa, Florida, USA
geni.us/DanAlatorreAuthor

I had not been to the house in a long time. The house I grew up in. The house where my childhood took place, or most of it. The best parts of it, I suppose.

And while a young girl's childhood has many best parts, most fade with time. Others are stored away, to be pulled out and quietly dusted off when the mood is right.

Dad's office is at the front of the house. Its two large windows look out over the grassy front lawn. Massive oak trees fill the spacious yard, clumps of Spanish moss dangling from their outstretched limbs, swaying in the gentle breeze. Dozens of squirrels, going about their business, hopping through the grass— and dashing away madly when a car pulled into our long gravel driveway. An occasional brown rabbit might be seen through the panes of his office windows, or a lumbering gopher tortoise, slowly making its way across the big lawn.

In the office were several things that always appealed to me. Its dark green walls were regal, decorated with paintings of an English fox hunt and many, many portraits of family. My artwork also hung there—crayon drawings at first, and then pencil sketches, until one day actual paintings made the cut. But none of the older, cruder art ever came down. Dad found room for it all.

The big mahogany desk, where I'd play hide and seek when friends came over—if Dad wasn't working at it—and the barrister's bookcase, with its shiny glass doors, holding many odd trinkets from faraway places.

The other bookcases in the office were filled with the classics of literature: leather bound volumes with gilded lettering on the spines, thick with heroes and dragons, lovers and rivals, cops and robbers, wizards and kings.

And in the corner by the side door, where the long bookcase from behind the desk met the smaller one lining the wall, was a gap where he stored items I could never touch.

Walking through the two French doors at the front of the office, an unknowing observer wouldn't notice the gap in the bookcases. From that angle, the far side of the smaller bookcase blocked the edge of the longer one. Actually, from almost any place in the room, the gap couldn't be noticed. Not unless you sat in Dad's chair.

I didn't notice it for many years, because kids don't notice such things. Not until it's pointed out to them.

Dad walked into his office, going straight to the gap in the bookcases. "Would you like to try?"

It was a tease, usually, because he said I wasn't magical enough to see or feel the objects that lay somewhere inside the gap. It opened into a big room, he said, and those with the powers could slide through the gap and stand in the space on the other side, gazing upon the wonderous items he'd stored there. It might not have only been him, either; I never asked. I just assumed he put the items there, because it was his office. The house was big and old. Who knew how many generations had stored things there?

"Yes," I said. "I'd like to try."

Every time I'd tried as a younger child, I was never successful. I'm not sure why I thought I'd be successful this time, but the same excitement bubbled up inside me on every rare attempt, ever since I was old enough to know the space between the bookcases existed and things had been hidden there. I hoped it would work each and every time, but it never did.

"No, it didn't work this time," he'd always say, sighing or shrugging. "You're not magical enough."

And my protests of when would I be magical enough were always met with the same explanation.

"One day."

As in, one day, things will get better. One day, things will make more sense. One day, you'll understand about the mirrors.

One day.

Now, I stepped to the gap, reaching my hands along the old wood.

The seam was about four inches wide, and maybe twelve or fourteen inches deep—not nearly big enough to hide anything—but it turned at that point and went to the left. There, it opened a little wider, but only a few inches. A shoe box might fit there, or a stack of them, but not much else. Not the heavy medieval swords Dad would produce from the gap, or a tall suit of armor. Not a room he'd disappear into and come back with trinkets from Italy or Spain or London. Not treasure chests filled with seashells and gold Spanish crosses inlaid with gems, or a brass candelabra from a haunted house. Not vases or brass lamps from India, not a Persian rug from the drum major of the imperial army marching band.

My hands found nothing.

The wall behind the bookcase, and nothing else.

I prepared for his often-repeated refrain: "No, it didn't work this time. You're not magical enough."

But instead, he stood by the desk, sliding his hands into his pockets. "That's okay. Maybe you're here for a different reason." He looked at the upper left-hand drawer of the desk. "There are candles here. In glass jars. Light three."

Even at age ten, I was wary of matches. But the thought that somehow the candles might lead to accessing the room between the bookcases, that was all the incentive I needed.

I tugged on the old drawer. The wood stuck a bit, groaning as it gave way and opened. Under some faded newspaper sections, a row of tall, thin votive candles rested. I took out three brand new ones and set them on the desk, rushing to the kitchen for matches.

Upon my return, Dad was in his chair, leaning back as he often did when I'd come down from my bedroom in the morning. He said nothing, just watched as I slid the blue-tipped match across the rough side of the box. It ignited with a puff of smoke and a yellow flame. One at a time, I held it to each wick of the candles.

"Now," he said, "place them in front of the mirror."

Our house had many mirrors, for some reason. In the bathrooms, of course, and in each dressing area of the dozen bedrooms, but also in the entrance hall, and the hallway by the back door. There was a giant one over the buffet in the living room, and smaller ones in the kitchen, the pantry, and the breakfast nook. There was even one outside by the pool. My playroom used to have the most: sixteen square mirrors arranged in rows of four, and two mirrored candlesticks on top of the game shelf. My parents' bedroom had eight or nine mirrors—a big one on the back of the bedroom door, and another one over the dresser; several adorned each wall of the suite.

Nearly every wall in the mansion had a mirror on it of some size or other, installed by my father four years ago, when I was six. I was probably eight years old before I realized my classmates' homes didn't have as many mirrors as ours did. It was as if the mirrors substituted for artwork throughout our house. Except for my father's office. No mirrors were ever in there.

Until today.

While I went to the kitchen, Dad must have taken the hall mirror from its hook and set it on his desk. A few thick books propped it up as it faced outward toward the side of the desk and the glassy doors of the barrister's bookcase.

"Put them here." He pointed to the mirror.

My three candles flickered as I moved them, each taking its spot along the bottom of the mirror's thick frame.

Sunlight streamed in through the two big office windows, turning dim as a cloud passed overhead. The Spanish moss swayed and danced as the wind picked up outside.

Soon, the room was dark, as if it was about to rain.

"Look through the mirror."

My father's voice was calm. Instructive, as it often was. It was the tone he took when we sat on the couch and he explained things he thought I needed to know. Like when I texted a boy I liked, why the boy might not text back right away.

"Kids your age don't all have phones. Or maybe he had to go out to dinner with his parents."

My disappointment would turn to understanding, and eventually the boy would text his reply, and all was right with the world.

Or when I needed to know about our cat dying.

"When we get old, our bodies wear down and give out, like your great grandmother's did . . ."

The tone was kind and soft, instructive but emotional. As if he felt the pain deeper because he was explaining it to me. "You're . . . sensitive," he'd say. "Like me."

He was good at that—explaining—in his own way.

"One day, things will get better. One day, things will make more sense. One day, you'll understand about the mirrors."

I leaned forward, gazing into the glass. Was this a trick? He used to play them often.

"Don't look *at* the mirror, look *through* the mirror," he said. "It will show you what's on the other side."

How can a piece of glass with silver on the back be anything other than a piece of glass with silver on it? It can't.

The reflection was of three candles on a mahogany desk, with a curious young girl's face behind them.

"You have to look to see an image. You can't just hope something's there. Concentrate."

The candles flickered again.

My father moved from his place beside the mirror, coming to stand behind me. The room grew darker.

"Look into the reflection. From any angle, a mirror only shows what you choose to look at *most*." He leaned close to my shoulder, whispering. "What do you *want* to see?"

I took a deep breath, focusing my thoughts on the room in the glass. It was dark and deep, bookcases and a chandelier, green walls that appeared to be almost black in the dim glow of the candles.

"I'd like to see Mom."

Dad smiled. "Good. Let's try." He stepped away, moving out of the reflection.

My eyes stayed on the mirror. Past my shoulder, the shiny glass of the barrister's bookcase reflected three yellow dots of light from the candles. Then, a shadow passed between the dots, blocking them from my view. The mirror showed my father's face, distant and smiling, his arm outstretched to a beautiful woman in a flowing dress.

He took my mother's hand in his and walked forward, growing larger in the glass, as if I were gazing at them both through a window.

And through the mirror, of course, they looked at me.

They spoke softly to each other, faintly, as if their words were carried on a wind I could not feel. I caught only glimpses, mostly from my father. The rain, a car crash . . . the words disappeared as soon as they were spoken.

My mother blew me kisses, as she used to when I was a little girl, her image already fading away, like the light on the movie projector was dimming before it went out completely. Dad lifted her hands as if to spin her around in a ballroom dance, and then they were gone.

Outside, the cloud moved past. The sun returned.

A delivery truck drove down the lane in front of the house.

I blew out the candles, lifting the mirror off the desk and putting it back on the wall. The candles went back into the drawer. Past last month's newspaper obituary with his picture, and the yellowed one from four years earlier, with hers.

From any angle, a mirror only shows what you choose to look at *most*. In every room of the house, my mother wanted to see her little girl. As much as possible, until her baby could finally see her, too. The thought made me warm in my heart.

I went outside, where my aunt waited in her van.

"Did you find what you were looking for, dear?"

"Yes, ma'am. Thank you for bringing me."

"Of course. I'm happy to bring you any time you want."

As the van drove down the gravel driveway and the squirrels ran for their trees, I stared out at the sky. It was a good visit. "One day" already seems to be getting closer.

Spellbound

"One day, things will get better. One day, things will make more sense . . ."

I suppose.

I understand about the mirrors, now. I guess the rest will come.

Spellbound

THE MIRROR

Adele Marie Park

UK

firefly465.wordpress.com/

Someone comes. Yes, yes. No, not mistress. She is gone. I told you she is beyond our reach. Be quiet! They come. They will see us. Back. Back.

A small blue car, polished to a high shine, stopped at the side of the road. It carried three occupants, Mr Drummond, his wife in the passenger seat and their daughter Fiona in the back.

Fiona opened the car door and stepped outside. Her boots crunched on roadside gravel as she made her way to the soft, overgrown grass path that led up to the cottage.

***

"This is a hovel!"

Fiona gazed at her mother who stood amongst the Highland wild beauty dressed in her own impeccable style. Rather than anger, a surge of love flowed through her and she hugged her mother. "I know but," she whispered into her ear. "I'll make it my palace."

Her mother sputtered complaints, but Fiona had moved onto her father, who under his daughters excited gaze sighed. "Let's have a look inside then."

***

The estate agent from the nearest city, Inverness, held the keys which would open the dilapidated cottage for examination. She hesitated, then passed the keys to Fiona.

"Do you want to do the honours?" she asked, in a melodic accent.

Fiona took a deep breath and inserted the key in a padlock. The sound of the lock tumbling vibrated in her ears and although she heard the others talking behind her, their words were meaningless.

I don't care what you look like inside. You are going to be my home.

***

They headed to the nearest village, Dubh Mon, translated from Gaelic, Black Mountain.

Fiona thought it suited the whole area which was dominated by great swathes of craggy mountains and moorland sweeps.

It was a short drive from the cottage to the village and Fiona smiled as the first houses appeared. This would be her village, a far cry from the outskirts of Glasgow, packed with people, fumes, and bad memories.

Lost in old thoughts she gasped as the car came to an abrupt stop.

"Moira, if Fiona is decided on this then we will support her and that's the end of it!" Her father's temper was slow to boil but once it did, it ended any more of her mother's arguments.

First impressions always count, Fiona's mother was fond of saying. The restaurant was a tourist's dream. A taste of Scotland brought to the masses but hidden here amongst the black mountains.

She gazed around the room, noting the tables which were occupied and those who sat at them. There was a policewoman and man who sat directly behind them and as Fiona caught the policewoman's gaze, they smiled at one another. The sense of welcome caused tears to prick Fiona's eyes. She sniffed them away, her smile fixed as an older woman came to their table, a menu in her hand.

"Hello there. I'm Mhari, the owner. Are you just passing through for the day?" her accent was softer than the estate agents, her hair would have once been as red as rowan berries but had now

170

faded, her cheeks were flushed and she wore a white apron over her dress.

Fiona had decided she liked her within the first minute. "I've just bought a cottage outside the village," she said and sensed her parents surprise, she felt it herself.

Mhari's smile broadened. "Oh, really? Which one is that now?"

"The broken down one with the orange roof," Mrs. Drummond replied with a scathing glance at her daughter.

Laughter came from Mhari and she placed a hand on Fiona's shoulder. "I know the one you mean. Still, it's a beautiful spot and those old cottages were built to last. It's not very big for a family though." Mhari's voice and gaze held only innocence but the question still caused Fiona to bow her head.

"It's just Fiona. She lost her husband a year ago," Mrs Drummond said.

"Oh, lass. I'm sorry. It's a tragedy but even more so when they're so young," Mhari held onto the back of the chair and her honesty caused Fiona to speak.

"He was a soldier. Afghanistan," she said, surprised that she managed to say those words without weeping. The sound of Mhari's indrawn breath produced silence at the table.

"You will be needing a builder then?" Mhari's question brought heads upward again and Fiona sighed as the practical question stopped the maudlin thoughts.

"A squad of them, I think," Fiona said.

"My nephew, Tommy, runs a building firm. I'll give you his number and if he doesn't do the job, he knows I'll be down on him like a ton of bricks. Now what can I tempt you with to eat?"

***

The meal was delicious and even her mother finished her plate of fried fish and chips. As Fiona stood at the bar waiting to pay, the conversation was like the drone of bees in summer. None of the harshness and noise of where she had come from. It was as if she had entered an idyllic bubble of calm.

She smiled as Mhari bustled along the bar towards her. "You enjoyed that, did you?" Mhari asked.

"It was delicious. I'll put on weight eating here."

"Are you staying while your cottage is being renovated?"

"I hope to, but I'll need somewhere else as all my savings are ear marked for the renovation work."

"Now you wait here. I'll be back," Mhari said and squeezed past the servers and bar man swinging the hatch up as she exited the bar.

Fiona turned her head and saw her stop to talk to the policewoman.

After a brief conversation, Mhari smiled and beckoned Fiona over.

"This is Alice our local policewoman and she has a spare room in her flat, don't you Alice?"

Alice rose and held her hand out towards Fiona. "I do, and I'd be happy for you to stay with me. The rent would be fair and it's clean and tidy, I promise," Alice said and a gentle smile at the end of her words caught Fiona off guard.

Her emotions surged upward, forcing her to gasp. She was so used to tying them down it surprised her when they broke free.

Mr. Drummond saved her as he stood beside her and squeezed her arm in comfort. "Thank you so much. You have made our Fiona feel welcome and it's a good start to a new life. Can we pay now, it's a long drive back to Glasgow," he said.

Fiona wanted to hug her father, his diplomatic speech had helped her to push down the emotions and take control.

"Well, consider your meal a welcome gift. No, I'll not take any payment for it at all. Let's just say that we'll see you again," Mhari said and the expression on her face was resolute, she was not budging.

***

Days ran into nights as activity kept her so busy, she didn't have time to dwell on anything but the renovation.

Tommy the builder had arranged to go with her, and after a restless night she set off early, determined to reach the cottage before he did. She wanted to breathe the clean air and let the atmosphere settle on her shoulders.

He arrived five minutes after she did, so her bonding with the landscape was cut short. However, she was impatient to get inside and listen to his plans for renovations.

A rush of giddiness infected both her and Tommy as she opened the front door and scraped it over the stone step.

"That will be the least of our worries, miss," Tommy said.

"Please, call me Fiona. We'll be working together for a long time, I think," she replied as they walked into the living room with all it's seventies clutter.

She turned around and grinned. "I brought coffee in a thermos?"

***

The coffee made things flow and they spent exuberant hours bouncing ideas off one another. The cottage rang with their laughter until the only space left to examine was the cellar. A sombre atmosphere draped over her, a fear of dark underground spaces.

"I'll go first," Tommy said and before she could protest, he opened the door and the bright light of his flashlight bounced as he made his way down the steps.

Fiona waited, her heartbeat thumping in her ears, she could have sworn she heard whispers. She shook her head and descended the stone steps with care.

Tommy had his back to her as he examined the walls, so she turned on her own flashlight and gazed around. A small chest of drawers sat in the middle of the room and an examination of its drawers yielded old rags, paintbrushes stiff with use and nothing else.

The floor was covered in remnants of peat which crunched under her boots. She swung the light into the corner and gasped.

A mirror was propped against the far wall and through the dust its surface winked at her caught in the beam of her torch.

She knelt in front of it and reached out to touch the frame. The wood was smooth and carved in shapes resembling waves compounded by blue paint. It was oval and turning it over, Fiona saw it had a stout iron chain attached which had not degraded.

She smiled as her fingers traced over the surface leaving trails through the dust.

"You're coming with me," she whispered then cocked her head to one side as a scratching sound as if some small creature like a mouse was on her shoulder interrupted her thoughts.

She glanced up at Tommy, but he was crouched in a corner studying the floor. A frown creased her forehead and she listened again but there was only silence.

As she placed the mirror on the ground Tommy's movements caught her eye. She rose and walked over to where he appeared to be digging.

"Have you found something?" she asked.

"Aye. Something's not right with the floor here and I think…" he grunted then pulled an object out of the ground.

Whispers buzzed in Fiona's ears, but she shook her head too excited to see what Tommy had found.

He held it up and they stared at it. It was a bottle covered in earth but as he rubbed the sides, they could see the contents. Old rusty nails, string, and other decayed matter.

"Oh my God! What the hell is it?" Fiona asked and took a step back. The hairs on the back of her neck stood up making a shiver run down her spine.

Tommy laughed. "It's what they call a witch's bottle."

"A what?"

"In the old days they used to put these in the foundations to keep away evil." He sat on his haunches and gazed up at her. "Did you know that the old woman who lived here was called a witch?"

Fiona shook her head her lip curled in a sneer.

"It's only superstition. What do you want to do with this?" he asked.

"Throw it out. It's disgusting." The scurrying sound filled her ears again and she turned around in a circle trying to find the source of the noise. "Are they're rats down here?"

Tommy rose to his feet the witch's bottle held in one hand. "I can hear something. I'll set traps," he replied.

He pointed to the mirror. "Is that for going out as well?"

"No. I'll take that to Alice's with me. I really like it."

***

Alice helped hang the mirror above the fireplace and both women stood back to admire it. It had taken a lot of soap and water to clean it but now it sparkled and shone.

Fiona accepted the glass of wine Alice held out for her and took a sip before she sat on the couch next to Alice.

"So, Tommy will start work tomorrow?" Alice asked as she kicked off her shoes.

"Yes. I can't wait to watch it take shape. My home."

They looked at one another and raised their glasses the rims chinking.

"To new beginnings," Alice said, and Fiona grinned.

***

Why did she take us? We are not allowed to leave the cottage. Be quiet. No, we will not. He will be released if we are not there. They took away the protection. We will make her take us back.

***

The shadows in the corners of the bedroom slid as if fog across the floor to surround Fiona's bed. As they grew in stature and thickened, Fiona began to mutter in her sleep. At the sound of a guttural growl, her muscles spasmed and she was jolted awake.

She opened her eyes. Fear shivered through her. A warning. Her heart battered inside her chest as her limbs remained leaden. With the physical flutter of her eyelashes, she moved her eyes left and right. The darkness around her swirled then coalesced into a humanoid shape.

Sweat broke out on her body sliding down her skin and into her eyes. Adrenaline rushed upward but made no difference. She was paralysed.

With increasing terror, she stared as the shadow poured itself over her body. Smudges of darkness appeared where eyes should be. A rudimentary mouth cracked into a toothless grin which kept growing. The shadow figure's mouth was a gaping void. A black hole.

Unable to close her eyes against the nightmare. Pain rumbled inside her chest as she exerted her lungs gasping for each breath. Sweat ran into her eyes again and she was forced to blink.

I'm going to die!

The shadow was the night sky without the comfort of stars. The seething darkness blotted her vision. Hairs trembled around her face as if a tiny breeze blew over her.

A sudden sharp noise broke the silence, but the shadow figure continued to hover over her. Then came a loud crash which vibrated through the walls and rattled the bed.

The shadow figure growled. It hesitated then slid away from her, a slithering snake like beast.

Free from paralysis, Fiona screamed as the adrenaline pushed its way out of her mouth and once released, she shrieked until her throat was raw.

The door burst inward, and Alice stood reflected in the hall light, a baseball bat held over her head.

"Fiona! Are you alright?"

Fiona shook her head, damp tendrils of her hair whipped around her face and stuck to her skin. She pushed herself upward and stared at Alice who still held the bat as if she were about to strike the ball.

"What happened? The television has been knocked onto the floor and our wine glasses are broken then you scream. I must check the house. Stay there," Alice backed out of the room then turned around with a swiftness that made Fiona shudder.

The realisation she was alone again crept over her slow and menacing. Fiona grabbed the bed covers in fists. Her gaze darted around the room with quick furtive movements.

She uncurled one fist then with a quick movement she fumbled for the bed side lamp. Its yellow glow cast eerie shadows.

"It was a nightmare. Just a nightmare." She repeated the mantra a few times until Alice stomped into the room.

Fiona closed her eyes as relief flooded through her and she groaned.

The baseball bat held low at her side, Alice sat with a flourish on the edge of the bed. "There's nothing in the house. I guess the television wasn't as secure as I thought." She grinned but Fiona saw her bite the bottom of her lip. "Your scream made me bolt from the room like I was in some tv cop drama."

Fiona bowed her head for a moment but already a smile demanded the terrors be forgotten and she gave in. "Sorry. I was having this terrifying nightmare. I dreamt I couldn't move, and this black thing was trying to suck my soul or something."

"Oh my God. That's terrifying. Would you like a coffee?" Alice asked.

Fiona nodded the need for coffee replacing terror and she stumbled out of bed to follow Alice.

Spellbound

The smooth plastered walls of the living room appeared alien at first. Fiona was used to seeing peeling wallpaper, cracks which ran like spider webs and as she glanced down the rotting carpet had been replaced with an exquisite wooden floor.

The windows were still dirty and needed replacing so light fell in weird patterns on the pristine walls. One shadow caught and held Fiona's attention as the movements of the clouds across the sky caused it to grow.

Flutters panicked inside her stomach as if they were trying to escape and spread upward to her throat. She swallowed but her mouth was dry as the dark shape loomed towards the ceiling.

"Hi Fiona. What do you think?"

Tommy's voice broke her terror and she turned towards him her legs shaking and her heart trembling inside. "It's beautiful, far more than I imagined. You've worked miracles, Tommy," the more words that came pouring out, steadied her voice and anchored her to this reality, not the shadow one which came every night as she slept.

"Are you coming down with something?" Tommy asked as he moved closer.

"No. I haven't been sleeping very well. Silly nightmares."

"Hmm. Well, the windows are due to be replaced later today and then we can start on the bedroom."

Fiona tucked a stray hair behind her ear a gesture which brought back memories of night's spent curled up in bed, heart beating too fast, waiting for the shadow man.

***

Alice couldn't understand why her keys, her police badge, and other objects kept disappearing one day and being found the next in the strangest of places. Yesterday her police badge had turned up inside the fridge.

These incidents put a strain on both women. Every night she would wake Alice with her hoarse screams. Fiona knew that Alice now slept with the baseball bat beside her.

When Fiona walked into Alice's flat a delicious smell wafted towards her. She frowned, hung up her jacket and walked through to the open plan living room kitchen.

"Hi, Fiona. Sit down, dinner won't be long," Alice shouted from behind a cloud of steam.

Fiona's heart thumped inside her chest as she sat on the couch and her nerves betrayed her as her fingers played with her hair.

This is it. She's going to ask me to move out.

"So," Alice began as she clutched two plates piled high with spaghetti and sauce. She sat beside Fiona and passed her a plate. "What's wrong are you feeling sick?"

Fiona shook her head.

"Okay. I've done some digging on who owned your cottage, the woman's name was Elizabeth MacLeod and get this…," Alice paused while she took a forkful of spaghetti. "In 1948 she was accused of witchcraft by the Laird who owned the land the cottage was on. The charges were dropped as the locals came to her defense. She lived in the cottage until she died of old age." Alice finished and stared at Fiona.

A sense of being hit by a speeding train tied Fiona's tongue. The relief which flooded her caused her to swallow and it turned into a cough. She picked up her glass of water and gulped half of it down before she was able to speak. "Oh God, Alice, I thought you were going to ask me to move out."

"What? Why on earth would you think that?" Alice asked.

"Because all of these stupid things happening since I moved in. The missing items, my nightmares, the television suddenly throwing itself off the wall. In fact, the only thing which has remained static is the old mirror."

The spaghetti lay congealed and cooling on their plates as they stared at one another in a moment where thoughts caught up and the truth was too much to believe.

"The mirror was in the basement but perhaps it was meant to stay in the cottage. I mean you hear about these things. Someone buys an antique and suddenly weird things start happening in the house." Fiona said and gripped the handle of her fork so tightly it vibrated in her shaking fist.

Both women turned their gaze on the antique mirror until a sudden thump caused them jump.

Fiona followed Alice as she strode to the bathroom and opened the door. She peered over Alice's shoulder and saw the heavy medicine cabinet lying on the floor the glass door open and beauty products strewn over the floor.

"That's it!" Alice shouted.

Fiona dived out of her way as she sped past her and back into the living room. She followed and saw Alice standing in front of the mirror.

"I've had enough! You are going back!"

***

Laughter spun around the living room of Alice's flat as the two women clinked glasses of wine together.

"They didn't break," Fiona said her comment startling more laughter from them.

Alice sighed. "I will miss you. I can't believe this is your last night here."

"Me either, but you'll come and visit?"

"Of course, and I'm coming with you tomorrow to help you settle in."

Fiona's smile twisted upward as the thought of moving into her new home at last played with her and caused giddiness, helped by the wine.

"I'll get a good sleep tonight, thanks to the vino," Fiona said.

The laughter and the second bottle of wine finished, and the women hugged before separating and going into their bedrooms.

"No nightmares tonight," Alice called out.

"No! Definitely not," Fiona replied as she slid into bed and pulled the light duvet over her body

***

Inside the cottage, moonlight slipped in through the new glass window, curtains stood at either side as if they were on guard duty. The beams of light illuminated polished wood and slid over the surface of the fireplace and the mirror.

The mirror glass rippled and sounds of groaning in child-like voices filled the empty room. The glass bulged and with the sound of a pop, a tiny black head poked out of the mirror and stared around its mouth open in an oval shape. It was joined by another and another until the surface of the mirror appeared to be covered in rotting *toadstools*.

We are back. Look. Our home is nice. Yes. Where is he? Not here. No. Oh they have thrown away the bottle. He has escaped.

A wailing and lamenting filled the room. High pitched and screeching it rattled the new window glass and a hammer which had been left in the room floated in mid-air.

***

Fiona whimpered lost amongst dreams and scattered memories.

"No!" Fiona fumbled with the duvet and slid out of the bed landing on the floor with a loud thump. She lay for a moment, gasping for breath, hot tears burning her skin.

After a moment, her skin rose in bumps and plumes of moisture fogged the air in front of her.

She shook her head, confused. Half of her wandered in the dream and did not want to come back, but the other, the logical part of her brain was screaming at her that something was very wrong.

A guttural growl from behind her caused her body to stop all movement and little breaths came faster than her heart could pump while her eyes slid from side to side.

"No," a whisper from her lips echoed in her ears but another growl changed her voice from a whisper to a scream. She scuttled on her hands and knees towards the door. With her back to the door she faced the shadow entity.

Blackness, holes for eyes and that mouth. An endless void stretched until it obliterated any semblance of facial features. This; this horror slid across the carpet towards her.

In madness there often comes a moment of clarity. The mirror had been protecting her and they had taken it away.

She screamed. Beat against the door. Rolled away from the solid mass of fear.

The door opened and Alice stood with her baseball bat aimed above her head. Alice screamed as she saw Fiona's nightmare. "Get out of my house!"

Head down Alice rushed the monster. Ran straight through it and out the other side. She pivoted and screamed at it. A pure scream of primal rage.

The entity bulged. The mouth stretched wider than before. There was a sickening crunch as if someone had stood on a snail. With a guttural growl the entity swallowed itself. All it left behind were two frightened women.

**

Like casualties of a disaster, Fiona and Alice sat in the living room. Fiona lifted a cup of hot coffee to her lips, but her hand shook so much she put it down again.

"It was the mirror. It was protecting us. Not the other way around," she said, the words coming in a rush of nervous stutters.

"Think, Fiona, was there anything else in that house that might have been part of all this?" Alice's logical brain which made her a good policewoman triggered a memory in Fiona.

"Oh no. The bottle we found. Tommy said it was a witch's bottle. It was full of rusty nails and God knows what else. We threw it away."

They stared at one another. The silence hung suspended as if from a spider's web. Quick thoughts went through Fiona's head parading in succession, teasing her.

"It only appears to you, well till last night," Alice said. "So, if you go to the cottage it's going to follow."

"Yes, that makes sense. Alice, have you got a plan?"

Alice grinned at her then bounded upward. "I might have. Get dressed you're coming to the library with me."

**

The room appeared much smaller now that electric light illuminated the smooth walls and the curtains shut out the darkness.

Fiona walked over to the fireplace and touched the mirror suspended above it. Her fingertips traced across the surface. "I'm sorry. I understand now. You tried to protect me."

A faint vibration pulsed through her skin. She took in a breath and her heart thumped. A prick of tears threatened to bring weakness, but she willed them away with a shake of her head. "I know. I must not fear. It feeds on fear."

Fiona turned her head as Alice stepped from the kitchen an empty mason jar held in her hands. She nodded. Alice returned the gesture.

They walked towards one another until the mason jar was the only space between them.

"Ready?" Alice asked.

Fiona swallowed and cleared her throat. "Ready."

They gazed at one another their breath matching, hearts beating in time.

"I bind ye with iron, ye foul spirit," they said.

Fiona heard the clink of the nails going into the glass jar. A faint hum filled the air around them, but they ignored it and carried on.

"With earth you will be buried." The thud of earth muffled the walls of the glass jar.

"With salt I banish ye. Back to the place of evil from where you came. You are not welcome here." The salt was the last ingredient.

A red ribbon was held between them and Alice began to wind it around the top of the jar.

A gigantic boom shook the windows. The hum grew louder.

Fiona glanced to where the sound came from. It was the mirror. Tiny black faces their eyes closed, and their mouths pursed filled the glass. They were helping. She turned her gaze back to Alice and together they chanted.

"By the power of Christ, by the power of air, earth, fire and water, get ye gone foul creature."

As their chant rose the door burst open. A powerful wind blew their hair and tugged at their clothes. They kept chanting, shouting to be heard above the noise of the gale.

Guttural growls. Loud stomping noises. Chattering teeth.

Fiona's heart thumped in time to the chant, her stomach rolled, and nausea rushed upward. She swallowed it along with terror and found strength with the thought that this was the shadow taking a mighty tantrum.

Together they held the jar aloft.

"Get ye gone foul creature! You are not welcome here!" They screamed together their voices strong.

From the inhuman demon came a wail which rent the air around them. The shadow figure appeared as solid and menacing as usual. It's black skin rippled and flowed taking on the shape of muscles which flexed in a horrifying human parody of movement.

Fiona mustered up her emotions. "Get back to where you belong!" she screamed at it. Anger gave her words strength and they flew towards the entity like knives.

The creature screamed and roared. Foul breath stinking of sulphur and decaying flesh made Fiona's eyes water.

The being wavered. It cast its rudimentary arms around as if something pushed it from behind. With a sucking sound like water gurgling down a sink the blackness sped towards the jar.

Alice slammed on the lid. A loud screech faded to a whisper.

"We got you," Fiona whispered.

***

Sunlight played over the white walls and the kitten true to its nature tried to catch the shadows dancing. It ran on spindly legs and jumped onto the couch. Tore like a tiger over the back and jumped its tiny claws outstretched.

"Oh, Fiona. He is adorable," at Mrs. Drummonds words laughter as bright as the sunshine filled the space.

"He is. Thank you, Mum. Thank you, Dad. He's the best housewarming present ever," Fiona said. She retrieved the kitten and it lay in her arms purring.

"You've done a grand job, love. I had my doubts, but this old place has been reborn," Mr Drummond said. "Were there many problems?"

Fiona glanced at Alice who sat beside her parents on the large soft couch. "A few, but nothing I couldn't handle with the help of my friends."

Spellbound

`

FAIRY RING

Frank Parker
UK

franklparker.com

John beckoned to me as he headed for the patio door. "There's something I want to show you."

I had begun gathering used plates from the dining table. "Let's clear up, it will wait a few minutes won't it?"

"It's okay, Dad, we can do the washing up, can't we Mum?" My daughter took the dirty plates from my hands.

Mary nodded. "Go on, let the boy show you whatever it is. We'll join you in a few minutes. It doesn't take long to load the dishwasher."

Was that a rebuke? I was trying to do the right thing; not leaving the dirty work for the women. I know she saw that as inconsistent with my refusal to buy a dishwasher for our retirement flat.

I followed my daughter's boyfriend across the neatly cut lawn, with its sharply defined stripes, to the area where he had created a pond and a small wildflower meadow.

"What do you make of that?"

At first, I thought he was seeking praise for his support for the environment; rewilding a small part of his suburban garden to attract wildlife. I opened my mouth to offer my congratulations then stopped. To the right of the pond, in an area of long grass and wildflowers, there was a clearly discernible circle of shorter but more verdant grass.

John was squatting down, pointing to something at the edge of the circle. He swept his arm in a wide arc, tracing the outline of the circle. As I squatted beside him, I saw what he was showing me, a ring of small brown toadstools.

"A fairy ring."

John looked at me, his eyebrows raised. "I didn't think you believed in that nonsense."

"That's what they are called. And, no, I don't believe in the supernatural qualities ascribed to them by some people." As I spoke, I stood up and John did the same. "There is a perfectly natural explanation. It probably means that many years ago there was a tree here. A pretty large one by the size of the ring."

"How do you arrive at that conclusion?"

"Honey fungus."

"What's honey fungus?" Mary and Janet had joined us.

"I'm sure you have seen it. Usually about knee height on the trunk of a very old tree. A kind of shelf of broad toad stool like fungus growing out of the bark."

"How does that connect to these tiny brown mushrooms?" John wanted to know.

Always the practical one, Mary asked, "Are they edible?"

"No. They'd likely give you a violently upset stomach. The connection is an underground network of fungal threads. Trees have a symbiotic relationship with them. When a tree dies, or is chopped down, they are still there. They flower on the tree bark whilst it is alive and again on the ground after it is gone."

We began walking back to the house. I stood still as Janet joined the conversation. "Siobhan is fey. She feels things when she is near those mushrooms."

Siobhan was the young woman John and Janet had let an attic room to. I did not want to be rude but could not help the snort that escaped my lips. "Fey? What does that mean?"

"Someone in touch with the spirit world."

"You know your Dad doesn't believe in that stuff." John came to the rescue.

"You can scoff all you like, but I saw the goose bumps on her arms and neck when I showed it to her the other day."

"Nothing to do with a breeze?" I could not help myself.

"It was a hot humid night. We were all in shorts and tee shirts."

"Mine was sticking to my back." John seemed to have abandoned his attempt to support me.

I didn't want to provoke a family argument, so said no more on the subject.

***

Later I thought about that word Janet had used: 'fey'. Didn't that mean near to death? Yet Janet had used it to imply that Siobhan could connect with the spirit world and see things. The sort of nature that would have got her charged with witchcraft in past centuries. Which in turn reminded me that there was at least one, very famous witch trial around here. I decided that as soon as I was home, I would look it up.

I also looked up honey fungus and fairy rings – I like to be sure of my facts and what I'd said about the connection between them came from a vague memory of something I'd seen on television years ago. It turned out I was only half right. Fairy rings are indeed caused by the same sorts of fungus that manifest as honey fungus on trees and shrubs. But what I had described is actually a bracket fungus which certainly destroys trees but is not related to honey fungus or fairy rings.

***

The more I read about women accused of witchcraft in the past, the more I came to realise that most of them were not guilty of casting spells. Rather, they offered remedies the efficacy of which would, in many instances, come to be recognised by modern medicine. Back in the mid-fifteenth century astrology and fortune telling were also highly regarded in the upper echelons of society. It seems that the woman I had in mind became entangled in a dispute between astrologers who disagreed about a prediction that the young Henry VI might suffer a serious illness.

She had done nothing more than assist other women to conceive. One of these women was the wife of a man who was next in line to the throne so could benefit were the prediction to come true. The men involved were accused of treason and executed. The women were accused of witchcraft. The woman with royal connections got away with life imprisonment. The woman who had provided her with gynaecological advice was burned at the stake. I shivered at the thought.

***

It was all a very, sad indictment of the ignorance of our ancestors. But what was the connection with the old tree in my son's garden and the horror that Siobhan felt was attached to it? I wondered if some kind of written accusation had been posted on the tree. In any case, the location was all wrong. The mid-fifteenth century case I'd discovered was enacted in and around Westminster. The 'witch' in the case was burned at Smithfield. My daughter's home is in Essex.

I needed to look for something from a later century. In place of the Wars of the Roses I needed to look at the English Civil War and the role of Matthew Hopkins and John Stearne in the middle of the 17th century. It is said that Hopkins and his associates caused more women to be executed for witchcraft in a three-year period than had been so treated in the previous 100 years. And their interrogation methods included techniques that would be outlawed as torture today. Some of the descriptions made my skin crawl.

Since Hopkins operated in and around Essex, if there was a connection to witchcraft in my daughter's garden it would most likely be from that time.

And then I received the phone call. I recognised my daughter's voice at once, despite it being distorted by anxiety.

"What on earth's the matter, girl?"

"You are not going to believe this. Siobhan's in hospital."

"The girl from the flat? What's the matter with her?"

"The doctors don't know." The line went silent for what seemed like a long time. I was about to prompt her when she spoke again. "Her body is covered in lesions. Almost as though someone has been pricking her with a knife point."

I felt the hair on the back of my neck prickle. I tried to keep my voice even as I responded. "She's been stabbed?"

"No, that's the thing. She lives alone. There was no break-in. She hadn't been sleeping well for several days. Ever since she saw the fairy ring in fact. In the end she resorted to sleeping pills. When she woke up, she discovered these marks all over her body, some of them bleeding."

The line went quiet again. I tried to think of something to say. Like most people, I have only a limited knowledge of diseases and their symptoms. What disease causes lesions to suddenly appear on a person's body? I refused to believe what the memory of my research was telling me.

My thoughts were interrupted by Janet's voice, lower, now, than before, almost a whisper. "There's something else Dad. Something really, strange. When she awoke her body hair was all gone and there were razor nicks everywhere, in addition to the deeper lesions."

Another jig-saw piece clicked into place in my brain. I forced myself to suppress my rising heartbeat. I took a deep breath, trying to stay practical. "Who found her? How did she get to the hospital?"

"We heard screams. I ran upstairs. When Siobhan didn't respond to my knocking, I used our spare key to get in."

"What do you think happened? Have you called the police?"

"No. Siobhan insisted she didn't want the police involved. I'm calling from the hospital. It's awful seeing her in such pain."

"Do you want me to come over?"

There was a brief silence, then: "No. When I rang, I was going to ask you, but now we've talked I can't see the point. John and I can manage. But, Dad, you are so good at research and I have stuff to do. Could you do some web searches for me?"

"Of course. Any ideas about where I should start?" I did not need to ask that question; my mind was already filling up with what I'd read about Hopkins and Stearne and their methods.

"Not really. Fairy Rings? Poisonous mushrooms?"

"You think she may have eaten some and hallucinated?" I was only trying to lighten the mood. It was not appreciated.

"Stop it, Dad. The woman is in a serious condition. It's not funny."

"Sorry, love. As it happens, I do have some ideas. I'll get back to you."

***

Hopkins and Stearne, I'd already discovered, used a technique called 'pricking'. The idea was that these women had sold their souls to the devil. Their bodies would contain a 'devil's mark', a place that would not bleed if pierced. They would prick the suspect's body with a sharp pointed instrument until they found some place that did not bleed. Often this would follow a search for a visible mark which involved the removal of all body hair. Sleep deprivation was another technique employed by 'Witch finders' of the period.

It was certainly worrying that, in Siobhan, there was lack of sleep, body shaving and piercing. The similarities were striking. Doubly concerning was the realisation that such abuse was usually followed by hanging. If this was some kind of possession, or haunting, we must do all in our power to prevent that.

But this is the twenty first century, not the seventeenth. The idea that some disturbed spirit from almost half a millennium ago had emerged to torment and, perhaps, execute a modern-day witch seemed absurd. There had to be a more rational explanation.

***

"How well do you know her?" My question was directed to Janet. We'd gathered at a pub just around the corner from the hospital. Siobhan was much improved, her lesions healing rapidly. According to Janet she fully expected to be sent home after the consultant and his team completed their afternoon round.

"Honestly? Not really that well." It was John who answered. I couldn't help noticing the look of annoyance that passed briefly across Janet's face.

"It's true that she has not told us much about her past. But from our first meeting I could see that she and I have a lot in common. I was more than happy to let her have the room. I thought then that she would be someone with whom I could share confidences. And that is how it has been."

"Any boy friends?" Mary rarely had much to say, but when she spoke it was always to the point.

"None that she has mentioned."

"Your exchange of confidences did not extend to that?" John's remark was equally to the point. I thought I detected a hint of sarcasm.

I did not want Janet feeling we were ganging up on her. "Maybe her past experiences with men were too traumatic to talk about?" I offered.

"She never struck me as the victim type. She was one of those people more interested in other people than herself. A good listener. Now I come to think about it, John, you are right. We were not exchanging confidences. I found it easy to open up to her. Apart from offering words of encouragement, she had little to say. I feel guilty now that I did not show the same interest in her as she did in me."

"So, we can't rule out the possibility of an ex-lover harassing her?" I stood up, draining my glass. "Same again?"

There were nods all around. I waited for Janet's response to my other question.

"I suppose not. But there would surely be signs of a break in?"

Mary ask the obvious question. "Could she have given him a key?"

I didn't wait for the reply. Instead I headed for the bar. They would surely work out for themselves the flaw in that argument. Why would a woman give a key for her new flat to an ex-lover who was harassing her?

When I arrived back at our table the conversation had moved on. I missed the question Janet was responding too, or the identity of the person who asked it. But she was directing her remarks at John and her tone was far from friendly. "Two things: first, I just don't see her as the type to indulge in self-harm. And, second, if she was she'd surely hide it. Cutters always wear long sleeves to hide their self-inflicted wounds. Her cry for help was loud and genuine."

Her eyes flared and she banged her empty glass down on the table. "You didn't see her. She was hysterical. To say she looked as if she had seen a ghost is a cliché, I know. But if that's how someone looks who has faced evil, she had."

It was time for me to reveal the results of my research. "Whatever is going on, whether she is being attacked by a spirit from the past or suffering some parapsychological hallucination, we have to guard against the final stage," I concluded.

***

We were preparing for bed when Mary voiced another theory. "Don't you think it's too easy to jump to the conclusion that Siobhan was being persecuted by an ex-boyfriend?"

"How do you mean? Surely you don't believe in all that supernatural stuff."

Mary, sitting in front of the dressing table, brushing her long auburn hair, eyed me in the mirror. "Of course not. You know me better than that." She put down the hairbrush and turned to face me. "But what if she was stalking someone? Someone who decided he had had enough?"

I slipped between the sheets. "The real problem with that theory is the fact that entry to the flat was not forced. Whoever the attacker was, they not only had to have a key, they had to climb past Janet and John's bedroom and enter the attic without waking them. Siobhan was out cold having taken sleeping pills. But surely John or Janet would have heard something."

***

Over breakfast the following morning I wondered aloud. "Where would Siobhan have got hold of such strong sleeping tablets?"

Mary's hand flew to her mouth. "You don't think?"

"Janet's boyfriend the pharmacist? It's the obvious thing. And why not? It doesn't mean he took the opportunity to inflict those wounds in her sleep. That's the action of a very, sick mind."

"Well. . . " Her voice trailed off. "You know I've never trusted John. But, I agree, I don't think him capable of something like that."

"We were saying yesterday how little either of them knows about Siobhan, but the same is true about John. How much do we really know about him?"

"We trusted Janet's judgement."

"She's always been a bit cagey, evasive even, when talking about him and his background."

They had met on holiday the previous summer. Janet had been working as a hostess in one of those nightclubs in a Mediterranean resort. We had both been shocked when she told us she was moving in with John. But he seemed to have a good job and the house had belonged to an aunt. Janet obviously felt she had made

192

a good catch, not that she would have used such an old-fashioned phrase.

***

Late that afternoon we got the call from the police station. When we arrived Janet was still shaking, her tear stained face painful to look at. She flew into Mary's arms and began sobbing uncontrollably.

I left them to it and went in search of coffees. When I got back, they had both calmed down and were sitting in an area the female sergeant called the 'victim support room'. Slowly Janet told us what had happened that lunch time. She had come home to collect some papers her boss needed. She had seen it from the kitchen window as she filled the kettle to make a cup of tea.

"They were struggling in the wildflower meadow. Right in the middle of that ring. The fairy ring."

"Who were?" Mary and I spoke in unison.

"John and Siobhan. He had his hands around her neck. She was trying to trip him up."

"What did you do?"

"Dialled 999 as I ran out the door to try and stop them. As soon as he saw me, John released Siobhan. She grabbed his wrists. Next thing I knew, he was in hand cuffs and she was reciting his rights."

Mary and I exchanged looks.

Janet continued. "It was horrible, Mum. He had never been violent towards me, and yet he was intent on murdering Siobhan." Her hands were shaking as she hugged the paper coffee cup.

"I've been such a fool. I'll never forget the look in his eyes. The evil. The hatred."

Mary hugged Janet's closer. "There, there. It's all over now."

"Where is he?" Part of me wanted to give him a taste of his own medicine. I'd have to restrain my anger whilst the authorities dealt with him.

"He's in the cells. Seems his name is not John at all. I still only have the vaguest idea of what he is supposed to have done. Turns out Siobhan is an under-cover cop sent to keep tabs on him. Befriending me was her way of staying close to him. I don't know how he found out, but when he did, he had to get rid of her."

"And I gave him a way of doing so by telling him about the activities of the witch finders."

"No, Dad. He must have researchcd that for himsclf."

"That's right," Mary added. "You didn't tell us any of that until after Siobhan was injured."

That was reassuring. It didn't stop me shivering at the thought that there are still men who are capable of inflicting such horrors on women.

LITTLE RED REVOLUTION

Ernesto San Giacomo

U.S.A.

Once upon a time, there was an ex-coal miner named John. He had spent twenty years in the mines before his union brothers elected him as their representative. John possessed the unearthly ability to whip a crowd into a feel-good frenzy. His clever speeches, biting humor, and booming voice became the highlight at any union meeting.

John relaxed near the back of the podium in the union hall, waiting to be announced. He grimaced, the audience fidgeted while the current speaker droned on and on. The man wrapped up his speech and introduced John, which generated a hearty round of cheers and whistles.

He strode to the podium and stood tall. "So, the company suits have the nerve to call the latest contract an offer." John shook his head. "Well, where I come from it's called an insult!"

The miners roared their approval.

With everyone's attention fixed on the podium, only John eyed a pasty-gray man near a shadowy staircase along the back wall. The figure flashed an impish grin at John before passing through the door under the staircase.

John did not recognize man and pondered if he had been sent to the meeting by the company bosses. He decided to pay the stranger no mind and continue. "People say you can't draw blood from a stone. Well, they're wrong! Energy is the lifeblood of the economy. And we provide that life blood every time we mine a load of coal."

Come here John. I need you.

What was that? Not a good time for voices in his head. John blinked and continued. "That's um…that's right! We are the most amazing people in this whole country! With our unified voice and fists, we'll make those bloodsucking bosses tremble in fear."

Led by John, the union leaders put forth a clear message: a seven percent pay increase or they would strike. A tough fight loomed ahead, but the miners were on board. "Can't they bargain honestly? A fair deal for everyone. That's the sort of world I want. Isn't that the sort of world you want?"

Cheers erupted. But that voice niggled at the back of John's mind.

Come back here John. I need you. Now.

The voice had become too intense for John to concentrate. Images of the gray man flashed through his mind's eye. Wanting to wrap up quickly, he led the group in a cheer. Ever the consummate showman, he chanted with the sure knowledge that his union brothers would join him. "Hey hey!" *Clap clap.* "Ho ho!" *Clap clap.* "This contract has got to go!" The strategy worked, repeated as a mantra, and the resulting racket rattled the walls.

The noise tapered off and John stepped down into the audience. People crowded around for the opportunity to shake his hand. He edged through the throng, smiling, and nodding along the way. Once he reached the back of the hall, he headed for the door under the staircase which led to the storeroom, where the gray man had gone.

He had trouble finding the light switch in the dark. His fumbling hand skimmed the wall and flipped it on, but nothing happened. The door swung closed, trapping John in pitch blackness. Too many years in the mines wouldn't make him panic over a little darkness. A footstep and a sinister laugh from behind made him freeze. After a sting in his neck, he tumbled to the floor.

***

John rubbed his eyes as he returned to consciousness. The aroma of fresh cut grass surrounded him. Loud crickets filled his ears. Too loud, he pinpointed their individual locations, even through the haze of awakening. He glanced side to side.

What the hell am I doing here?

He bolted up.

How did I fall asleep in the field?

Footsteps drew near.

"Are you feeling better?"

The same silky voice he'd heard during his speech. Except now it wasn't in his mind, but in his ears.

"Yes. I'm better." John took a deep breath and stretched, then sprang to his feet with the vigor of a young man. He took another breath and flexed his muscles. "More than better. I haven't felt this good in years. It's like I'm twenty-one again."

"And now you shall always feel young."

John stared at the face that belonged to the voice, the face of the gray man. He wore a cape and crisply pressed clothes. His hair was jet black and slicked back. "Who are you, and how do you know my name?"

"I'm Victor. And I've been watching you for some time now."

John weighed the potential danger of the situation. "Spying on me? You work for the mining bosses?"

"No. Only to be certain that I had the right man for the job."

"I already have a job. Fighting for the rights of my union brothers and negotiating on their behalf."

"Yes, and you were quite good at it. But now you'll work for your blood brothers."

"Blood brothers? What the hell are you talking about?"

A thin grin lit Victor's face. "I've given you the gift of immortality. You're a vampire – a creature of the night."

"Oh, now I've heard everything." John stared at the man and pointed off into the distance. "There's a free mental health clinic a mile or two down the road."

Victor laughed and clasped his hands.

A porch light shone in the parking lot, illuminating the lone car left – his car. John beckoned Victor and said, "I'll give you a ride to the asylum."

Victor laughed again.

"Honest, there are some nice people in white coats to take care of you."

"I assure you, I'm fine."

"No, you're not. Now I don't mean to be rude or anything, but I can tell you're sick by just looking at you."

"As if you're any different than I." A sly grin crossed Victor's face.

John examined his hands, his skin had turned pale gray. "Well, I'll be damned."

"Now that's the first correct thing you've said."

"This can't be true. You knocked me out and put make-up on me or something." A mirror. Where's a mirror? Of course, the car! Though it was a hundred yards away, John scampered over in three bounding strides. He stopped by the passenger door, so shaken; he had to sit on the ground, feeling faint. He glanced over his shoulder at Victor and shouted, "What the heck?"

"Another benefit of our condition, my friend!" In less than a second, he strode to where John sat, and lifted him to his feet.

John steadied himself and stared at the side mirror. The reflection showed trees swaying against the night sky, but no image of himself. "Must be something wrong with this thing."

"Nothing's wrong with it. You're different now."

"No reflection. Like in the movies." John rubbed his face, trying to take in the reality of the situation. And that led to another surprise. Hours had passed, the stubble of a five-o'clock shadow should've grown by now, but his face was soft and smooth.

John ran his tongue over his dry lips. *What! Did I feel fangs?* "How can this be?" John bared his fangs at Victor and resorted to his main defense whenever threatened — sarcasm. "No reflection isn't very practical is it? How will I know if I've got a piece of asparagus stuck in my teeth or something?"

After a robust laugh, Victor said, "You won't be eating vegetables ever again. You'll feed on living blood now."

"Oh yeah? Well – we'll just see about that. I'll be the only vampire who eats a T-bone or chocolate pudding with whipped cream!" John paced back and forth, frustrated, and confused.

Victor gave him a stony glare. "The gift of immortality should not be mocked."

"Gift? You call this a gift?" John stopped pacing and returned Victor's indignant gaze with his own. "You made a big mistake making me immortal."

"I don't believe so."

"Oh, yes you did. Because now I get to slap the crap out of you for the next thousand years, you lousy bastard."

Victor folded his arms. "Lesson number one. Vampires don't poop. Honestly, John you're not making this any easier."

"I'm sorry, Victor. So sorry for not putting on a happy face and a party hat and jumping for joy about your so-called gift." He kicked at some gravel. "Usually I return rotten gifts!"

"Perhaps when I introduce you to the others, you'll better understand the reason for your fate."

"Reason? What reason?"

"I chose you above all others for a particular task."

"You're gonna have to convince me. And I'm warning you, I'm a tough sell." John released an exasperated breath. "This is the worst day of my...*un*life." He paused, considering his options, and figured he didn't have any. Part of him was even curious about these 'others' but he didn't intend to make things easy for his new companion. "Fine. Maybe I'll feel better if I meet a bunch of people who are just as miserable as I am."

"Oh, I nearly forgot," Victor said. "Lesson number two. The sunlight is dangerous for you."

"Well hell, I know that. Doesn't everybody?"

"Not the younger generation. I transformed some co-eds a few weeks ago. They ran out into the sun to see themselves sparkle. What a mess."

"Where did they ever get an idea like that?" John asked.

"Perhaps they read it somewhere," Victor said. "Come, let me introduce you to the others." He led the way into the forest.

John shrugged and followed. The landscape blurred past as the pair travelled at vampiric speed. He had to admit, being undead did have its perks. They crossed several miles in under a minute, until Victor stopped at a cave entrance.

"My fellow conspirators are eager to meet you," Victor said. "After you."

John took a breath and stepped through the cave's mouth, following a dim winding passage until it opened into a larger cavern. Torchlight illuminated the space, casting ephemeral light onto the rough walls. Music filled the room, bleeding from the craggy surfaces. After a moment, John identified the song – *Venus in Furs* by The Velvet Underground.

Across the room danced a scantily clad female vampire, undulating sensuously to the slow, dirge-like rhythm. Long raven hair fell to her waist. She wore thigh-high black patent leather boots with stiletto heels, and a thong bikini to match. As John and Victor approached, she stopped her dance and slapped a riding crop into her palm. "Ah, fresh untrained meat."

Victor made the introduction. "John, this is Mistress Vanessa."

John dragged his lustful stare away from Vanessa's naked torso, "I bet you give new meaning to the word *necking*."

She stroked John's face with the crop. "I never bite victims on the neck. It's not painful enough."

A pregnant pause ensued as John alternated his gaze between Victor and Mistress Vanessa. "I've got the uneasy feeling you're going to tell me how you do it."

"A victim-lover never expects my bite." Her eyes glistened as her gaze fixed on John's crotch. She bared her fangs and bit down, her teeth snapping, and then made a slurping sound, like sucking the bottom remnant of a milkshake through a straw.

"Sounds charming." John moved away.

"We don't kill merely for the sake of feeding," Victor said. "Some of us enjoy turning it into an erotic tryst. The others call us lymphomaniacs, but we scorn the term. We prefer vamperotics."

"Others?"

"The vampires in this cave are a minority, a small part of our population. The main populace ridicules us for our erotic feeding habits. We've been shunned from their society, treated as second class. But it's not the others' fault. They're being influenced."

Spellbound

"By who?"

Victor put up his hand to halt the conversation. "Mistress Vanessa, I need a moment alone with John. Please excuse us."

As John and Victor strode away, a *smack* sounded near Victor's butt. He spun around, Vanessa pointed her crop at Victor. "Make sure you see me later. Do not disappoint me."

"Later, later," Victor said with a dismissive gesture. "My business with John is more important right now."

"I bet she spends many weekends home alone, wondering why her dates don't call back," John whispered to Victor as they walked away.

"She's a vampinatrix," Victor said.

"This isn't making me feel better about what you did to me. Are you going to get to the point soon?"

"Patience, my friend."

The scene around the cavern was laced with vampire couples in passionate embraces. Some danced erotically while others caressed in coffins. John eyed the two males in one of the caskets.

"Hemosexuals," Victor whispered in John's ear.

"What do you call the girls, lesbloodians?"

"No, shemosexuals."

Among the caskets were tables and leather chairs. Skeletons and mummified bats dangled from the ceiling. There was even a black Christmas tree, decorated in red ornaments and clear plastic fangs as icicles.

"Love what you did with the place, Vic," John said. "I once read an article about this in *Better Graves and Coffins*." John stopped and stared at Victor. "I think we're done here."

"They're mistreated, John. The Master is unfair to us. He is the one who began publicly denouncing us, turning the others against our way of life."

"Who?"

"The Master is the darkest of us all. The oldest and most powerful – and we all must bow down to him and pay tribute."

"I bow down to no man," John said.

"He can destroy any one of us in single combat, and so we do as he wishes. But what my people need to understand is, if we all linked our minds together, we could defeat him, and clear the way for a proper leader."

John scanned around at the number of vamperotics. "Looks like you already have enough troops."

"No, we are too few here. We'd need the majority of the whole vampire community."

A small winged goblin carrying a plastic shopping bag entered the chamber and waddled toward them. "What the hell is that?" John asked.

"A plastic bag."

"Not the bag. The thing carrying it."

"That's what happens when a human isn't strong enough for the transition."

"You mean I might've ended up as a three-foot tall goblin? With wings?" John asked.

Victor. "A chance I had to take."

"Now I really want to slap the -- former crap out of you."

With a finger, Victor beckoned, and the goblin hurried over.

John put his hand out to the creature. "Hey little fellow. How are you?"

Grunt bowed to John.

"No, don't bow to me," John said.

"Sorry, bro," Grunt said. His voice had a peculiar quality, like a sped-up recording. "A habit burned into our minds by the Master." He extended his hand to John. "Put 'er there, pal."

Victor chimed in. "If you witness the Master's treatment of these little ones, you'll become livid."

"Yeah, the Master's pissed off at us 'cuz of yesterday," Grunt added. "We ain't supposed to be seen by humans." Grunt took a small scroll from his bag and handed it to John.

John opened the scroll and read, "By order of Master Key...Keym..."

"Kee-mee-ya," Victor said.

John continued to read, mumbling to himself.

"They need blood like the rest of us," Victor told John. "So, they hunt in the forests."

Grunt interrupted, "But sometimes there ain't much game and we gotta go to a farm to feed." He snapped his fingers and used his thumbs to point at himself. "Ever heard of chupacabras?"

"This Keymia moron shouldn't get angry at you guys because you ate," John said.

"Yeah, well, fat chance of that. The thought of what the Master is going to do tomorrow makes me wanna party tonight." Grunt dug through his shopping bag and took out a tee shirt with black and white horizontal stripes. The back had been cut off and he put it on like a smock, leaving room for his wings. "Tie this for me?" While Victor tied the back of the shirt, Grunt donned a beret, sunglasses, and a red bandana. "Well whaddya think? I'm going for the Parisian artist look tonight."

"You're certainly one of a kind," Victor said.

"Hope I get lucky." Grunt scanned the room. "Wow, babe fest. Check out the jack o lanterns on those two." The goblin lit a cigarette and let it dangle from his lips as he swaggered over toward two well-endowed female vampires.

"He's serious, isn't he?" John said.

"He'll get slapped twenty times tonight. But he is a persistent and horny little creature."

Grunt made his approach. "Ladies, wanna check out my *oui oui*?"

John shook his head. "So, what was he talking about? Why is he dreading tomorrow?"

A grave deadpan expression crossed Victor's face. "Tomorrow is the full moon. We must go and pay homage and tribute to the Master. It's a sort of pep rally, I suppose. A chance for the Master and his underlings to brandish their authority, and to soak up the praise of the masses. Of course, public humiliation of us vamperotics is always part of the festivities. The goblins will be put on display tomorrow as well, to pay for their transgressions."

"I've dealt with Keymia's kind before." John's new purpose came into focus. This community needed a leader, someone to galvanize them into action against this Master. That's what Victor meant when he said John was the right man for the job. He'd been transformed to bring unity to his new blood brothers and sisters. The anger of injustice surged through him; this was what he was born to do. "Let's go talk some treason."

***

On the night of the full moon, the entire vampire community gathered in the largest cave of the complex.

John supposed two hundred miners could work comfortably and not get in each other's way. Stalagmites and stalactites had been left in their natural pattern, with the crowd filling the spaces between. A stage was carved on one end, where Master Keymia sat upon a black throne. John examined the Master's tall, lean presence. His complexion matched that of the other vampires, but his hair was long and straight, which accented his thin long face. His eyes were narrow, black, and merciless.

Goblins performed for the Master. They fell and tumbled like circus clowns while other vampires laughed and threw tomatoes and cow pies at them. The Master cackled and howled with glee.

Hatred at the sight of such injustice welled up inside John, making his stomach clench. Suppressing his aggravation for now, John moved about the cavern, introducing himself to his blood brothers. While some gave the impression of gladness to be there, the majority had a sullen appearance, like those who would rather be somewhere else. When he spotted a group of shriveled old vampires in a corner, he approached one of them and extended his hand.

The old vampire stared at John's hand in disbelief, then extended his own and shook. "I don't know you," he said.

"Well, I know your suffering," John said. "Had a little chat with Victor last night. He told me all about your condition."

The old vampire smiled through his wrinkles. "Victor made you?" He slowly turned toward the other elders. "Victor made this one last night."

They raised their bowed heads and struggled to smile at John. "He's the one come to save us," one of the elders said to another. Eyes filled with desperate gleams of hope fixed on John. Their confidence and trust inspired his heart. He turned back toward the stage and glared. Master Keymia, entertained by the cavorting goblins, never took his eyes off his performing underlings. Now was the time to act.

John spotted a large stalagmite with a flattened top, a miniature Devil's Tower, in the middle of the cave. Confident and filled with the anger of injustice, John climbed to the top of it and stood tall. He found Victor among the crowd and winked a signal to him. Then John stretched out his arm and pointed his finger directly at the throne. "Master Keymia!" His voice had lost none of its bass authority and echoed off the curved ceiling.

The crowd hushed as all eyes went to John. The goblin 'entertainers' stopped their antics. In the silence, John distinctly heard an "Oh, crap!" from one of them before they scurried off the stage. Grunt spread his wings and landed next to him.

John's posture and voice were an open challenge. "Who undied and made you boss?"

Keymia stood up from his throne. His dead eyes narrowed and fixed on John. "How dare you, you insignificant little worm! I'll squash you out of existence!"

John didn't back down. "You're a clot in the flow of progress. Time to step down."

The Master stretched an arm toward John, but John stood firm and unwavering. Keymia's mouth dropped opened, eyes widened, and his head tilted.

Thank God, John thought. The conspirators had joined their minds, blocking the Master's power, preventing John from being burnt to a crisp right then and there. Their small numbers couldn't defeat the Master, but for mere minutes, they had the capability of blocking against his attack.

"We call each other blood brothers, but we don't act that way toward our brethren." John put his hand on Grunt's shoulder. "My blood burns and boils when you make sport of these little goblins, and call them shrimp-imps, gob-lames, or wing-things. Those names are hateful, offensive, and plasmically incorrect. His name is Grunt, he's a Hemogoblin, and he's my friend."

While some in the crowd nodded their heads, others averted their eyes from John's gaze. *Ashamed of themselves. Good.* He stole a glimpse towards Keymia struggling against an invisible force. The Master acted as if he was screaming, but no sound emerged. *Wow, Victor's better than I thought.*

"Up at the crack of dusk to serve a thankless 'Master.' It's nothing but an endless daymare of drudgery and servitude if you're not one of his favorites!"

One of the vampires raised his fist and said, "Right on, blood brother!"

Another pointed at the Master. "We've taken enough of your nonsense, Lew!"

Lew? John thought. The vampires were addressing the Master by his first name. A sure sign they were fed up, losing their fear, and ready to revolt. Another glance at the throne, the mind link was still working. The Master's arms had dropped, and he stood frozen. Victor had told John that the conspirators could hold him for a short time, and Keymia's mind must be working overtime to break their hold. John continued, "And just look at the condition of our elderly. Why aren't they being fed properly by Lew's regime?"

More vampires edged closer to John.

"The elders might challenge Keymia for leadership, if they had the strength - so he weakens them."

One among the crowd yelled, "That's why he won't let me feed my auntie!"

John pointed and said, "One sad story among many. The humans take care of their own. Why can't we? We'll start a Social Suckurity program to collect proper meals for them. Who among us would hand a starving blood-brother an empty platelet?"

Many in the crowd cheered and some pumped their fists.

"And as for the lymphomaniacs, stop using those hateful names. The proper term is vamperotics." Their smiles and rapt gazes told John that he was getting through to more of them. "Keymia has corrupted all of you by turning you against each other."

Some of the vampires glared at the Master with hate-filled eyes. Others at the edge of the cavern skulked away. John supposed they were Keymia's lackeys.

"Who made up those silly names?" John pointed at the Master. "He did! From now on don't say butt-biter. Say hemosexual or shemosexuals." John spotted Mistress Vanessa and pointed at her. "She's not a crampire or fangpanger, she's a vampinatrix!"

The crowd erupted. Some applauded while others stamped their feet and howled.

"Why should any of us care about how they feed?" John said. His speech was growing more rapid. "As long as they're contributing for the greater good, I'm all for it. That's the sort of dark world I want! Isn't it the sort of dark world you want?"

John turned his attention back to the still-frozen Master. "Your nights are numbered Lew!" He stretched out his hands. "Everyone join with me." He led them in a cheer. "Hey!" *Clap.* "Ho!" *Clap.* "Lew Keymia has got to go!"

The entire crowd joined in the cheer, and the noise in the cavern turned deafening.

"Join the vamperotic mind link and bring him down," John yelled.

The cheering subsided as one vampire after another linked their minds together.

Master Lew Keymia collapsed, writhing in pain. He slowly shriveled and wrinkled, releasing horrid moaning sounds. He tried to stand in a last effort to show his defiance but then fell hard. The thud echoed throughout the cavern.

Two vampires rushed to examine Keymia. John recognized them as the hemosexuals in the casket the night before. The pair examined Keymia, then faced the crowd and said, "Ding-dong, the lich is dead!"

The crowd danced and cheered. John jumped down from his perch.

Victor's exhausted face sported a wide smile as he approached John with a covered bowl. He removed the cover and displayed the contents.

"Chocolate pudding sausages?" John asked. "A little too dark to be chocolate."

Victor smiled. "No, it's not chocolate. Authentic English blood pudding. Best I could do on short notice."

And so, they danced and sang the night away, reveling in a vampiric way. And they all unlived happily ever after.

Spellbound

WINDOWS OF THE SOUL

Joanne R Larner

UK

www.joannelarner.wordpress.com

There was someone else in her mind. Apart from Lukas, of course. Lukas was still there, she could sense him, but his voice was fainter, like a whisper, drowned out by the interloper.

"Lukas, what is going on?" Marie was curious rather than alarmed. Her previous mental conversations with spirit people other than Lukas, her spirit guide, usually took place at her own invitation.

"Marie, it is a lost spirit. Be careful, he –"

"I LOVE YOU, MARIE! I WANT TO BE WITH YOU FOREVER!"

She clenched her teeth trying to block out the noise in her head. The voice was strident and so loud, powerful. It was not a physical voice but internal, like the ringing in your ears after a loud music concert, only a hundred times louder.

"I can't hear you, Lukas. He's talking over you."

"I cannot prevent it. He is too strong. <u>You</u> must block him. You could try sending him to the Light."

Lukas's voice was so faint she could barely hear him. She sensed his energy withdrawing, diminishing and another's moving forward eagerly, almost as if he had shouldered past Lukas, taken over from him. Was that even possible in the spirit world? She didn't know, she was so new to all this.

"Who are you? Do you need help finding the light?" She needed to know, perhaps then she could work out what to do.

"I AM PUBLIUS. I DON'T WANT TO GO TO THE LIGHT, TO LEAVE THIS PLACE. PLEASE! LET ME STAY! I JUST WANT TO WATCH YOU AND LISTEN TO YOUR BEAUTIFUL VOICE, IT'S LIKE MUSIC TO ME!"

"Do you have to speak so loudly? I can hear you very clearly, no need to shout." Perhaps, if she made the effort to converse with him, she could get rid of him more quickly.

"Sorry, is this better?"

She nodded, although in some ways it was worse; this stranger seeming to whisper right into her ear. She shivered as if a cold hand was running over her body. She swallowed.

"What is it you want from me? Is there a message you want me to deliver to someone?"

"No! I just want to be here with you. I love you."

"But I don't know you. How can you love me? I don't understand." She was confused. Why had this spirit chosen her?

"Let me into your mind and I will show you."

"No! Look, you need to go into the Light. Your family and friends will be waiting for you. It's beautiful there."

"I'm content to remain here by your side."

"Well, Publius, will you just be quiet for a moment then, please? It is exhausting when you keep talking like this." She attempted to calm her thoughts, to order them without this unwanted visitor's jarring interruptions.

"Sorry!"

One word and then there was silence, as swift as a door closing. She paused, relishing the sudden peace.

She decided to call Caroline, one of her psychic medium friends. She would know what to do.

***

"It sounds like a negative attachment. There are various ways to deal with it, don't worry." Caroline had reassured her and went on to give her numerous suggestions. In spiritual circles they used white sage or incense, grounding crystals, sea salt and visualisations. More powerful, traditional aids were white candles, Holy water and prayers to Archangel Michael, the Archangel of protection.

She decided to start with what she already had in the house: crystals and sea salt. She placed the grounding crystals - haematite and tiger's eye - in her pocket and sprinkled the sea salt all around herself. She visualised a white sword of light sweeping around her and cutting any unwanted attachments.

"Why are you doing this? You know me, Marie, my love."

He sounded hurt and anxious and her heart went out to him. He must be confused. Perhaps he had been insane before he died.

Finally, she lit some incense which she had found in the drawer alongside the crystals.

"My love is stronger than these silly spells. I remain here with you."

"Lukas?"

There was no reply.

***

The next day, after managing to get only a couple of hours of sleep, she went out and got some holy water and a crucifix from the local Catholic Church. She also visited the closest Wiccan shop and purchased some white scented candles, clear quartz crystals and white sage. The whole time she was struggling to hear clearly because of his voice inside her head.

"I love you!" "Don't do this to me." "Why don't you remember me?" He wept and pleaded with her, sobbing, panting. At times she felt his breath on her face, even his tears. Were they real or was it her own mind tricking her? She was unable to escape him, he was constantly present, wearing her down, exhausting her.

She had to find a way to block him. Not even waiting to get home, she ripped open the paper packet from the church, opened the plastic box and placed the delicate, silver crucifix around her neck. He was quiet then, for all of ten minutes.

Arriving home, she positioned the clear quartz crystals in the corners of the room. She lit the sage stick and, with trembling hand, smudged it all around the house: the windows, doors and herself, allowing the pungent smoke to cover everything.

"Our love is unbreakable! You will not be rid of me like this! I am part of you, your soul mate!" His voice echoed in her head, resonant and impossible to ignore, like the tolling of a bell from a church that was too close. She had even developed a headache from the lack of sleep and the stress.

She closed her eyes, visualising white light surrounding her, protecting her. But, she knew it was to no avail. She could still sense him close to her and Lukas seemed to be completely absent. She still had the holy water and prayers to try, though.

She dripped the blessed water everywhere around the room, on her own head, over her heart, her hands. She paused, a few drops left in the vial and drank them down. She lit the pure white candles and intoned a prayer to Archangel Michael, which was designed to help unwanted spiritual attachments leave and go to the Light.

"I ask you, Archangel Michael, to use your Sword of Light to clear me of all negative attachments. I ask that they leave me now and go somewhere safe within the universe without harming anyone. So be it, may be so. Amen."

She visualised the spirit travelling upwards with the smoke from the candle.

She breathed a sigh. It felt good, the prayer. She was sure it had worked.

"I'm still here, Marie. I won't go to the Light. Not until you can come with me. We belong together."

She clenched her fists, tears pricking her eyes. She was so tired. Then she took a deep breath and squared her shoulders.

"I command you to leave. I do not want you here. Be gone!"

"Please, Marie, just listen to me. Let me tell you about our life together. Then you can send me away if you don't believe me. I promise." His voice was gentle, reasonable.

A tingling sensation travelled from her shoulder to her hand, making the hairs on her arm stand on end. Didn't this kind of phenomenon mean a spirit was very close, even touching?

"Stop that right now! I didn't say you could touch me."

There was a pause, but the tingling feeling receded. She let her breath out in a sigh of relief.

"You used to love it when I did that…" He sounded sad now. Wistful.

212

"You mean in this past life you keep talking about?" She was genuinely curious about this. Past lives fascinated her.

"Yes, you were my wife, Paulina, in the first century. We shared an idyllic life. We were soul mates." His voice was breathy and soft, full of emotion.

"Why have you come to me now? Why have I never had any inkling about you?"

"You just visited Rome, didn't you? I was there, waiting. We lived in Rome – and Macedonia. We were happy until HE came between us." He paused and let out a low moan. "He stole you from me!" Plaintive now, with a hint of anger.

It was true, she had just been to Rome and it was also a fact that she had felt slightly odd after that, as if her brain was fogged. And then the voice had begun.

"Who stole me from you?"

"Lukas! He was named Gaius in that life. He caused us to part – it wasn't my will!" His voice was tight now, clipped.

"Lukas has never told me about a life in Ancient Rome. I need to check this with him. I have no memory of such a life."

"You don't need to ask him – he will only lie. Allow me to show you our past life and you will remember."

His voice sounded despairing. Perhaps she should let him show her. She was intrigued by past lives and she had to admit she did find what he said familiar, as if he had awakened a real memory.

"OK, you can show me."

She gasped as his spirit entered her head, intolerable pressure filling her skull as if it was about to burst.

"It's all right, my love, relax."

She took a shaky breath and, as the pressure eased, vivid images flashed across her inner vision, one following the other in a weird procession of scenes. In one, she was holding a bronze mirror, the face within different from hers but the eyes, the same. So, the old saying 'The eyes are a window to the soul' must be true.

More images invaded. Riches, wealth, a wedding, she was getting married to a tall, handsome man. His name was Publius. Her eyes fixed on her new husband's, she smiled, joy filling her at the thought of the happy life they would have together. Her feet were decorated with pearls and her clothes dripping with precious jewels.

Her rich garments shimmered like the scales of a fish and were heavy, they were so laden with wealth. Her new husband was a powerful man, a consul.

Abruptly, the scene changed, and she was in agony, reclining in a birthing chair. She clearly saw a bracelet on her wrist, marked with mysterious symbols, an amulet, she knew somehow. Her head was swimming, though she was vaguely aware of other women about her, instructing her what to do and then, with one last pain-filled push, her son was born. Flashes of different scenarios came thick and fast, mostly happy times, her husband presenting her with gifts, his reputation rising as he became governor of Macedonia, the start of a family. Sunshine, jewels, laughter.

Then the news of a new emperor back in Rome. Gaius. He was going to visit them in Macedonia. As he was escorted in and shown to the seat of honour, normally occupied by Publius, his eyes met hers and they lit up in delight. All evening he barely stopped gazing at her and she shuddered as a dark, foreboding engulfed her. He turned to her husband.

"Publius, my friend, you have not yet celebrated my accession by offering a gift. I have a suggestion."

"Anything, Most Sacred Emperor. As you can see, I have precious jewels, horses, gold, perfumed oils, the best delicacies. Pray choose whatever you will."

Gaius smiled like a cat, his eyes glittering greedily as he made a show of examining all the treasures on display, finally coming to rest on her. She lowered her gaze.

"Of course, the greatest treasure you possess is your wife, Paulina. I choose her!"

The blood drained from Publius's face as he stammered a reply.

"But, Sacred Emperor, I –"

"I hope you are not going to refuse your Emperor?" It was worded as a question, but there was only one possible reply and his grin of triumph showed he knew it.

"I will divorce her immediately, of course." He couldn't look at her, his hands were shaking.

Tears filled her eyes as the Emperor held out his hand…

Her attention was flung back into the room as Publius's mind withdrew from hers. She was shaking, her heart hammering. It was true then. She remembered the happiness she felt with Publius, his loving embraces, their laughter. And, if Lukas was Gaius in this life, he had, indeed, forced Publius to divorce her. Everything fitted. Lukas had tried to keep this from her! Publius had really been her soul mate!

"I believe you, Publius. But why are you showing me this?"

"I will go to the Light, but only if you come with me. We can be together, forever, in Heaven."

She felt dizzy, confused, but the memory of their life together, their love, was so vivid. She realised she longed to be with him again.

"Yes, I want that too."

As soon as the thought entered her mind, Publius was back inside her head and the memories with him. They began with Gaius taking her hand, leading her away to his bed. She submitted, tried to pretend she was happy to be chosen by him, but, inside, her heart was broken. Another wedding, even more lavish than the first, but poorer in joy. Gaius was young and handsome, and she might have even grown to love him if only he had been slightly kind.

But he was mercurial, she never knew what kind of mood he would be in. He lavished gifts on her one moment and then, if he was angered, he would take it out on her. Her body, once voluptuous, grew thin and bruised, her eyes lost their sparkle. The bronze mirror told the tale only too clearly: fear had replaced love.

Then a shocking procession of images and a jumble of scenes, one after another, endlessly, each more horrible than the last. Beatings, verbal abuse, and she helpless, enduring, growing ever more desperate until one day which she would do anything to forget.

She had walked in on Gaius with another woman. This was nothing new, just one of the ways he liked to humiliate her. But as the woman turned, she recognised her. It was Agrippina, his own sister! Agrippina smiled triumphantly but, from then on, her life as Paulina was hell. Gaius divorced her after six months, accusing her of infertility and yet forbade her to return to Publius. The end of her short life came when Agrippina accused her of sorcery and forced her to commit suicide.

Paulina lay in the warm bath and took a shaky breath. The knife gleamed in the last rays of the setting sun, her last evening. Twice she brought the blade to her wrist, twice she could not bring herself to use it. The guard took a step forward, his hand gripping the hilt of his sword.

"No! I will do it; I'll do it now."

Before she could hesitate again, she swiftly drew the sharp edge along her vein, gasping as the water began turning red. Then, as if in a nightmare, the other wrist, her blood ebbing away with her life.

Marie's heart thumped madly, and then came a crushing pain and her spirit floated gently out of her body too. Disorientated, she glanced around and her spirit eyes finally met those of Publius. She froze. The eyes are the windows of the soul. And the eyes that met hers were not those of her love, Publius, but Gaius, her torturer, the cruel and debauched emperor who had stolen her.

"You're not Publius!" she gasped.

"No, sorry, I lied about that; Lukas is your Publius. But you are mine now. And we won't be going to the Light, of course. They won't have me there, I'm afraid. Not the Emperor Gaius, or as I have become known to history… Caligula." He smiled as he took her hand…

AUTISTIC GIRL AND THE KILLER LAWN GNOME

Dabney Farmer

Charlotte, North Carolina, USA

www.webtoons.com/en/challenge/life-with-lee-/list?title_no=1013

6:15 A. M.

Leila was the first to find the groundskeeper's body, and she knew right away he was dead.

I'm not sure what tipped her off, but it might have been the giant pink pointy hat sticking out of his chest, for the groundskeeper had been impaled by a lawn gnome.

Not just any lawn gnome, but Skippy, one of the five lawn gnomes spread throughout the back garden. It was most unfortunate for the groundskeeper to have landed on a lawn gnome with such a pointy hat.

Also, it hadn't helped that Skippy was also made of solid concrete, whereas the other gnomes were made of clay and hollow inside. If the groundskeeper had fallen on a different lawn gnome, he would have been fine. Well... maybe not fine, as if you land on any lawn gnome it would hurt. But he would be alive, more or less.

Leila didn't enjoy looking at the dead groundskeeper, not because she was squeamish about blood, which there was a lot of.

What bothered her about this most grisly scene was that the groundskeeper was getting sticky blood all over Skippy, who was her favorite gnome in the garden. Leila didn't even like the other lawn gnomes, as the rest had big cheerful smiles painted on their cheeks.

Which she found most unsettling. Skippy had been the only non-smiling gnome, and no one could see him with the groundskeeper lying on top of him.

Now, don't get the wrong idea about Leila. It wasn't that she didn't care that a man was dead, it just hadn't registered with her at that moment. On TV, when a cartoon dies by falling off a cliff or blowing themselves up, they always come back to life.

No questions asked in the next episode, or even the next scene. So, as absurd as it might sound, she assumed the groundskeeper would be okay later. Which was why Leila was more concerned for Skippy. With Skippy covered up, all she could see was the cheerful lawn gnomes with the big cheeky smiles staring at her.

Even if you didn't share Leila's dislike for the other gnomes, anyone else in her place would have had to admit seeing their cheery faces on such a grizzly scene was unsettling.

It wasn't that Leila was against people, or gnomes smiling; she just simply didn't like smiling herself. It hurt her mouth. Which was why she liked Skippy, as Leila always felt he was only frowning because he didn't feel like smiling, just like her.

Although Leila didn't really frown, she usually had a somewhat expressionless look on her face, which often gave people the wrong impression she was disinterested in them.

Leila's eyes were another story. Where the rest of her face stayed blank, her eyes showed brightness and curiosity. Maybe too much curiosity.

Unfortunately, few people noticed this as Leila wore her dark blue sunglasses everywhere, even inside and at night. Her eyes were oversensitive to lights, so she almost always covered them up. Except right at bedtime, as she couldn't sleep with sunglasses on (although she had tried).

She also always wore a Yankees baseball cap facing backwards. Originally, she was given the hat to keep the sun out of her eyes. However, one day her brother turned the hat backwards and said she looked cooler wearing it that way. After that, she never wore it facing forward again. It was funny she could be so adamant about how she wore her hat when otherwise Leila didn't care what she had on. When it came to other clothes, Leila wore whatever she was given, as long as it was comfortable and not itchy.

She didn't care about fashion and preferred to go barefoot, and never wore shoes or socks unless she had to.

Today was the first day in a long time she had wished she had shoes on, since she had gotten a little bit of blood on her feet—since there was a pool of reddish brown stuck all over the sidewalk. Some had seeped into the mud, and she hadn't noticed until she examined her feet.

She wiped her foot off in the grass. Nothing worse than sticky stuff on your feet. Well, almost nothing worse; it could have been worse. At least, she wasn't the groundskeeper, who was not going to be happy when he woke up and saw he was dead.

6:33 A. M.

Leila couldn't help Skippy as the groundskeeper was too heavy to move, and if she did, she'd get her hands all sticky, which she hated. She would just have to wait for someone else to find him. So, she decided to go back inside before anyone saw her—seeing as how she wasn't supposed to be outside anyway.

Leila lived in a special group home for special needs, called Safe Haven.

At the moment, everyone else was still asleep inside. There was a house rule that you were not supposed to go outside without a special aide helper. That was a staff member that kept an eye on the people who had special needs.

Leila was the only one that knew how to open the locked doors to the garden without any help from an aide.

So when she woke up early (which was very often) she would go out to visit the garden with the outdoor trampoline so she could jump without anyone telling her not too high, not too close to the edge, and give other kids a turn.

This day, however, she decided she would go back inside.

Although the groundskeeper had not been a nice man, the adults were going to be very upset when they found him. Leila did not want to be around when that happened, as she had seen that kind of thing happen before.

6:35 A. M.

Making sure to not slam the screen door behind she stepped back inside, Leila let out a little sigh.

One of the benefits of sneaking out in bare feet was having quieter footsteps. Normally, when Leila was forced by the staff to put on shoes, they would stick these big, clunky boots on her. They say it's to keep her safe, but she thought it because they give her loud footsteps they can hear better in every room.

But without shoes, Leila's footsteps were as quiet as a mouse, making it easy to go up the stairs. Once safe inside her room, Leila forgets about being quiet and turns on her TV.

Leila has her own taste in movies and had over three hundred old VHS tapes in her room. Along with her own old but effective small TV and an even older VCR.

Her favorite things to watch were old cartoons. The one she put in was called *G.I. Joe.*

Leila didn't understand the show at all. She wasn't even sure who were the good guys and bad guys, since they all dressed very similar. That was okay, because Leila only watched it for the theme song anyway. "G.I. Joe, American heroes!" her TV blared.

She loved cartoons, even if they didn't make any sense. Like how a tiny little yellow bird could pick up anvils and throw it on a cat's head without killing him. Or how when a cartoon dies, they suddenly show them as an angel playing a harp with wings in a white dress and with a floating gold hula hoop over their head.

The nice thing about *G.I. Joe* cartoons were that even though they kept shooting at each other, no one ever died in the show. The worst thing that happened was someone falls into a coma after being stabbed with a snake in the chest.

Maybe the groundskeeper wasn't dead after all; maybe he was just in a coma. If getting stabbed by a snake was any different than stabbed by a lawn gnome, that is.

For a moment, Leila wondered if maybe she should tell someone what she saw? But only for a moment, then she just replayed the theme song about five more times, got bored and put in another tape. This one was the old *Care Bears*. Pretty soon, her VCR was blasting "I wanna be a Care Bear!"

"Oh, sweet Jiminy! Not the Care Bears again!" shouted Rob from his room.

Rob could hear every tape Leila ever put in her VCR when he was awake, as his room was, unfortunately, right next to Leila's room. Rob was a special aide, and the house rules were that each aide should have a room between two residents. Rob had been trying to switch rooms for years, but everyone else was aware of Leila's early morning movie routine and wouldn't do it. Leila was not fond of Rob, either, but he was a heavy sleeper, which was how Leila could sneak past his room every morning unnoticed. Rob could sleep through almost anything except for a loud TV blasting and 80's cartoon.

Leila didn't like to talk, and avoided it every chance she got. She knew if she were to try and explain what she saw she'd have to talk, not draw it out on her little dry erase board.

Leila knew there would be a lot of trouble coming later, as death caused a lot more drama around the house then any cartoon theme song.

By this point, it was slowly starting to occur to her the groundskeeper might not be coming back. For if he did wake up from being dead, he might not get up right away. He'd always been a lazy man who made excuses, and having something stuck in your chest is the very good excuse to use.

She found herself wondering if the groundskeeper would wake up, curse about Skippy being stuck in him and having to clean up his own blood. Then he would be calling in sick feeling, it's too much work to do. Then he'd drive to the bar and we wouldn't see Skippy all day.

Leila found herself thinking about the time Kevin found Molly's pet gerbil dead in the cage, he did not break the news to Molly well. He had picked up the departed gerbil by the tail, showed it to Molly who was eating oatmeal and said, "It's dead."

Then, feeling his point had been made, he let go of the gerbil to leave it on the table, but it ended up falling in her oatmeal.

I don't know who was more upset that day, Molly or her aide Miss Jill, who screamed when she turned around to see why Molly was crying and saw the gerbil floating in her oatmeal.

Leila did not want to think how loud it would be over a dead person versus a dead gerbil. She had a bad feeling it would be about a million times worse. Especially since a person was a lot bigger than a gerbil.

Leila hoped whoever found the groundskeeper wouldn't try flushing him down the toilet.

7:00 A. M.

Leila replayed the Care Bears theme song sixteen more times, then replaced it with another tape of the *ThunderCats*.

"Thunder! Thunder! ThunderCats!" She really liked this one and turned her TV up as she rocked in her bean bag chair harder. By then she had started to hear other people in the house get up and leave their rooms.

"Oh, for . . . It's those ThunderCats now!" Rob moaned "That's worse than the Care Bears. If I have to hear that stupid theme song one more time…" Rob grumbled angrily from his room.

Rob always opened his closet door by throwing it open against the wall. Leila hates that sound, so she turned the TV up even louder so she wouldn't hear it.

"Gah! Now it's getting louder," Rob shouted, sounding like he was in a bad mood. Which was no surprise, as Rob always sounded like that.

7:15 A. M.

Eventually, Leila's aide Gerald peeped his head in her room.

"Breakfast will be ready soon. Why don't you get dressed?" he told her.

Leila slunk back on her beanbag chair and thought momentarily about telling Gerald what was out there in the backyard. She knew if she did, they would get to work removing Skippy from the groundskeeper. Then they would clean Skippy up, so he would be put back in place. Leila had no idea where they would put the groundskeeper. Maybe he'd be put in the shed with the other broken lawn ornaments, like the pink flamingos that had been run over, or the racist lawn jockey.

Maybe he'd get buried in the backyard with Molly's gerbil. If he was buried in the backyard, would the neighbor's cat try and dig him up like the gerbil.

In the end, Leila decided she would go down to the kitchen, if not to tell Gerald, but for waffle day.

7:30 A. M.

"Can't that old, drunk groundskeeper ever keep the squirrels from uprooting the flower bed?" Miss Jill complained while stirring up her oatmeal. Miss Jill was often grumpy in the morning, although thankfully not as vocal as Rob was. Instead of yelling, Miss Jill would take out her grumpiness on her oatmeal. She stirred it up like she wanted to punish it.

Leila loved waffles, as long as no one ruins them by putting syrup on the top. She only enjoyed them plain and crunchy, as she hated when her food got gooey or moist. As long as they weren't sticky like blood.

"If he's not drunk, what is he, then?" Miss Jill asked staring at Leila's waffles with what can only be described as envy. Miss Jill was always on a diet, so she only ate oatmeal.

"He just has… problems," Gerald said.

Leila agreed with Gerald, as she felt having a lawn gnome stuck in your chest was a big problem. She even nodded her head up and down for yes, but no one noticed as they just thought she was stimming.

"He's just lazy. I wish Miss Charity would fire him," grumbled Miss Jill, looking at her oatmeal discontentedly. She started stirring it up again, as if to say, *take that, oatmeal.*

Miss Charity was the one who owned the group home and many others in town. Everyone loved her. If Miss Charity had been impaled by a lawn gnome Leila would have talked for her, or considered it. But not for the groundskeeper.

"I will talk to him about the squirrels later," Gerald said while trying to get his breakfast ready.

"See that you do. The garden was a mess yesterday," Miss Jill said. When has that old drunk ever fixed anything on time?" Miss Jill scoffed.

"So, you mean you went out and checked this morning?" Gerald asked, one eyebrow raised.

Leila assumed when Miss Jill did see the Groundskeeper, she would be complaining about him being dead and bloody more than squirrels.

Leila raised her own eyebrows, but as she already had her sunglasses on, no one noticed. Miss Jill and Gerald tried not to look right at her face anyway, unless talking to her, since they knew she didn't like it.

"Well…No, I don't have to. I know he didn't do it," Miss Jill said.

"Maybe he did. He might surprise you," Gerald said optimistically.

Oh, you will both be surprised, all right. Leila thought to herself, wondering what they would say when they did look outside. Leila shifted in her seat.

"I have too much to do to check the garden," Miss Jill said, sliding her oatmeal away and leaving the room.

"But you have enough time to complain about it," whispered Gerald under his breath, but not quietly enough, because Miss Jill stormed back in the room.

"What did you say?" she asked.

Gerald jumped, but didn't turn around "Oh, uh… I said you have enough time to take good care of yourself."

"Oh. Well, I try to," she said, smiling, and left.

7:55 A. M.

No one mentioned the groundskeeper again for the rest of breakfast.

No one looked outside in the garden, either, since none of the other special aides went outside the house until everyone was fed and dressed—which took a while, because some people needed to be fed separately, like Leila, or simply ate slowly.

Even if they were to open the drapes, they wouldn't see the groundskeeper unless they opened the window and stuck their head way to the left to spot him.

Leila was uneasy, but not for the same reasons most people would be, thinking about a dead body.

Leila was more worried about the yelling being involved. She remembered when the neighbor's cat had dug up the dead gerbil buried in the backyard. Leila had taken Gerald's hand and led him to the cat and what was left of the gerbil. Gerald had made a gagging sound as if he was sick. Then he ran inside the house to get the other aids to help… by help, all they did was start shouting about what to do.

Some said they should just let that cat have the gerbil, others said it was a matter of principle and they had to get it out of the cat's mouth. With so many aides shouting, it caused a chain reaction. Soon, the other residents got uneasy and worked up—since they weren't used to seeing their aides get so angry—which caused them to become anxious and make noise themselves.

The aides that had stayed inside tried to keep everyone calm, but it was no use. That had been a most unpleasant morning, one that Leila didn't want to repeat any time soon.

8:30 A. M.

As soon as breakfast was finished, Leila went back to her room and put in a *Casper The Friendly Ghost* tape, as well as put on her headphones. The ones that connected right to her TV. She rarely used them, but Leila was hopeful that when they started shouting, she wouldn't have to hear them with the headphones on. Unfortunately, the morning was not the time to watch TV, since after breakfast, Leila was supposed to go downstairs to get her reading lessons. So, it wasn't long before Gerald tried to coax her out of her room again.

"Oh, Leila, don't you want to go down to your reading class?" Gerald asked nicely.

Leila shook her head hard for no, making it clear she wasn't going.

Gerald sighed a little louder than last time, but did not force her. So, Leila was allowed to stay in her room.

Which she was pleased about, until Rob showed up.

8:45 A. M.
"Hey! Why aren't you in class?" Rob sneered, barging into her room.

Even with her headphones on, Leila could hear him.

"Maybe if you ignore him, he'll go away," she thought. It was wishful thinking.

She turned around to look at him, then put in another tape.

"That better not be another *ThunderCats* tape," Rob said.

It was.

"You better not play it," Rob said.

She did.

"You better not turn the volume up!" Rob said.

She did. How else was she going to listen with Rob yelling?

"I'm going to take a nap! A nap I have to take because of your six bloody A. M. TV watching." He sneered so hard, snot flew out of his nose.

Leila pointed to her headphones, it was her way of saying she wouldn't wake him up from his nap with them on, but Rob was too mad to notice.

Rob stomped over to the TV, slammed his finger on the eject button and grabbed the *ThunderCats* tape. He held it up over her head so she couldn't reach it.

"You know what I'm going to do?" There was a moment of silence as if he thought she'd answer.

"I'm going to throw this out the window and see if the bloody ThunderCats always land on their feet."

Leila wished she could have told Rob that if you did throw a real cat out a window, its feet would get bloody. She had seen this kind of thing happen before, with the neighbor's cat.

But she couldn't. The best she could say was, "Ewww," which was her way of saying "Uh, gross." She didn't want to think about blood after seeing poor Skippy.

"That's right. Eww!" said Rob, clueless about what she meant. "Now say goodbye to Prince Adam."

If Leila could have talked right then, she would have told him Prince Adam was from *He-Man*, not *ThunderCats*! When you watch something a billion times, you learn all the names. But Leila didn't talk, so she didn't say anything. She wasn't worried, anyway. After all, she had five other *ThunderCats* tapes she could put on when Rob left. So she was okay if he threw one out.

Rob had trouble opening the window, since it was one of those heavy-duty safety kind you're only supposed to open in an emergency, but with a few mighty grunts that would have impressed He-man and She-Ra, he got it open.

Then he leaned out her window and dropped the tape.

"Geronimo! So long you lousy piece of crap . . . what the?" Rob trailed off.

He leaned back inside Leila room, his face white as Casper the Friendly Ghost. Rob rushed out of the room, and down the stairs while Leila went back to watching TV—but she could still hear Rob.

"Uh, say . . . Miss Jill, did we take in all the Halloween decorations from the backyard?" Rob asked, sounding oddly nicer than he'd been earlier.

"Of course, we did. Halloween was months ago," Miss Jill said.

"So, what you're saying is... we don't have a Halloween decoration of a dummy laying on one of the lawn gnomes?" Rob said.

"No . . . Why would anyone own something so morbid?" Miss Jill asked.

"Could you look in the backyard for me?" asked Rob.

"Why? I have a lot of work to do today."

"You might have a lot more work for us if what I think is out there is really out there," said Rob, breathing hard.

* * * * *

The screaming got worse, and worse as the weeks went on.

The groundskeeper's death was ruled an accident. As it was assumed that he'd simply gotten drunk and fallen on Skippy, end of story.

Only it wasn't the end of the story, far from it. Not where the lawn gnomes were concerned.

* * * * *

A week later, Rob was found dead with a lawn flamingo stabbing him in the back. At first glance, it looked like the flamingo

227

was just sitting on his back, like in those nature documentaries where birds sit on rhinos' backs. Or it would have, had it not been for all the blood. Who would have thought little metal stick legs could punch through a body and do so much damage?

No one could figure out how such a thing could have happened. As he hadn't fallen on it like Skippy and the groundskeeper, more like the flamingo fell on him and impaled him somehow.

Leila had her suspicions, as Skippy who was still in the garden, cleaned up of course, had just the slightest smile on his face. No one noticed it but her.

The next week, there was an annoying old neighbor—a cranky lady who had hated kids and everyone else—had her large bird house fall on her head, killing her instantly.

This wasn't as odd as Rob's death, as it had been a large bird house, but it had been on a sturdy tall pole, so it still seemed odd it would fall over on its own when it wasn't even windy the day it fell.

On further inspection, it looked as if something had been cutting into the pole, but what? No one knew.

Meanwhile, Leila had noticed Skippy's small smile was a little bigger now. Not only that, the axe was, too. Another lawn gnome "BoBo," was missing, along with his axe and the arm that held it.

It hadn't been a real axe, but if you were going to split hairs, these were real lawn gnomes, and it seemed awfully coincidental that the day a pole had been chopped down, another lawn gnome was missing his axe arm.

The week after that, the cranky lady's husband somehow managed to trip on one of those hide-a-key rocks and fell face-first in the cement bird bath and drowned. How exactly a grown man can drown in less than an inch and a half of water was confusing to everyone. But it didn't seem to bother the birds, who were found splashing in the water next to his face.

Skippy's smile was bigger than ever.

So, even though Skippy was still her favorite, Leila decided to take a break from going in the garden for a while.

THE TOYMAKER

Geoff Le Pard

South London UK

geofflepard.com

Geppy Parsons was a chameleon: those who knew him called him 'toymaker'; those who didn't, but benefited from his model-making expertise called him 'genius'; and those bereaved by the application of his uniquely crafted weaponry called him 'monster'.

Geppy lived for his work. He hand-tooled beautiful mechanical devices, using only wood and twine. The children who received a 'Geppy Gift' cherished them for their clever tricks and their parents for their robust construction and the modest prices he insisted on charging. Many such models would be loved into adulthood and bequeathed to future generations to enjoy afresh.

But there was another side to Geppy. His placid uncomplaining nature made him the perfect uncle, but his amoral indifference to the lives of those from outside his hillside town made him highly suitable for the role that was to make him comfortable, loathed and hunted by the forces of law and order across many national boundaries.

Never one to resist a challenge, Geppy was tasked by the mayor of his small town to use his skills to craft a unique weapon for the local passion: boar hunting. Geppy exceeded the brief by

229

building an all wooden dart gun that was small, powerful, and accurate.

When the mayor proudly showed off his new 'toy' to one appreciative guest who had visited to enjoy some hunting, he had no idea that the guest was a member of a significant crime syndicate. The guest, Torens, was intrigued by the weapon's apparently innocuous construction and lack of anything that the now ubiquitous metal detectors would reveal.

"Who made this?"

"Ah, that's Geppy. His is a special talent,"

"He's a gunsmith?"

"No, a toymaker."

Torens pondered this stroke of luck. After debating with his superiors, he had a terrified Geppy kidnapped, threatened, and propositioned. Could he build a totally anonymous and undetectable, yet fully functional weapon?

Geppy thought through the logistics and developed three prototypes, the final one, in the shape of a small wooden doll that delivered a deadly wooden dart, capable of piercing both a human skull and most Kevlar, was perfect for his new clients. They took it and tried to replicate it, but, without Geppy's skill, the copies were never as effective as the original. No, the syndicate would have to retain Geppy for themselves.

Geppy understood the commission was one he wasn't meant to reject. And indeed, he didn't want to. If whoever was the intended target was from outside his region, it didn't interest or concern him. And the parochial life Geppy led suited his paymasters. An untraceable system for collection and payment was devised and refined so that, by the time the world awoke to the novel way in which assassins delivered their terminal messages, Geppy was once more just a small-time model-maker, lost in the mists of the remote hills.

Geppy's 'Pinocchio' - nicknamed for the way its deadly dart resembled the original's nose - became the weapon of choice for the syndicate's dispensers of their form of justice. Infinitely variable in design, undetectable by all security systems, small enough to be secreted in a handbag and capable of being swiftly burnt to remove all evidence, the violent way the 'nose' exploded from the model's head to deliver its message never failed to bring about the desired impact. The syndicate's local successes led to its being commissioned for bigger and better paid projects, its infamy spreading rapidly.

Occasionally Geppy would hear tell of some famous leader's untimely end at the hands of an assassin or terrorist or freedom fighter and understand that death came via a 'Pinocchio'. He would listen to the news reader's approval or approbation, with equal indifference and retire to his workshop to consider his next commission.

While assassins were caught and terrorists exposed, the anonymity of the mysterious maker of these tools of death caused increased vexation amongst the powerful and the moneyed. How on Earth were they to stop this?

Geppy's grandniece, Dolphi, loved her uncle's little house, carved into the hill. Its dark cool rooms held a myriad of toys and machines to delight and intrigue the young mind. And, as Geppy grew old, he enjoyed letting the little girl roam around after school finished or when she stayed during the holidays, bringing some much-needed life to the old building. While he worked and she played, he told her stories, both real and imaginary. One day, after a particularly brutal multiple killing of a royal family had been in the news, each member relieved of their existence by a Pinocchio, he recounted the old fable of the woodcarver and the animated doll whose nose grew when he lied. "Please, please uncle, make me a Pinocchio!"

Sweet thing, he thought as he turned to his old lathe and crafted a small figurine for his Dolphi. She was asleep when he finished his task and he propped it by her bed for her on waking. Tired and rheumy-eyed, he poured himself a large beaker of the local spirit and took himself to bed.

When Dolphi awoke she found the gift. As she inspected it, she realised with growing horror that her uncle had made the wrong doll. No, this wasn't right. She wouldn't allow this. Hurrying to his room, where the old man slept, she cried, demanding he fix things, repair his error. Her doll was no liar; hers would be a good Pinocchio.

He refused to stir as the increasingly agitated girl's desperation to wake him grew. "Please, Uncle, please. You need to fix this."

He shifted, moving away from her pleadings. His head hurt and he just needed a little more sleep.

She shook his shoulders and poked his arm, anger now adding to her frustration. How could he be so thoughtless? She lifted her doll and used the unwanted nose to prick the old man's neck, determined that he wake and deliver his promise.

The might of thousands and the wealth of nations over more than a decade had failed to stop Geppy, the anonymous, yet malevolent force behind the 'Pinocchio'.

It took Dolphi seconds. As she lifted her Pinocchio and brought it down with such force as she could muster in order to deliver a second, and sharper message with the doll's unwanted 'liar's' nose, the old man twisted his head to deliver a rebuke of his own.

The beautifully tapered and varnished nose had no troubled passing through Geppy's outer ear, eardrum, his inner ear and into the brain's soft tissue.

Death wasn't instant. Geppy had enough time, as thick arterial blood oozed out of the newly crafted hole and ran into his mouth to realise the irony that he was the latest and last victim of one of his Pinocchios. As Dolphi cried and the world sighed, Geppy died.

GOTHAM ON PAUSE

Anne Marie Andrus

New Jersey, USA

AnneMarieAndrus.com

Tiny tremors escalated to an eerie quiver that whipped whitecaps over the dead calm river of onyx. Colossal anchor chains of a resurrected heroine groaned under the strain of a northern tempest. In her hull, far below the waterline, a crystal coffin shifted on its pedestal. Like a phantom, the occupant slid the cover back as though it were a feather. A glance around with lost eyes did little to clear fog from his stirring mind.

The man raised pale knuckles in front of his face and wiggled his fingers. *Pins and needles.* Blinking orange lights lurked behind steel framework, casting just enough glow to reveal panes of dark glass in an oval perimeter. A disembodied hand with ruby nail polish beckoned for his attention. *Reminds me of the Haunted Mansion on the boardwalk. I hate Halloween.* He cautiously bent his knees. *Like walking on someone else's legs.* Footsteps fell in silence on the faded deck. As he shuffled from mirror to mirror, each one leapt to life and the ominous black holes sparkled into a ring of vivid memories—movie clips of an extravagant life.

My life. He retraced his path to the first mirror, the opening scene. He remembered the party, the champagne and the orchestra. *My first inauguration. Must have been well past midnight.* A bow tie hung loose around his collar and the woman in his arms had confetti in her ink black hair. *I have three ex-wives and she is absolutely not one of them.* He struggled to see her face but it remained hidden, as if the reflection magically turned her deeper into the past as he stepped closer. *Who are you?*

The man balled his fists and glared around at futuristic trash. *And where the hell am I? Looks like a derelict starship.* He stomped back for a closer look at the storyline. Moonlight surfing on the Big Island, skiing in the remote Alps, racing vintage cars on condemned tracks, scuba diving Tahitian caves…the scenes went on and on. The only thread that tied them together was the endings. Accidents—lethal ones. *Were there really so many?* He massaged his forehead and squinted at a horrific helicopter crash. *Never should have flown in that weather—officials warned me and I ignored it.* He froze mid-step. Amidst the mangled wreckage, a murky silhouette stood with crossed arms. *How did I not notice that person before? The eyes...*

A frantic review of the other mirrors revealed the stranger at every site, flashing unmistakable emerald eyes. *I had no business surviving any of these events, yet somehow...* His gaze was drawn toward two blurry mirrors at the end of the storyline. One hung crooked, partially obstructed and undecipherable, while in the last pane shadows drifted beneath a glittery veil. *This must be the closing scene.* He tapped the glass and a picture flickered in and out as if begging him to remember. He concentrated, allowing his eyes to focus on the center and make sense of the emerging shapes. *The skyline...my penthouse. Is that—*

The portal reluctantly revealed a man in a midnight blue suit staggering through a heavy door. He kicked it shut behind him, leaving a row of bolts open and locks unchained as he stumbled to the bar to splash caramel liquor in a tumbler. He nearly gagged on the first sip and stared into the glass. Hints of metal and ash seared his tongue. *That bourbon was revolting. Th*e man slammed the rest of the drink back before grabbing a plum from a polished bowl and wandering to the balcony. *I look defeated.* Behind the glass, his likeness slouched against the railing, crumpling papers in one hand. *Why? My approval ratings were sky high.* One page floated in the breeze and he slid closer, struggling to decipher the print. *A police report. Burglary?* He nearly tossed the plum away but took an impulsive bite instead. The picture sputtered and lurched like old time film spinning off a projector wheel. Firecrackers exploded inside his skull. His real-time howl bounced off steel walls as the picture withered and flashing orange lights picked up speed. He frantically searched his wrist for a pulse. *Seriously?* His hands flew to his neck, hunting for any kind of beat. *Am I—*

"No!" The air rippled like a bomb's shockwave, knocking the man to his knees. A woman strutted to the center of the compartment. "Arrogant, definitely." She crossed her arms with precision. "But not dead, Governor. Not yet."

"You know me?" He staggered to his feet. "I'm sorry I don't recognize—wait—your eyes." He spun back to confirm that the silhouettes all now had facial features and hourglass curves. Facing forward again, a smile tugged at the corner of his lips. "It was you who danced with me at my inauguration." Behind him, the woman with confetti in her hair turned and smiled.

"A tango to be specific." She tucked her grey collar over an ornate black chain around her neck. "Since you've forgotten, I'm Victoria."

"Governor Bell." He stepped forward and offered his hand. "Grayson Bell."

Victoria held out her hand and watched as he struggled to grasp it, his palm passing through hers like smoke several times before giving up. "You said I wasn't…"

"You aren't dead, sir. But that's not your real body either." Victoria gestured from his feet to his head and back. "Is this your normal attire?"

"Looks like a sooty toga." He groaned and shook his head. "Where is my body and how do I get back in it?"

"I have a lot to clarify." She pointed behind him at the coffin. "Though you may be looking for him."

The Governor forced himself to peer through the crystal lid at a figure in a midnight suit. Not pasty enough to be a corpse, yet way too still to be alive. On his lapel, a golden eagle held a flaming torch in its enameled beak. "My campaign pin—that man looks much older than I remember."

"It was a rough time—before—don't you remember any of it?"

"Very little." He rubbed his chin. "There was the plague, of course and it was awful, but we beat it. Things were nearly back to normal."

"About that." Victoria slumped onto a pile of iron girders in the corner. 'Maybe if I'd been present and not made idiotic schoolgirl mistakes."

"Victoria, I don't care what you did or didn't do." The Governor took two erratic steps back and clenched his jaw. "And, I don't mean to sound short or arrogant, as you so flippantly called me before." He turned his head just enough to glare at her. "Explain. Now. All of it!"

"Of course." Victoria flashed to the first mirror and placed her hand on the glass. On the other side, her twin in grey matched the gesture while strains of violin and piano echoed from the past. "You recall this gala?"

"My first win. To say I was the underdog in that election is an absolute understatement." He smiled and brushed a single piece of confetti off his toga. "Damn, that night was sweet."

"I'd only surveilled you from a distance until you asked me to dance." Victoria drifted to the next scenes, stopping to acknowledge her reflection in each one. "Then the story turned darker."

"Clearly this is you at every accident scene." The Governor caught up and tried to intercept her. "Why?"

Victoria evaded his moves as a blur, finally stopping short to confront him. "To save your sorry reckless ass. This Hawaii fiasco—" She jabbed her thumb at the picture. "Was *the* worst judgement I've ever witnessed from a human and somehow people still voted for you. Trust Grayson Bell, they said, he's the future of our country, they said…three terms and counting."

The Governor raised an eyebrow.

"Never mind that surfing off a beach famous for shark attacks was insane, I almost couldn't pry that leviathan's jaws off you. Fun fact—he wasn't hunting alone." She flipped her shirt up to reveal mutilated black skin. The white of several ribs peeked through ragged tissue. "I lost so much blood, it was you or me—almost neither."

"So, you rescued me from all this." He swept his hand back at the carnage. "No offense, but how? You're a wisp of a thing who had the nerve to call me untrustworthy. Nobody speaks to me like that."

Victoria stomped up to him and then past to the pile of steel girders. She lifted a piece of metal twice as long as she was tall with one hand, tossed it and caught it with the other. She laughed at his wide eyes and snapped the beam in half like a toothpick. "Need more proof?" Her eyes flared an impossible green and instantly she was an inch from his face. A wide smile revealed razor sharp fangs. She slammed him to the deck with one finger.

"I apologize." He cringed away. "For questioning you and whatever other garbage I said. Holy—what are you?"

"I'm sorry—the truth is, between all the daredevil nonsense you were a once-in-a-lifetime leader." Victoria held both hands up. "I know you don't believe in monsters."

"I was more of a skeptic." The Governor's body flickered. "What now?"

"Must hurry." Victoria grabbed for his arm and cursed. "I keep forgetting you're…we sort of conjured a storm and used its energy to resurrect 'ghost you', but the magic is expiring. I'm not a witch. A friend from home—New Orleans, he actually saved you."

"Please help me understand." The Governor staggered to his feet and crumpled again as the deck pitched. "Who the hell is piloting this spaceship?"

Victoria rolled her eyes.

"Can't you just give me your blood or something?"

"That body, yes." Victoria nodded over her shoulder. "Not this one. Sorry."

"Same suit. Same lapel pin." He pointed to the final mirror. "How did I go from my penthouse to a coffin?"

"A last-ditch effort to remedy my unforgivable screw up." Victoria sank to the deck next to him. "Remember when I said the plague came back? I wasn't there to warn you or protect you after the vaccines were stolen and the drug companies got annihilated in court."

"No—wait…the treatments failed? All of them? Are you saying I'm—" He crawled to the mirror and touched the surface.

The action rewound and restarted. "Make it stop, please! Before I die again."

Victoria knocked his hand away from the glass. "Brace yourself, from now on everything gets scarier." She nudged her silver collar aside to reveal the heavy black necklace.

"Your jewelry is moving." He scuffled back. "Oh terrific, it has eyes."

"I mentioned that I had help with the spell." A snake unfurled from around Victoria's neck, slithered behind her back and rested its diamond head next to her cheek. "Meet my friend." She whispered to the serpent. "Can you give us a few more minutes?"

The snake flicked his forked tongue, coiled back and sprayed a puff of venom over the ghost.

The Governor stared at his hands. The dim white mist filled in and his form stopped flickering. "Am I sick?"

"That man on the balcony was." Victoria nodded and frowned. "The man in the box still is but it's not too late. That's the reason I took you. I'm sorry it hurt so much. I was on my own with the fruit trick."

"So, that was the mistake?"

"I wish it was so innocent."

The Governor pointed to the last blurry mirror. "Show me the final puzzle piece."

"Please go back to the box."

"No. I demand to see what happened—please."

"My sworn duty was to guard you." Victoria crushed her eyes shut and the snake nuzzled her neck. "And you don't know what you're asking me to re-live."

"Tell me the truth, then I'll get in the—wait, I have to climb on top of a corpse?" He tossed his hands in the air. "Fine, I'll do it, just..." He looked over her shoulder. "I'm sure that's something important I don't want to forget."

"I've tried to erase it, but my mind won't allow the mercy of escape." Victoria glided to the mirror and bowed her head before dragging her finger across the middle. Like paint dripping down a wall, the room rippled into focus. Candles danced against paneled walls and a jacket lay crumpled on the gleaming floor. One high heel, a sapphire tie and the shoe's match beckoned like a trail of teasing clues. At the end of a long hall, tasseled pillows were scattered across plush carpet.

"That looks like the lake house." He stepped closer and shrunk back. "And my bedroom." At the top of the mirror, figures slowly moved in front of a crackling fire, materialized and faded again. The Governor's jaw dropped. "Is that you—us? Victoria!" He grabbed his head and neck as memories of wine and silk sheets flooded back. Pinpoints of fire pierced his throat and a bright red puddle grew around his feet.

A lone heartbeat thudded from below the deck.

Inside every mirror the characters flew to their side of the barrier and hammered on the glass as if desperate to escape a collapsing prison.

The heartbeat accelerated, pressurizing the air until Victoria screamed and covered her ears with both hands. Shards of mirror exploded from around the room, passing through the man's ghost but slicing her alabaster skin to ribbons. Thunder crashed outside as black blood poured down her face.

"You're hurt." The Governor stepped closer and nearly disappeared into thin air.

"If the shark didn't kill me, this won't either." She wiped blood away with her sleeve as the cuts began to knit themselves from the inside out. "But you need to get in the coffin before all this effort goes to waste."

"Vicki, what happened?" He grabbed for his chest. "The scene with us…that was no mistake."

"The hell it wasn't. I got fired—some incompetent vampire was assigned to guard you and here we are. The whole world went straight to hell." She tried to shove him and pressed her palms together instead. "I'm begging you."

"Why did you go to so much trouble?" He scrambled over the crystal edge. "Will I know what to do if I wake up?"

"When, not if, and I sure hope so because that was the entire point of the memory cage." Victoria gestured wildly at the shattered mirrors. "You're the only future we have left."

Alarm sirens exploded in the distance. The snake bolted up from the floor, hissing and spitting. The rumble of stampeding footsteps above escalated to a roar.

"Gray, get in the damn box!" Victoria barely had time to slam the lid shut before the serpent drenched it in scarlet venom.

Through blood splattered crystal, Gray watched Victoria slump against the head of the coffin and sob with the snake curled in her arms.

***

Inside the crystal casket, Grayson's finger twitched and his eyes flew open. *Is this a dream?* He swallowed, clawed at his burning throat and thrashed against the lid. *Nightmare!* All the strength in his arms only slid the cover back an inch at a time until he finally hooked an elbow over the rim and hauled himself up. The compartment around him was thick with charged silence. The mirrors had disappeared to reveal the sweeping v of a steel skeleton. *The bow of the ship.* He turned his head to see rows of creatures standing in formation. Their stillness was where the similarities ended. "None of you could be bothered to help me?"

"That was my call." Victoria slipped through the forest of soldiers. Her drab gray dress had been replaced by a skin tight sleeveless blouse and leather pants. Black hair decorated with intricate braids and jade beads hung past her waist. "Some things you need to do on your own."

"Any chance I can get a drink?" A cough wracked his frame as his eyes traveled up and down her body. "Vicki, you look so different."

"Because you only saw glimpses of me, back when I was trying to pass as human." She held out her hand and a glass bottle appeared in her palm. She walked to the coffin with deliberate steps. The snake swirled behind her like the train of a fancy gown. "And stop calling me Vicki in front of the elders." She held the drink just out of his reach and relented. "Enjoy the water Gray, as if these were your final sips."

"What does that mean?" He gulped, climbed out of the coffin and crashed to the floor. His attempts to stand were unsuccessful until her iron grasp pulled him upright. "Thank you. I feel like I was hit by a train."

"I know you don't want to hear this again, but time is not on your side." Victoria snapped her fingers and soldiers closed ranks with a collective grunt. A man with gold bars on his collar and huge biceps straining his sleeves slammed down a table and chair.

"Thank you, Lieutenant." She unfurled a map that looked like a satellite photograph and stared at Grayson. "Sit."

"I'd rather stand." He traced a twisted coastline, tilted his head and narrowed his eyes. "What was in that stupid plum?"

"Seven years of poison." Victoria met his mahogany eyes as he silently mouthed the word seven. "It was an emergency."

"Governor Bell, if I may?" The Lieutenant huffed, straightened the map and nudged Victoria's shoulder. "Captain, he looks disoriented and we don't have time for a geography lesson."

"Captain?" Grayson eyed Victoria. "I thought you were fired?"

"I started over. Now, I'm in command."

"Pay attention, sir." The Lieutenant pointed to the top of the West Coast. "Portland Proper."

Victoria tapped the southern canyons. "Los Angeles Territory.

"I assume this is Chicago?" Grayson ran his fingers across the shiny paper and stopped at the base of the Great Lakes. "A few bright hubs with nothing but darkness in between. Where are all the other cities?"

"Not many left, but Chicago Land is much too dangerous to travel through. The Denver Zone is safer, at least for my kind." The Lieutenant rubbed his salt and pepper beard. "It's wolf headquarters."

"I don't see any state boundaries or even highways." Grayson shuffled nervously. "Where are all the people?

"What's left of the humans..." The Lieutenant paused. "They're hiding out in the wilderness."

Grayson looked back and forth between Victoria and her soldier with a blank stare.

Victoria sighed and caught the Governor's gaze. "After the second wave of the plague wiped out most of the human race, others took over."

"Russian invaders?"

"No Governor, the supernaturals slaughtered each other for a few years and finally called a truce." The Lieutenant pointed to the southwest desert. "They met in the remnants of Las Vegas and drew lots to divide the land up."

"Follow along." Victoria's fingers zigzagged across the chart. "Chicagoland—zombies. Nashville Realm—fae. Atlanta—witches. She paused and drew a sweeping circle at the mouth of the Mississippi River. "The Empire of New Orleans—safest location in the entire country."

"Let me guess—vampires?"

Victoria smirked. "Vampire royalty already ruled the Crescent City so all we did was fortify the borders."

"Does the government system work? It seems scattered."

"All these cities are their own kingdoms and very exclusive to their race and kind," The Lieutenant said. "They operate on a brutal and archaic caste structure."

"There is no unity, only savagery and bloodshed." Victoria turned her back. "Bad news, slavery is legal again. Humans are property or prey. Hate is the endemic culture."

Grayson shook his head and pointed to the middle of the east coast. "Who controls D.C.?"

Behind Victoria, a murmur flowed through the uniformed crowd.

"Washington is gone, sir," The Lieutenant whispered.

"Gone, how?" He finally slumped into the chair. "Where's the President?"

"Gray, the capitol is a wasteland—nothing left except stone stairs leading nowhere." Victoria gently massaged his shoulders. "The government was overthrown—so many humans fell ill and perished at once."

The Lieutenant pulled out a dagger and pierced the map on a black stain just north of ruined Washington. "You are here."

Grayson traced the familiar borders—rivers, lakes, mountains and islands. "What's the name of my home state now?"

"We don't have one." Victoria leaned on the table. "We're the resistance. Every misfit, cast-off and rebel is welcome here. Our tribe includes members of every species and bloodline—all committed to freedom and equality, like the original founding fathers."

Grayson's neck sagged. "So, no President. Who's in charge of the cities? Governors?"

"You're the only Governor left. It's mostly kings, emperors, czars, war lords...despot of the day." She shot a look at the Lieutenant and nodded toward the stern of the ship. "Not exactly the land of the free you grew up in. May I show you something?"

"Only if someone explains to me how I fit into this disaster."

"We will, but first, your jacket." Victoria held out her hand. "And lose the pink tie. That's not the image you want to project."

He shrugged the suit off his shoulders and slipped into the black leather and brocade coat he received in return. "The fit is impeccable, but..." He adjusted gold cufflinks. "What are we, pirates?"

Victoria traded glances with the soldiers and chuckled.

Grayson followed her past screens of digital code and graphics. "Is this some new radar or space scanner?" He climbed steep steps, stopping to cough and wheeze several times while the army followed in silence. "I still want to talk about what happened with us—that night."

"Later." Victoria spun the five-spoked vault handle and nudged a hatch open. Murky night loomed on the other side.

"Can I breathe out there?" He stepped into the salty air and did a double take. "I, I thought we were in outer space."

"Clearly not." She cupped her ear to listen to a hushed message. "Excellent, Lieutenant. Three minutes. Spread the word."

Above Grayson's head, the tower of a battleship loomed like a skyscraper. He turned to face the stern. A sweeping number sixty-two was painted across the deck. At the mouth of the harbor, remnants of the setting sun glinted off graceful suspension cables. "How does one acquire a decommissioned ship like this?"

"Taking one was easy." She pointed to the southern horizon beyond the majestic bridge. Two more superstructures were silhouetted against the clouds. "Stealing three was harder."

"Is that?" He squinted into the twilight haze. "A carrier? Which one?"

"You thought we were *on* the Enterprise?" She tapped her foot on the teak deck and tipped her head toward the fleet. "Almost."

"No way." He raked both hands through his hair.

Rumbling began in the east. Red and green lights were only visible for seconds before two jets cruised in from the sound. With wings swept back into a delta, they roared low over the ship as a matched pair of warriors.

Grayson watched them disappear behind the crown of a dark statue. "Tomcats?"

Victoria nodded and pointed to the sky. "Wait for it."

Another smaller fighter blasted into the airspace, fired both afterburners and shot into a vertical climb until it disappeared. Applause erupted around the harbor as a fleet of smaller boats flashed their lights in appreciation.

Victoria scooped up the snake and handed him to a tall woman with rich olive skin. "Ensign, we'll meet you on the bow. Be ready." She spun around. "Lieutenant, with me."

"Ready for what?" Grayson chased Victoria up two sets of metal ladders.

"The ritual."

"I beg your pardon?" He tripped on the final rung and toppled forward. "Where are we going?"

"You'll see." She hauled him to his feet and dragged him to the catwalk in front of the bridge. Straight ahead the harbor's water ended at a sheer cliff of dark buildings. "Take this."

"Something is crushing my heart." A bronze cylinder wobbled in his grasp. "Is this an antique?"

"Here." She whipped the telescope out to its full length and held it up to his eye.

"People?" He scanned the perimeter of buildings along the sea wall. "Thousands." His gaze snapped to Victoria and then back to the city. "They have spyglasses and binoculars. All those eyes staring."

"Right at you." Victoria placed her hand on his sleeve. "They've been waiting a long time."

"So...seven years ago, you abducted me with all this in mind? Genius."

"No, Gray. The truth is I took you for myself." She slumped against the railing with her head in her hands. "I was desperate—my heart was crushed, too."

The Lieutenant stepped forward. "Permission to speak freely?"

Victoria nodded weakly.

"Governor Bell." The Lieutenant plucked the telescope out of his hand. "The Captain saved your life. There was no cure for the infection then and there wouldn't be one for years. She gave you the gift of time—which is about to end."

"So, I'll be healed."

"Sir, your human body is already dead."

Grayson brushed off his chest and flicked his wrists. "No."

"It's only magic." Victoria groaned. "The ritual is to turn you into one of—us."

"You can't be—" Grayson looked between the two. "Come on, there must be another way."

"Sir, I'm a wolf. I lead my pack and speak my mind." The Lieutenant's voice dropped to a snarl. "Everything you see around us, the buildings and harbor, was preserved by her." He pointed at Victoria and then at the Governor. "For you. She crisscrossed the country at great personal peril to recruit soldiers. For you. Your legacy is not only alive, she whipped the story into legend and gathered disciples by the thousands. Humans, vampires, wolves, witches and more…banished from other cities because they weren't pure enough or wouldn't bow down to dictators or evil kings."

Grayson's jaw hung open.

"All these followers remember what America stood for and they're willing to fight to reclaim it. You're standing on a floating fortress. The Captain stole guns, ships and aircraft to build a militia. For you." The Lieutenant slammed his fist down on the railing, buckling the metal. "She hid your body, snuck back into New Orleans searching for magic elemental enough to keep you alive and came home with that." He pointed down at the bow of the ship where the serpent weaved around the soldier's legs in an erratic pattern. "An overly dramatic snake, who spits on everyone every day and still thinks he'll grow up to be a dragon."

Victoria chuckled and raised her hand. "That vampire serpent's ancestors have been vessels of royal blood and magic since the beginning of recorded history. He dreams big."

Spellbound

"I'm sorry Captain." The Lieutenant turned away. "I worry this old man won't understand the sacrifice you—"

"We. We all made sacrifices." Victoria took Grayson's trembling hand. "The ritual only makes your body immortal. Compassion, wisdom and honesty are gifts from the soul." She tapped on the center of his chest. "The country has never needed the inspiration of your voice as much as we do right now."

"Since we're laying all the cards on the table, I'm terrified." Grayson forced his shoulders square. "But I'll do it if you show me the way."

The Lieutenant stood back and swept his hand out. "The elders are waiting on the bow in front of the big guns."

After descending several ladders, Grayson tugged the back of Victoria's shirt. "What's up with the snake now? He's dancing."

Victoria paused and shook her head. In front of the assembled soldiers the serpent was bobbing its head and swiveling as if he had hips. "He likes show tunes. What do you think vampires do all night in the big city? Read spooky manuscripts and finger paint in blood?" She turned and patted Grayson's cheek. "We dance."

"Good to know." On the main deck, Grayson ran his hands over the base of massive gray gun barrels and whistled.

"We're fully stocked with sixteen-inch shells, sir." The Lieutenant thrust his chest out and stepped into the formation. "Firepower and freedom."

The elders raised their hands to salute the Captain. She returned the gesture with a crisp snap. "Lieutenant, has everyone donated blood?"

"Yes ma'am." He swiped a black droplet from his own wrist.

"My turn." Victoria stood motionless. The snake swirled around her body until their eyes met. "Ready? You've waited for this your whole life."

The snake opened his jaws wide and buried his fangs in Victoria's neck. She swayed and sunk to one knee as the serpent drank.

"Oh, sh—" Grayson stumbled back, covering his eyes and gulping for air.

The snake disengaged, floated to the deck and rolled onto his back as if in a deep slumber.

"Gray." Victoria flashed to his side. "Relax, I'm fine. Look around." She pointed to the dark edifices that loomed like waking giants around the harbor. "The message has been delivered."

He hesitantly moved his hand from his eyes, first focusing on her unmarked neck and then on the scene beyond the ship's rails. Through the telescope's lens he found every inch of space along the streets, in the windows and on the rooftops filled with living creatures. Even the bridges were lined with spectators jostling for the best view.

Victoria motioned to the Lieutenant. "Do you have the vial?" A long cylinder appeared in her hand. "Stay still Gray."

"Vicki, I think I'm dying."

"I know."

"We never talked about it—you and me."

"Have faith." She flashed back to the snake, pried his mouth open with her fingers and poured crimson liquid down his throat. Vacant, black eyes sparked with green.

The Lieutenant rushed across deck. "That's her human blood from before she turned." He met the Governor's wide eyes. "Keep breathing, just a little longer."

"The box!" Victoria spun around as the Ensign flipped open a wooden container. She grabbed a dark orb and knelt next to the stirring snake. "It's time!" In a flash she was holding Gray in her arms. "Hang on."

On the polished deck the serpent flipped over and began to writhe, coiling like a spiral pyramid until he was two stories tall. He arched his back and the hood of a cobra flared behind his head like a wicked circus tent.

"Whoa." The Lieutenant shuddered when the snake tossed a languid look in his direction. "If I ever said anything to offend you, I take it back."

Victoria held the orb up and the snake wagged his tongue like a panting dog. She shook the shrinking man in her arms. "Gray!"

"Please don't let that thing kill me, Vicki."

"I won't. He won't. Just stay awake." She slapped his face. "When the snake gives you this—bite it."

Grayson's eyes focused on her hand. "The plum again? Seriously?"

"Yes." Victoria hurled the plum into the dark sky. The snake shot up like a missile. High above the battleship's deck, he caught the plum in his fangs and punctured the ripe skin. Venom, magic and the blood of every species flowed into the fruit as he somersaulted through the night air. He dove down and landed like a feather on the gun turret.

The plum dropped gently into Grayson's palm. He raised it to his lips, hesitated, rubbed his chest and shivered. "I'm so scared."

"It won't hurt. I promise." Victoria steadied his hand. "Just wait until you see what's on the other side."

Grayson bit into the fruit. Red nectar exploded into his mouth and down his face.

"Come on, come on. Drink it all." Victoria held his body tighter as he shriveled in her arms. "More!" She grabbed the plum and squeezed, forcing the remaining elixir down his throat. The drained plum dropped to the deck.

"I'm sorry, Vicki." Grayson raised his shaky palm to stroke her face.

She clasped his hand and kissed his knuckles. "For what?"

"Everything, the accidents, my arrogance..." He grabbed both her hands as his vision went black. "For crushing your heart."

Grayson's body fell limp and time gasped. The crowd surrounding the harbor plummeted into silence. Every eye, human or supernatural, remained fixed on the Governor and Victoria's clasped hands.

The army of elders sunk to their knees, bowed their heads and silently chanted individual prayers. The snake drifted toward the stern without touching the deck.

**

The waters of New York Harbor caressed his skin like a silk blanket. Grayson floated to the top and walked on the surface as if it were black glass. From the tip of Manhattan, he looked past the ferry terminals and flowers of Battery Park, up to the familiar jagged skyline. He rose higher in the air as if climbing invisible stairs.

Lights blazed in the windows of every apartment and office building. A few blocks west, one gleaming skyscraper stood where two had fallen.

He crossed his heart and froze in respect. *Home of the brave.* Sweeping his gaze east across the cityscape, he paused to admire the art-deco facade of the Empire State Building and the many church spires that peeked above the rooftops. Straight up Fifth Avenue, the grandest cathedral faced a giant tree with twinkling lights. Childhood holiday memories flooded his mind. Every street was alive with music, neon signs and endless brake lights. A slow turn revealed bridges ringing the city with a barrier of steel and electricity. Fireworks exploded over the rivers and a legendary lady stood guard over America's open door.

How did we lose all this?

The vision faded and he sunk into the gloom of uncertainty that awaited him in the future. Deep in his chest, his heart winced. *Victoria thinks I can fix it.* He fought to keep his eyes shut. *What if she's wrong?* Velvet breezes caressed his face and a hissed murmur of French scripture brushed past his ears. Slender fingers grasped his palm like a steel vise. *Victoria!*

Grayson's hand clamped around hers and his eyes flew open to the full moon, a blanket of pulsating stars and Victoria's timeless smile.

"Welcome back, Governor." She nodded to the hovering snake. "Mission accomplished."

The serpent tripled in size as his endless body of metallic scales wrapped around the tower of the battleship. He arched his neck back and lunged forward with a full-fanged thundering hiss for the entire harbor. Deafening applause erupted and bells tolled from every shore.

Grayson stood and glanced up at the Lieutenant. "Sure looks like a dragon to me."

"Big dreamer?" The soldier shrugged one shoulder. "He's in the right place."

Grayson turned to Victoria. "Do you have the telescope so I can see my people?"

"Let me look at your eyes." Victoria stood on her tiptoes. "Lieutenant, do you see what I see?"

The soldier sauntered over and flashed vicious canines. "Oh yes, your bloodline's emerald fire."

Victoria turned Grayson toward the city and raised their clasped fists in the air. "You don't need any telescope."

He peered into the crowd. "Looks like New Year's Eve in Times Square and I can see every single person." *They're dancing in the streets.* "Every detail." *Strangers hugging each other.* "Unbelievable." An elderly man lit a match and offered to light the taper of a child beside him. As if it had been rehearsed for years, the original spark spread through the crowd and intensified from small candles to blazing torches. "What's happening?"

"You are living a unique moment in history." Victoria urged him over massive anchor chains to stand at the tip of the ship's bow. "Yes, I memorized all your speeches. The good ones, anyway." She stepped back to give him the moon's blazing spotlight.

Grayson glanced over his shoulder with a sly smile and a wink.

The progression of shared flame zipped around the harbor and across the bridges until both edges met high above the Verrazzano-Narrows. A solid ring of unified fire. A flurry of red rockets exploded over the vessels beyond the bridge.

"Governor Grayson Bell." Victoria tapped him on the shoulder and pointed west. The final torch burst to life in Lady Liberty's outstretched hand. "Showtime."

THE SELECTION

Christine Valentor

Chicago, Illinois, U.S.A.
witchlike.wordpress.com

Jeremiah Wells aimed his scythe at the corn stalks. He sliced, clean and rigid, sending the dry ears tumbling to the ground. The field stretched before him like a blanket of rust. He hated September. It was the worst of seasons, with its backbreaking work to bring in the harvest. Fruit withered on the vine, daylight waned, and nights lengthened. Worse yet, the autumn equinox was near. And Lizzie had come of age.

The yellow sun sank, melting like a drop of butter on the horizon. Jeremiah put down his scythe and made his way back to the farm shack.

Inside, he found his wife Morwenna sitting with their two daughters at the kitchen table. They were making corn dolls, little toys fashioned from the husks. Morwenna had done this in the old country, too. Jeremiah remembered, in their courting days, how each autumn she'd sit for hours with her mother and her aunts, fingers lacing gold sheaths, creating the small figurines. He never understood it. Waste of time. Especially now, with so much *real* work to be done. How could they trouble their hands with such nonsense?

"The harvest is sparse this year," he said. "Not likely to get us through winter."

251

Morwenna looked at him placidly. "Nothing here is guaranteed, husband."

Jeremiah sighed, placed a hand on her shoulder and bent down to kiss her cheek. It was true. This New World offered no certainty. It was a wild, unexplored land. Their survival was dependent upon weather and luck and the whims of Ananias Dare, the plantation master. But at least Jeremiah had escaped the gallows. Coming to Roanoke was not his first choice.

"Papa, look!" His youngest daughter Kerry held up the poppet she'd made, a sheath torso, the bent husk that formed its head and two arms that stretched like claws from its shoulders. The eyes were two corn kernels, dried red as poppies, staring boldly from the scrawny face. It was a silly thing, really.

"Wenna," he said to his wife, "why must you teach the children this nonsense? They have chores of their own to complete."

"Ah, husband. You never did understand the old ways."

Jeremiah shook his head and helped himself to the grits that boiled in the kettle over the fire. He cut a slab of bread.

"Don't eat too much, Papa," Lizzie said. "The Corn Full Moon Festival is tonight. There will be tables of sweets. Goodwife Henley has made sugarplums and cherry pies. Oh, Papa, I cannot wait!"

"We're not attending." Jeremiah looked at his daughter. At age fourteen she was the image of her mother, a stream of golden hair and eyes blue as sapphire. "Ananias has forbidden it."

"Ananias Dare is a pompous man," Lizzie said. "He may control our indenture, but he cannot control our lives."

"The girl speaks truth, husband," Morwenna added. "We labor his land from sunrise to sunset. The nights belong to us. The man has no right to claim our free time."

"But the Croatan… Ananias has prohibited all contact with the Croatan."

"Oh please, Papa, please?" Kerry pleaded. If Lizzie was the image of her mother, Kerry was the image of Jeremiah's mother. Sleek brown hair, gray eyes, and a sharp wit. At age six she was already learning to read. United together as they were, a trio against him, Jeremiah knew he'd lose this battle.

"Very well, then. We shall attend. But only for a few hours."

"Long enough to see the full moon rise?"

"That and no longer."

He spoke the words, but he was wary of his decision. It was foolish to tempt Ananias' wrath. Jeremiah was, perhaps, wary of every decision he'd made in the past two years.

***

The Corn Full Moon Festival was one of the few exciting occasions at Roanoke. The native people hosted it, a tribute to the moon, and settlers were welcome to attend. Here was dancing, a swish of red and yellow robes, headdresses of feathers and beads, jewelry of turquoise and goldstone. Men wore thick wooden masks with painted eyes, crooked teeth, and straw hair. There was singing and chanting, a blur of soft moccasins on the grass. The Roanoke settlers slinked through, plain as barn mice in their clothing of brown and gray, but as the night wore on, bonnets were removed in favor of feathers, boots traded for moccasins. Drumbeats mesmerized the crowd. Chores and duties were forgotten.

"A man who'd forbid this has no love of life," Morwenna said as both Lizzie and Kerry joined in the tribal dance. "Ananias is a fool."

"I don't like risking bad measure with him," Jeremiah said. "Not with Lizzie come of age."

Morwenna eyed her husband. "The Selection is a thing of chance. It is the reckoning of Baphomet. We've no control over its outcome."

How could she be so indifferent? They were speaking of their *child*. Sometimes Jeremiah did not understand his wife at all. "Do you not remember Silas Dunlap?" he blurted. "Last year – after his daughter…"

Jeremiah could not say it aloud. But he remembered, how he had found the body of Silas Dunlap hanging from a tree, noose wrapped around his neck, after his daughter had been chosen for the Selection. His was the second suicide of the colony.

"You, husband, are stronger than Silas Dunlap."

"Mama, Papa!" Lizzie twirled breathlessly out of the dance. "May I play games of chance with Hester Greenly and Samuel Jones?"

Jeremiah scoffed and shook his head. "Most certainly not." Hester Greenly and Samuel Jones were slovenly children, with parents who let them run wild. And games of chance? Surely, she'd rack up a debt from dicing and cards. How would he pay it? The indenture gave him no allowance, merely food and shelter.

"Come now, husband." Morwenna moved closer and gripped his waist. "Is the girl not entitled to some fun and entertainment?" Her eyes met his and immediately Jeremiah knew. Was she not entitled to some fun and entertainment when very soon… her every joy might be ended?

"Very well then. But meet us back here within an hour. I'll not have you cavorting about all the night with those two hellions."

"Thank you, Papa!"

In a whirl she was gone, clutching the hand of Samuel Jones. The thought persisted in Jeremiah's mind. *After the equinox, we may never see her again.*

The Roanoke settlement held one hundred and fifteen inhabitants. Of these, only nine were girls that qualified for the Selection. Past age fourteen but not yet turned twenty, pure and healthy. Only nine. The odds; one to nine. What percentage was that? Jeremiah wracked his brain, thinking of the arithmetic. How likely was it…

"Look there!" Morwenna steered him toward a booth cluttered with sweetmeats. Goodwife Henley had outdone herself. Here were plates of molasses biscuits, purple sugarplums piled high, bags of nuts, pies bursting with cherries and peaches.

"Have a plum, Jeremiah?" Goodwife Henley asked, and before he could say no, Morwenna brought the fruit to his lips. The sugar particles were like tiny daggers on his tongue. Jeremiah rarely allowed himself such indulgences.

Morwenna settled herself in the booth beside Goodwife Henley and the two began an elaborate chatter of gossip. Kerry was chomping merrily on her third molasses biscuit.

Jeremiah could not endure it. This game playing, this sweet eating, this – this façade of normalcy! How could they act like this when they knew? They *knew* of the impending doom! He had to get away.

"I'm going for a walk, Wenna. I shall be back shortly."

In the distance, the Croatan tribe had begun another dance. Jeremiah hoped it was for rain. The plantation had been in drought this year, the wheat fields faded to dust. With sparse crops, there was real concern for the coming winter. Jeremiah imagined diseases, gnawing stomachs, bodies reduced to skin and bone with the threat of starvation. Ah, but never mind winter. This coming week would bring things more abysmal.

Jeremiah thought of the past. He'd always intended to do the right things. And yet, they all turned out so wrong. It had begun two years ago, back in Southampton.

That scoundrel deserved death. And worse.

It was not murder, but defense of his beloved. Any man worth his salt would have done the same. Nobody, *nobody* could attack Morwenna and go unpunished. Luckily, Jeremiah had come to her rescue before the deed was done. He'd found Morwenna with her eyes blackened, bruised and crying, but still – thank the stars – unpenetrated, unviolated. The lumbering body of Elias Dangerton was atop her.

Jeremiah never regretted wielding his dagger, nor the deep slice he'd made through the villain's throat. He never thought twice as Elias Dangerton rolled over, blood spouting from his neck like a fountain. Dangerton made an attempt at words, mouth gaping like a fish washed to shore. With one hard kick of his foot, Jeremiah silenced that mouth forever.

He felt no remorse as Dangerton sputtered his last breath, stared out with the vacant eyes of the dead.

The rest was a blur of constables and shackles, the condemning brick walls of the gaol. Two months later came the trial. He had no money for a solicitor and his plea of innocence meant nothing. The jury did not sympathize with men like Jeremiah, working men of singular morality. And so, he was convicted of murder. Powerless over his fate, Jeremiah braced himself for the hangman's noose.

But on his walk to the gallows, it all changed.

A man named Ananias Dare approached him.

"Seven years of indentured servitude in the New World," Ananias said, "will buy you a lifetime of freedom. You need only work the Roanoke plantation, where you'll be given room and board."

It was an offer too lucky for words. Morwenna could have an indentureship, too. Lizzie, at age twelve, was fit for cooking, cleaning, and mending. Little Kerry would be able to help soon enough. As he escaped death, it seemed the heavens had opened before him.

What followed was a six-week sea journey over the turbulent Atlantic. The ship was full of criminals, undesirables, and never-do-wells. Outlaws and thieves, rogues and vagrants, prostitutes and fallen women. The New World, apparently, would be populated with England's rejects. Jeremiah did not care. It meant a fresh land and a fresh start.

Sea sickness was a vile thing. It afflicted every passenger. Days and nights of wrenching stomachs, vomiting and the trots. Some died. One poor woman threw her live self over the ship's rail, too ill to go on. But Jeremiah and his family braved it, all the while eating ginger candy Morwenna had brought along, as well as sipping ginger teas and some noxious bottled drink that went down like slime but eliminated the illness.

It was only after they'd reached the Virginia shore that Jeremiah realized he'd made a devil's bargain.

***

Now at the festival Jeremiah strolled through the crowd. Music rose from crude instruments, a banging of stones, a rustling of seashells, the chanting of tribal dancers as they jumped from foot to foot. Clouds drifted across the moon, casting shadows over the grounds. There were trades and deals, bartering and bargaining as settlers and natives argued, their faces serious as grindstone.

Jeremiah walked. In the jostling of the crowd someone pushed him. Nearly losing his balance, he brushed up against a bear on a leash. The animal rose on its hind legs. Its face met Jeremiah's, cheek press close and it roared, a thundering bellow that drowned out the music. Jeremiah gasped and staggered backwards. The bear's trainer, a Croatan brave, pulled on the leash, taming it to submission. The brave shouted a command in a language Jeremiah could not understand.

Jeremiah pivoted in the opposite direction, but it was no better, for a few steps forward he nearly tripped into a pack of vicious dogs. Maniacally they barked, teeth bared, white as pearl and sharp as his scythe. Jeremiah jumped away, barely avoiding a bite as another Croatan brave pulled on their leashes. These, Jeremiah knew, were bait dogs, trained to torment the bear, once the animals were placed in the pit.

Bear baiting was a cruel sport. How could the natives have adopted it, this diabolical game, brought from England? Its result was always the same; a bloody mess of fur and teeth, flesh torn apart, senseless brutality. All for a bit of entertainment and coin.

"The Croatan have, for better or worse, learned some tricks from the settlers."

Jeremiah turned to see who had spoken. She was an elderly woman, dressed in worn buckskin. Her grey hair fell in plaits down her back. She stared at Jeremiah as if assessing him. "You have a worried mind, newcomer." She spoke perfect English.

Jeremiah gave a nod and moved to walk away, but the woman gripped his arm. "You'd do well to hear your fortune."

Before he could refuse, she led him into a teepee and motioned for him to sit upon the blanketed floor.

"Call me Hattera." She lit a candle, illuminating the tent. "I know what you're thinking. What could a mere Indian squaw know of your problems? But the Corn Moon reveals all." She grabbed a pitcher and poured a cup of clear liquid. "Have some corn water."

The heat of the busy festival had made Jeremiah thirsty. He gulped the sweet, cool liquid. Hattera poured a second cup and he drank it eagerly.

"Your troubles are many, newcomer, but I will tell you this - do not let her cross the hayfield at setting of the sun. If she does, she will be among the chosen. And once chosen, there is no turning back. Baphomet demands what he demands. A young woman, come of age, pure as winter snow. Your Lizzie fits the picture as well as any."

"You know her name? And of Baphomet? But how…"

The woman moved closer. Her ancient face was an oval of wrinkles, high cheek bones and bronze skin. She smelled of horses and leather and sweat.

"I know men of your kind. The sins upon your souls are black as night. Murder and mayhem. A temper too big for your body. A series of bad judgments, and now you find yourself in this strange land. A land that does not belong to you. A land you have taken from me and my people."

Suddenly Jeremiah felt dizzy. The teepee had become stiflingly hot and its walls seemed to spin. He thought he might vomit. It was not unlike the seasickness of the ocean.

Hattera reached in her pocket. Jeremiah's vision was blurred, but still he could see what she clutched in her hands – a tomahawk, its silver blade glinting in the candlelight.

"Such fine hair you have, newcomer." Her voice was a low purr.

Only then did he notice them. A series of human scalps hung upon the teepee wall. Hair of all colors and textures dangled from withered skin, blood dried in red-brown crusts.

"Nice slayings, aren't they?" Hattera smiled. Her teeth were yellow corn kernels.

Jeremiah shuffled to his feet. The woman was half his height and probably twice his age. The idea that he'd have to fight her was absurd. He exited the teepee, but not before Hattera stuffed something in his pocket. "There's for your trouble, newcomer." She cackled a laugh, loathsome and vulgar. That laugh seemed to follow him all the way back to the plantation and he feared he was losing his mind.

When he arrived home, Jeremiah checked his pocket to see what the old hag had given him. It was a packet of pins, large and sharp, glinting silver as her tomahawk and wrapped neatly in thread. Jeremiah tossed them in the trash basket. He was not about to trust a woman who displayed human scalps on her wall.

Morwenna watched, peeking into the trash. "These are perfectly good pins, husband. And so often we lack them for our mending."

Jeremiah was too tired to argue.

***

The next day, he reaped the fields, aiming his scythe, trying, with all his will, to concentrate only upon his work. He wanted to forget the events of the night before and avoid the events which were to come.

He had no chance of doing either.

Before the noon hour, Ananias Dare came riding through the field.

"Wells!"

Jeremiah pretended not to hear, but the voice only became louder.

"Wells! Come forth, I'll have a word with you."

Jeremiah put down his scythe and walked toward the master. Ananias eyed him with suspicion. "I knew…" he said, "that I took a lame chance on bringing you here." His voice dripped with distain, as if Jeremiah were some defective, runt-of-the-litter animal.

"I gave you a brilliant opportunity, Wells. And what have you done with it? You and your greedy family are scarcely worth the space you occupy!"

"We do our work, sir. We fulfill every obligation in our contracts."

"It's not contracts I speak of! It is respect. Of which you have none."

"I know not what you refer to."

"Don't play coy with me." Ananias scowled, corners of his mouth inching downward as if he had eaten a bad oyster. "Have I, or have I not, forbidden contact with the Croatan tribes?"

"You have forbidden it, sir, but my daughters – they lack diversion. Roanoke, I'm sure you might agree, can be a dreary place for the children."

"I'd agree to no such thing! Attending the moon festival, cavorting with natives, it is an act beyond forgiveness. As punishment, I shall add two years labor to your contract."

"But sir! The festival was a mere amusement. No harm was done, and you see we are all back to work this morning."

"Silence!" Ananias' voice boomed like a rifle shot, causing the other field hands to pause. "Get back to work, you lazy-legged scoundrels!" Ananias turned to Jeremiah. "Don't cross me again. If you do, the price will be more than a mere two years' servitude."

That evening at the farm shack Jeremiah found Morwenna and Kerry grinding cornmeal for bread. Jeremiah began to think he would rather starve than eat anything of corn again.

"Where's Lizzie?" he asked. "It's nearly nightfall and she…"

At that moment he looked out the window to see his daughter, plodding through the hayfield alone. The sun, red as carnelian, sank over the meadow just as Lizzie crossed. When she opened the door of the farm shack the blue-gray twilight was already behind her.

Hattera's words haunted him.

Do not let her cross the hayfield at setting of the sun.

***

On the morning of the Selection, all workers were spared from their labors. Jeremiah walked, with his wife and daughters, to Dare Hill, a large knoll in the eastern corner of the plantation. With one hand, he held Morwenna's hand. With the other, he gripped his dagger, hidden deep within his pocket.

They climbed the hill to find the other families gathered at the summit. They formed a circle. In the center were Ananias Dare, his wife Elinore, and their tiny daughter Virginia. The child, now two years old, had been the first baby born in the New World. Beside them sat a giant statue of Baphomet. It was an ugly thing, with the head of a horned goat and the torso of a man. Wings sprouted from its back. Its feet were goat's hooves. The monstrosity sat upon a throne like a royal entity. Before coming to the New World, Jeremiah had never heard of Baphomet. Now, the hideous creature ruled his every fear and nightmare.

"We are assembled here today," Ananias began, "to perform a ritual of sacrifice to the deity Baphomet. It is *he* who has made it possible for us to inhabit this great colony. There is nothing reaped that is not sown, nothing received that is not earned, and nothing given without a price. This is the law of the land. As such, if we, the people of Roanoke, hope to continue the success of our settlement, something must be sacrificed at every autumn equinox."

Jeremiah looked at the crowd around him. One hundred and fifteen people, eighteen of which were parents of the girls in question. It was a dreadful, inhuman practice. If Queen Elizabeth knew Ananias ran the colony with such repugnant acts, she would surely take this settlement from him. He had no right to claim innocent lives!

But the Queen knew nothing. How could she? The ship that had been sent back to get supplies from the old country had left two years ago and never returned. For all the Queen knew, the colonists could be dead.

"Pass the hat, please." Ananias spoke to his wife Elinor, who handed the hat to Maude Greenly. She was the mother of Lizzie's friend Hester, who had also come of age that year.

"As you know," Ananias continued, "Each parent of a candidate must place their daughter's name in the hat. I will then retrieve only one. The Selection, as always, is done with no influence from myself. It is the great Baphomet who shall decide."

"Master Dare!" Maude Greenly descended to her knees. She was a feisty woman, a London thief who had served time at Newgate prison, plucked, just as Jeremiah had been, for the Roanoke crew. But she loved her daughter dearly.

"Master Dare, I beg you, do not continue this madness! Queen Bess would never allow it. In the name of the crown, I implore you, stop this lunacy."

Ananias glared, his eyes dark as soot. "Goodwife Greenly." His voice was a treacherous growl. "You have the *audacity* to question *me*, the lord of this plantation? You will pay for this insolence. I hereby add two years to your servitude."

Maude Greenly's face was a ribbon of tears. Silently, she placed the parchment with her daughter's name in the hat.

Jeremiah bit his tongue to keep from speaking when it came his turn to enter Lizzie's name. He hoped with all his being the victim would not be her. But if not Lizzie, who? There were eight others at risk, eight innocents. Eight that did not deserve this fate.

Ananias continued his ceremony, praising Baphomet, uttering prayers in a strange language, a mass of gibberish that nonetheless sounded official and intimidating.

Jeremiah found Morwenna's hand. Sweat coated his brow. He wished it had never happened, that he had never killed Elias Dangerton, never put his family in this – this *impossible* situation.

Finally, Ananias reached into the hat. He read the name silently to himself. His eyes scanned the crowd, moving salaciously from one face to the next. The corners of his mouth turned up in a gloating grin.

"The maid to be sacrificed this year shall be… Elizabeth Wells."

Breath caught in Jeremiah's chest. Tears began to form in his eyes, but he willed them away. His Lizzie. His baby. It could not be. It *would* not be!

He pushed past the crowd. Everyone was silent as he bolted toward Ananias, all the while clenching the dagger in his pocket. When he was close enough to see Ananias' eyes, he stopped.

There is a split second of time in which a predator decides it will kill its prey. Animals do this. A snake will pause for a moment, gather all its strength, then jolt its head toward the target, embedding fangs and poison exactly where intended. In that moment, the animal is certain to defeat its victim. Jeremiah knew this and paused for that brief instant.

And in that brief instant, Ananias gasped. His body bent backward as if he had been punched in the spine. He cried out in pain, a yell that pierced Jeremiah's ears. Ananias then bent forward, as if he had been struck in the chest.

"My heart! My heart!"

Ananias descended to his knees, crumbling like a branch of withered leaves. He lay there for a moment, then cried out again, this time more subdued, like the yelp of a punished dog. His eyes began to bleed. The trickling liquid flowed, bathing his face in blood. Soon his entire head was the color of raw meat.

Jeremiah let go of the dagger, still in his pocket. He had never even used it.

Ananias lay on the ground. His legs flailed one last time. A putrid smell rose as he soiled himself. Finally, he was motionless, his body stiff with death.

Elinor Dare watched without sadness. "Good riddance," she muttered. When some of the people looked at her questioningly, she answered simply, "I, too, have a girl child."

Jeremiah ran back to his family. Lizzie and Morwenna stood, clutching one another in a hug stronger than the baited bear. Jeremiah had never seen a more glorious sight.

Lizzie was safe.

But where was Kerry?

His youngest daughter sat, cross legged on the grass. The corn doll she had made lay in her open palms. Three long, silver pins had been inserted into it. One was to its back, right where a human spine would be. Another was to its chest, right where a human heart would be. The third was to a corn kernel that formed its eye, red as the blood that now trickled from Ananias' head.

Kerry looked up. She grinned a sinister grin.

"Husband," Morwenna said. "You never did understand the old ways."

Spellbound

.

ENDS AND BEGINNINGS

Dan Alatorre

Tampa, Florida, USA

geni.us/DanAlatorreAuthor

Chanticlaire smiled at Madeline as she closed the book and set it down. "You are magnificent, child. Far beyond where I was at your age. Your instruction will go fast."

"And your fee?" Madeline said.

"That which you will bear, and that which bore you." Chanticlaire clutched the old book to her bosom. "Two lives, I require for your instruction."

Madeline looked at her mother. "Her life?"

The girl's mother gasped as she lay on the floor.

"And your firstborn," Chanticlaire said. "What I do with them is not your concern. Besides, you have no use for this woman now. You belong to the spirit of the coven."

Madeline took a deep breath and let it out slowly. "This is your price?"

"This is my demand," Chanticlaire said. "You must pay it willingly."

"Life, in exchange for instruction. A dark request."

The witch shrugged. "It is what I require." She turned her head but kept Madeline in the corner of her eye. "It is a fair price."

"But . . ." Madeline got to her feet. "Do you know of the *effusio*? Where a master enhancer is able to absorb the powers of another?"

"Rumors. Lies, told to keep children and the *antiquuum maleficos* in line." Chanticlaire swallowed hard. "I—I know it to be false."

Madeline shook her head, stepping toward the blonde witch and gazing into her eyes. "You know it to be true. That is why you hid the book before I arrived."

"How dare you speak to me that way!" Chanticlaire stepped away. "Who—who do you think you are?"

Madeline's mother stood, sweeping her hands out and casting the room in an orange glow. "We are those that rule the night, like you. Spellbound and coven-born, to flush out and rid the world of the darkness that the darkborn bring."

Chanticlaire's forehead grew lines across it. Her teeth yellowed and her back curled into a painful stoop. She howled, grabbing the wall to keep from falling down. "Get out. Get away from me!" Her eyes widened at the sound of her cracked, warbling voice. "You will leave here at once!"

"We will. You will not." Madeline stretched her arms out, pulling flames from the fireplace.

The fires swept over the hearth and wrapped around the old witch, clinging to her like a burning tornado. Chanticlaire screamed as the flames engulfed her, dropping to her knees. The blonde strands shriveled and turned black, smoldering and then bursting into flames. She fell backwards, kicking and writhing as the fires penetrated her eyes and mouth, leaping upward in an orange plume as the energy left her body and fueled the heating inferno. Chanticlaire screamed, her robe turning to ash and her skin shrinking and pulling away from her bones. Her flesh turned black and cracked open, her blood boiling in the flames.

In a howl from Hell, the fire consumed her, rising up to the ceiling and then crashing down again, bursting forth and disappearing into the air.

The flickering flames returned to the fireplace. The room was quiet.

Madeline went to her mother. "Are you okay? Did she hurt you?"

"Not a bit," her mother said. "Her powers were strong—nearly as strong as yours. But her arrogance was stronger. It blinded her."

Her daughter smiled. "And I did well?"

"You did well, my child. As always." She patted her daughter's head. "Now let us get to the work of burning this house and all the darkness it keeps within its walls." She walked to the fireplace, pulling out a long, thin log. Holding it up, the flickering flame at its tip illuminated her face. She pushed open her coat and withdrew the book from Madeline's vision at the burned-out shop. "Bring the mate to this, and all of the dark witch's other forbidden volumes. The powers that have been released in their reading must be recaptured again. We have much work to do."

THE END

If you enjoyed stories in this anthology,
please post a review on Amazon.

It's okay to post a review that's only about
the stories you read.

Thank you!

Other Books In This Series:
Nightmareland
Dark Visions
The Box Under The Bed

and COMING SOON in this series:
Wings & Fire – PREORDER IT NOW!
Shadowland

Printed in Poland
by Amazon Fulfillment
Poland Sp. z o.o., Wrocław

64005946R00164